Five boxes f

lawyer who j

Atmospheric, is the story of a man who tried to walk away from the law, only to find it waiting for him in the California sun.

It's 1992 in Los Angeles. The riots are over, the Menendez brothers are on trial, and Charlie Trust is living in a borrowed beach house in Malibu right next door to Farrah Fawcett and Ryan O'Neal and trying to figure out what comes next.

After inheriting a little money and a lot of burnout, Charlie left Virginia to run the Pacific Coast Highway in a cherry red 1969 Mustang. Now he spends his days reading Raymond Chandler paperbacks and watching the gulls on Carbon Beach.

But his quiet life of reinvention is interrupted when the friend who loaned him the house asks for a little favor in return. Talk with Emma Scott, a woman trapped in a divorce from one of Hollywood's most powerful television producers. Just one conversation. Just some friendly advice. How could Charlie possibly say no?

It turns out that Emma Scott isn't just a scorned wife looking for casual advice. She's the keeper of her husband's darkest secrets.

When she drops evidence of a huge international money laundering ring operating in the American television business right into Charlie's lap and then disappears into thin air, Charlie is left holding the bag. Literally.

What follows is a classic LA mystery with a modern twist. Charlie is dragged from his life on the beach into a world of high-priced fixers, old-money Brentwood estates, and shady PIs operating behind storefronts on Normandie Avenue.

With no backup but a crusty eighty-year-old retired legal legend, an even older private investigator who swears he was Chandler's inspiration for Philip Marlowe, and the loaded Glock he keeps by his bedside, Charlie is just trying to survive long enough to find a way out of what that simple favor for a friend has gotten him into.

For readers who like their heroes flawed, their lawyers cynical, and their body count rising, this is a darkly funny California noir thriller that combines the high-stakes contemporary tension of Michael Connelly with Raymond Chandler's world-weary vision of Los Angeles.

Charlie Trust is a fresh voice in legal thrillers. He's a true noir hero.

What the critics say about Jake Needham

"If there is a living writer whose work makes me think of the great Raymond Chandler, it's Jake Needham. He's a prose master in the same vein." —**James David Audlin, author of THE TRAIN**

"This is a best-of-the-best crime novel with a lawyer hero. Charlie Trust wrestles with the most difficult ethical issues that a lawyer can face in the search for justice. A great read!" - **Michael Tigar, legendary defense attorney and author of SENSING INJUSTICE**

"Jake Needham is a smooth operator and his writing skills show that. He handles this change-of-pace novel with aplomb. This is a fun, fast read that is cleverly plotted and well executed." — **George Easter writing in Deadly Pleasure Mystery Magazine**

"Tight and atmospheric, Needham's novels are thrillers of the highest caliber, a perfect combination of suspense and wit." — **The Malaysia Star**

"Jake Needham has a knack for bringing intricate plots to life. His stories blur the line between fact and fiction and have a ripped from the headlines feel. Buckle up and enjoy the ride." — **CNN**

"Jake Needham is in a class of his own." — **The Bangkok Post**

"Mr. Needham seems to know rather more than one ought about these things." — **The Wall Street Journal**

"No clichés. No BS. Thrillers written with a wry sense of irony in the mean-streets, fast-car, tough-talk tradition of Elmore Leonard." — **The Edge, Singapore**

"Needham knows where a few bodies are buried." — **Asia Inc.**

CONTEMPT OF COURT

The Charlie Trust Legal Thrillers
Book 2

Jake Needham

For Aey.

Always.

"The TV business is uglier than most things. It is normally perceived as some kind of cruel and shallow money trench, a long plastic hallway where thieves and pimps run free and good men die like dogs. There's also a negative side."

— Hunter S. Thompson

CONTEMPT OF COURT

1

Los Angeles is the lover who gives you a kiss and a key, and then changes the locks.

It teases a future that both inspires and frightens. It's a trick of the light, a con man's ruse, a gypsy switch.

LA may be a place where men talk tough, and women say they know the score, but that mostly turns out to be either a lie or a delusion. It swallows people whole. Buy the ticket, take the ride. Los Angeles is America seen through refracted light.

Like almost everyone else I knew in LA, I was there because I was on the lam from something, and nearly every single day I had been there I had wondered how much longer I had before my key stopped working

But all that had just changed for me.

I stared at the letter in my hands, reading the words for the third time. This time, just to be sure I had it right, I moved my lips.

> *Congratulations. You have successfully passed the California Bar Examination.*

I wasn't just a runaway any longer. Now I had official standing here. I was a duly licensed lawyer in the State of California.

A little over a year ago, I had walked out of Pritchard, Wells & Monroe in Arlington, Virginia, a suburb just across the river from Washington, DC, that is mostly a bedroom community for people who live off the federal government. With my less than inspiring record at the University of Virginia law school, I had been lucky to get a job there, but if I'd had the slightest idea how much of my soul that job would suck out of me, I would have run like hell right at the beginning.

Eight years at Pritchard, Wells & Monroe, grinding away as the firm's one and only divorce lawyer, had not only soured me on the idea of being a lawyer, it had even left me wondering if remaining a member of the human race was all that attractive a proposition.

I swore when I left Virginia that I'd had enough of the whole lawyer thing, but now here I was, sitting on the deck of my safe house on Malibu's Carbon Beach, holding a letter from the State of California announcing that I was now officially empowered to start the lawyer thing all over again here in California. The irony of the moment wasn't lost on me.

The prep course I had to take to prepare for the bar exam had been pure humiliation. Thirteen weeks of four nights every week stuck in a windowless classroom in Santa Monica, surrounded by eager twenty-somethings fresh out of law school. They arrived with color-coded highlighters and pristine outlines, energy radiating from them like heat coming off concrete. I showed up with a beat-to-shit leather portfolio and the distinct feeling I was too old for this nonsense.

Taking a bar exam when you've been out of law school for ten years in the company of a crowd of kids who have been out of law school for about ten minutes is a humiliating experience.

If there's anything more humiliating, I hope I never find out what it is.

"Has anyone here actually practiced law before?" the instructor had asked during the first session.

My hand was the only one that went up. Thirty-three pairs of eyes turned toward me, sizing up the old guy in the back row.

The instructor nodded with a patronizing smile. "Well then, you'll find California law quite different from wherever you practiced before."

Virginia, I wanted to say. I practiced in Virginia, where I learned that being a lawyer could hollow out your heart and leave you questioning whether humanity was worth saving. I imagined it did in California, too. But I didn't say that. I just kept my mouth shut and opened my study guide.

The kids around me formed groups to prepare for the bar exam together. They met at coffee shops, shared notes, and created elaborate charts mapping the relationships between various aspects of constitutional law. I studied alone on my borrowed deck, watching the waves roll in while memorizing the differences between California law and what I had known back east.

The exam itself was three days of pure torture.

Day one was the multi-state bar exam, six hours of multiple-choice questions designed to test whether you remembered anything from law school. Day two was devoted to obscure essay questions on California law, five hours of writing about subjects I'd crammed into my brain over the previous six months. Day three required more essays, plus some kind of flaky California performance test that required you to pretend you were a real lawyer doing real lawyer things.

I sat in the convention center in downtown LA with fifteen hundred other hopefuls, the air conditioning struggling against our collective anxiety. My hand cramped during the fourth hour of day one. By day two, the kid next to me was slamming energy bars and muttering under his breath.

"Why are you doing this?" I had asked myself when I was driving home at the end of the second day.

It was a damn good question. Did I have a damn good answer to go with it? Not really.

Maybe I just hadn't been able think of anything better to do. Maybe it was a matter of having too much time on my hands and not enough purpose. Maybe I simply wanted to see if I could do it.

I folded the letter and slipped it into my pocket. The surf was high today, and the waves kept rolling in completely indifferent to my newfound status.

I listened to the hollow booms of the surf crashing onto the shallow slope of Carbon Beach, and I watched the salt spray shooting high into the air. A seagull skimmed the surface right in front of me, black eyes hunting the foam for something. With a shrill squawk, it suddenly spun up and away and flew off into the distance.

I guess it didn't find whatever it was looking for. I hoped that wasn't a bad omen.

I feel your pain, pal, I thought.

But this wasn't a day for feeling pain. I'd passed the goddamn bar exam. I really had. Somehow, despite everything, I'd passed.

I decided that was more than enough justification for me to go inside and get myself a beer.

I popped the tab on a can of Budweiser and settled back into one of the deck chairs. The beer was cold, and the first sip carried the sense of satisfaction that comes with marking a major personal achievement. And it *was* a major achievement.

I knew that. Even if it wasn't one I was entirely certain I wanted.

The waves had settled into a steady rhythm, four-foot sets rolling in from the northwest. I counted the intervals between the larger swells, a habit I'd picked up over the months of watching this stretch of water. Seven waves, then a pause. Seven waves, then a pause. The ocean kept its own time.

I had met the owner of the house I was living in here on what the locals called Billionaire's Beach three years ago when I was still grinding through divorce cases in Arlington. Harry Wells had walked into our offices on a Thursday afternoon in October looking like a man who had been run over by a bus, which, in a manner of speaking, he had been. His wife had moved out of their Manhattan apartment a month before, gone back to Lexington, Virginia, where she had grown up, and filed for divorce there.

That meant Harry needed Virginia divorce counsel. Somebody he knew had referred him to Pritchard, Wells & Monroe in Arlington, and when Pritchard, Wells & Monroe in Arlington had a divorce client walk in the front door, I was the designated hitter.

"While I was away for a week working on a show, she left and took everything," Harry told me during that first meeting. "She took all the furniture, she took the coffee maker, she even took the cat. All she left me with was a mattress on the floor and a note saying she needed space to find herself."

I had handled scores of Virginia divorce cases by then. The details changed, but the core of all of them was always the same. Two people who had once joined together in a partnership to stand back to back against the ravages of an uncaring world were now screaming at each other about who got the blue chair.

Harry's case was messy. He and his wife had no kids, so

there were no custody issues, but Harry had been a successful composer of music for television for decades. His major assets were royalties that went back thirty years, and his wife wanted half of everything he had ever been paid to write music, including royalties from shows that wouldn't yet air for another year or more. Just trying to do the math dragged everything out for months.

But somewhere during those long conferences, Harry and I had done more than talk about asset division and settlement negotiations. We had developed a friendship of sorts. When it was finally all over, Harry insisted on taking me to dinner. We went to Old Town Alexandria, the next chunk of Northern Virginia south of Arlington, and ate at a place called Landini Brothers that I'd heard about but never been to before.

On my third glass of red wine, I confessed to Harry how much I hated doing divorce work. I'd never been a huge fan of humanity in general, but whatever tiny bits of optimism I had mustered about our species had been utterly decimated by eight years of handling divorce cases. I'd done a little criminal defense work when I first started practicing, and I'd quickly discovered that even criminals were more honest than most people going through a divorce.

"You got a girlfriend?" Harry asked.

I just looked at him.

"Figured," Harry had said. "You need to get out of this stuff before you're burned to the ground."

"Easy for you to say. You're a successful composer. You'll have royalties coming in for the next century. I'm a lawyer who gets paid by the hour to help people destroy their lives."

"I've got a house in Malibu," Harry said. "It's been sitting there empty for a couple of years now. I keep telling myself I'll use it, but I never do. New York's my life now. Go out there.

Move in. Stay as long as you like. Watch the ocean and figure out what comes next for you."

I thanked Harry for the offer, of course, but I didn't take it very seriously. People didn't just hand over Malibu beach houses to lawyers they barely knew. Besides, I wasn't much of a beach guy. I didn't surf, I didn't even swim very well, and the idea of sitting in the dirt all day doing nothing held no appeal for me at all. Okay, you can call it sand, but sand is dirt, isn't it?

On top of that, I still needed a job. A house on the beach was great, but life required me to have a certain amount of cash money in hand, and the only money I had came from the salary Pritchard, Wells & Monroe paid me to keep anyone else at the firm from having to suffer through handling divorce cases. Maybe, I thought to myself, if I win the lottery or inherit a fortune, I'll reconsider.

And then that was pretty much exactly what happened.

My mother passed away suddenly and left me a tidy little nest egg. We had never been close, and I had been equally surprised by her passing and the inheritance she left me. It certainly wasn't a fortune, not by any means, but it was enough to finance a few years of living without Pritchard, Wells & Monroe, a few years of not practicing divorce law, a few years of repairing whatever passed for my soul these days and figuring out what I wanted to be when I grew up.

It had been six months since Harry had thrown out his expansive offer for me to squat for a while in his Malibu beach house if I pulled the cord and walked away from divorce law, so I called him with some hesitation. He probably didn't even remember who I was, and surely his house was occupied now after all this time.

But he did remember who I was.

And the house wasn't occupied.

"Stay as long as you want," Harry said. "Place needs someone living in it."

So that's where I've been for nearly a year now, here in Harry's house in Malibu, but most of the time I still feel like a squatter. I'm just an ordinary guy, a former divorce lawyer on the run from his life, living on one of the most beautiful beaches in California and surrounded by Hollywood glitterati. When I discovered that Farrah Fawcett and Ryan O'Neal lived right next door, I was staggered. What was I going to say if I heard a knock on my door one day and found Farrah standing there asking to borrow a cup of sugar?

That's never happened, of course, and I certainly haven't become anything like pals with Ryan and Farrah, but I see them when we're both out on our back decks at the same time, and we always greet each other with neighborly little waves and the odd call of *How you doing?*

Harry stays in touch after a fashion. I got a Christmas card from Manhattan, and a postcard from London when he was there for some music industry conference, and he telephones me occasionally. Each time he does, I listen carefully for hints that he wants his house back, but I have yet to notice one.

The sound of the front door opening and slamming closed again abruptly put an end my reverie.

What the hell?

Nobody had a key to Harry's house except for me. At least not that I knew of.

I twisted around in my chair trying to see back inside the living room. The sun glaring off the windows was too bright, and I couldn't make out a thing.

But I knew what I'd heard. Someone had just opened the front door and walked straight in.

2

I heard footsteps moving through the living room and coming toward the back of the house. I put down my beer and stood up.

"Who is it?" I called out.

"Charlie? That you?"

It was Harry's voice.

There's one hell of a coincidence, I thought. Here I am musing over my history with Harry Wells, and he walks through the door for the first time since I'd been living here.

"Out here," I called.

Harry stepped through the sliding glass door onto the deck, and I saw immediately that the past year had aged him. His hair had gone mostly gray, and he had lost weight in a way that made his clothes hang loose. At least his smile was the same. We embraced warmly, and I thought again about what a friend he had been to me.

"Look at this," Harry said, gesturing toward the ocean. "Still the best view in Malibu."

His voice had the same slightly gravelly tone it had always had, but something in it sounded tired to me.

"Harry. Jesus, this is a surprise. What are you doing here?"

"I had some business here in town for a few days, and I just thought I'd come out and check on the old place."

My stomach dropped. This was it. He was being polite about it, but he wanted his house back. I had gotten too comfortable and stayed too long. The free ride was over.

"I can pack up and be out of here by tomorrow morning," I said. "I should have asked before now if you needed the place."

Harry laughed and waved his hand dismissively. "Relax. I'm staying at the Beverly Hills Hotel. Just wanted to see how you were doing."

"You're staying in a hotel? That's ridiculous. This is your house."

"It's a house I never use. You're the one who's made it a home again."

He walked to the railing and looked out at the water. A gull swirled through the wind off the ocean and glided toward the deck. It hovered for a moment, looking us over, but it saw nothing of interest in either of us and allowed the wind to carry it away.

"Besides," Harry said, "the hotel's got room service and a bar that stays open pretty much as long as you want it to. I'm too old to rough it at the beach."

"This isn't exactly roughing it," I said, looking around at the deck, the view, and the house that had become my sanctuary.

"It is for me. I've turned into a New Yorker, Charlie. I actually like noise. Traffic. People arguing in the hallway."

Harry waved a hand at the sets of breakers rolling in to the beach.

"Hanging on to the edge of the continent by my fingernails like this makes me nervous."

I pointed at my can of Budweiser sweating away on the little metal table next to the deck chair.

"You want one? I've got plenty."

Harry made a face.

"Budweiser? Seriously? Why are you drinking crappy beer? Buy some decent stuff, for God's sake. Have you run out of money already?"

"I *like* Budweiser, Harry. I'm a Budweiser kind of guy."

He chuckled.

"No, you're not," he said. "You're just drinking it out here because you get a grin out of giving your high-hat neighbors the middle-class finger."

Maybe he had me there.

"How long are you in town?" I asked, shifting the subject away from my humble status on Billionaire's Beach as quickly as I could.

"Four or five days. Maybe a week. Depends on how the business goes."

"Music business?"

"Yeah, the usual. Somebody wants me to score a pilot. They think they've got the next big police procedural drama, something that will leave *Law and Order* in the dust. They need music that sounds important, of course, but not *too* important. Today's television audience isn't that big on important."

Harry settled into the other deck chair, the one I don't think I'd ever used. It creaked under his weight. He peered closely at me.

"You don't have much of a suntan for a man who lives at the beach," he said. "What have you been doing with yourself?"

I reached into my pocket and pulled out the letter from the California bar and passed it to him.

"Well, goddamn," he said after he had skimmed it. "You're a lawyer again."

I tried to look modest, which I found wasn't all that hard under the circumstances.

"I thought you swore you were through with all that shit. I figured you'd become a sculptor, or maybe a yoga instructor."

I chuckled.

"Well, goddamn," Harry repeated.

Well, goddamn, indeed.

"Since you're too snobbish to drink my Budweiser," I said, standing up from my chair, "let me at least get you a Coke."

"I'll take it."

I went inside and grabbed a can from the refrigerator. When I came back out, Harry had moved his chair closer to the railing so he could prop his feet up on the lower rail. The sun was starting its slide toward the horizon, painting the water in shades of gold and orange.

"Since you're going to be around for a while, I should start looking for my own place," I said, handing him the Coke.

"Don't be silly. I told you the house is yours for as long as you want it, and I meant that."

Harry popped the tab on the Coke can and took a long drink.

"Besides, I'm happy to have somebody I trust living here. LA's a different place since the riots. Break-ins are up all over the city. Even out here."

I hadn't thought much about the riots recently, although I'd certainly thought a lot about them when they happened back toward the beginning of the year. Most of the worst of it had been in South Central, many miles from Malibu in distance and even further away in culture. But Harry was still right. The whole city felt different now. Anxious. On edge.

"This is going to make me sound like an old man, I guess, Charlie, but I don't recognize this place anymore. I've been writing music for Hollywood for thirty years, but everything here is suddenly different."

Harry glanced over at me, and I nodded. I wasn't really certain what I was agreeing to, but nodding seemed the polite thing to do.

"The music business has gone completely corporate now," he said, settling back in his chair. "Used to be you worked with people who understood music, who cared about it. Now it's all MBAs and focus groups."

He stared out at the ocean.

"The money's less and less, and they want everything faster and faster. Last month, I got a call from some kid producer who told me they were looking for something youthful and cheap for a series he was producing. Those were his exact words. Youthful and cheap."

A seagull glided past us, wings motionless, riding the air currents along the beach. It banked and disappeared down the beach.

"I've scored everything from cop shows to soap operas, but now they want twenty-something composers who work for half what I get and think synthesizers are actual musical instruments."

The waves kept rolling in, but the light was changing. The bright afternoon sun was softening into the golden hour that made everything in Malibu look like a postcard.

"You know what the worst part is? Maybe it *is* time for youthful and cheap. Maybe I'm nothing but an old relic."

"You're not about to tell me you're retiring, are you?" I asked.

I sipped my Budweiser and watched Harry wrestle with his thoughts.

"Hell, I don't know. Maybe it's time to admit I'm washed up. Maybe I should sell the New York place, move somewhere cheap, and learn to paint watercolors."

Harry laughed, but there wasn't much humor in it.

"Pathetic, right? A grown man sitting here feeling sorry for himself because the world is leaving him behind."

The twilight was coming on fast now. The sky had turned deep purple, and the first stars were beginning to show. Down on the beach, a couple walked hand in hand along the water's edge. Their voices carried on the evening air, but I couldn't make out the words.

"I used to love this business," Harry said. "There was something magical about creating music that would become part of people's lives. Someone would be watching a show twenty years later and hear my music and remember exactly where they were the first time they saw that episode."

He took another drink of his Coke.

"Now it's all about demographics and market research. They test-screen everything. They focus-group the music. Can you imagine? Sitting a bunch of people in a room and asking them to rate musical themes on a scale of one to ten."

I found myself only half listening. Harry's words were drifting over me like the sound of the waves. His fears about an uncertain future, his doubts about relevance, his questions about what came next. I might be thirty years younger, but I'd been asking myself more or less the same questions for months now.

What was I going to do with this new California law license? Did I really want to practice law again? Could I stomach going back to the world I had walked away from? And if not law, then what?

"The thing is," Harry went on, "I'm not ready to be put out to pasture yet. I still feel like I have good work left in me. But how do you convince people of that when they've already decided you're yesterday's news?"

The couple on the beach had stopped walking. They stood facing each other, silhouetted against the last light on the water. Even from this distance, I could see they were arguing about something. Their voices had gotten louder, sharper.

"Sorry," Harry said. "I'm being a real downer here. This should be a celebration for you, right? You passed the California bar. That's a big deal."

"It is, I guess."

Did I really believe that? I wasn't sure.

The couple on the beach had gone in opposite directions. The woman was walking back toward the houses, and the man was drifting slowly along the water's edge.

"You know what your problem is?" Harry asked.

I looked at him. "I have a problem?"

"It's the same one I have. You passed another bar exam, but you still don't know if you want to be a lawyer. And I've been composing music for thirty years, but I don't know if I still want to do it."

He raised his Coke can in a mock toast.

"Here's to middle-aged men who don't know what the hell they're doing with their lives."

I was a good deal short of middle age myself, but I thought it would be ungracious to point that out. Besides, if Harry wanted to group himself with me for whatever reason, I figured it put me in pretty good company.

"Speaking of practicing law," Harry said, swirling the Coke in the can, "I mentioned your name to someone."

I looked at him sideways, but I didn't say anything.

"A friend of mine," he went on after a moment. "Her name's Emma Scott. She lives down on La Costa Beach."

The name didn't ring any bells, but La Costa Beach was

just south of Carbon Beach. Close enough that I probably walked past her house at one time or another.

"What kind of friend?" I asked.

Harry gave me a look. "Not *that* kind of friend. Just a friend kind of friend."

"Right," I said, and Harry grinned.

"She's a singer," he went on. "Or was. Had a couple of records back in the day. Good voice, but the business chewed her up and spit her out like it does most people."

"And you mentioned my name, why?"

"She's going through a divorce. Her husband is Zachariah Scott."

Now, that was a name I recognized. Zac Scott was one of those guys who showed up in the papers here all the time. He was a big-time showrunner with a string of television hits, a Hollywood player of the first order. He was the kind of guy who probably had lunch meetings about lunch meetings.

"Harry," I said, "I came out here specifically so I wouldn't have to do divorce work anymore. Remember? That was the whole point of leaving Virginia."

"I know, I know. I already told her that."

"Anyway, I doubt her lawyer would be too happy to have her talking to me."

"She hasn't hired anyone yet, not as far as I know."

"Look, Harry, there is no way—"

"Relax, Charlie. She's not looking to hire you. She just wants someone to talk to. Someone she can trust."

Harry leaned forward in his chair. The last light was fading from the sky, and his face was mostly in shadow now.

"The thing is, her husband's got serious juice in this town. I mean, serious. And she's convinced that means she can't trust anyone in the local divorce bar. Figures they're all either working for him, or hoping to work for him someday, or simply afraid of him."

"So she just wants to talk to someone who's not in the local divorce bar?"

"Exactly. Someone who understands the law but doesn't have any skin in the Hollywood game."

I took a drink of my beer and thought about it. The woman on the beach had disappeared, but the man was still standing at the water's edge. From this distance, he looked like a statue.

"Is she one of the needy ones?" I asked.

"Nope. She's smart. Tough. And probably getting screwed over by her husband's lawyers."

Harry finished his Coke and set the empty can on the deck railing.

"Look, Charlie, I'm not asking you to take her case. I'm just asking you to have a conversation with her. Hear her out. Give her some straight talk about what she should look for in representation. Maybe help her ask the right questions."

"Just a conversation."

"Just a conversation."

I thought about all the mornings I had spent sitting on this deck, drinking coffee and watching the waves. All the afternoons spent reading books I had been meaning to read for years. All the evenings like this one, nursing a beer and wondering what I was going to do with the rest of my life.

Harry had been letting me live in his house for almost a year now. He had never asked me to pay rent, never asked when I was leaving, never asked for anything at all in return. The least I could do was have a conversation with someone he cared about. To refuse, no matter how much I wanted to, really was unthinkable.

"All right," I said. "I'll talk to her."

"Thanks. I figured you would, but I didn't want to put her in touch without asking first."

"So when is this conversation supposed to happen?"

"She said she could call tomorrow if that works for you. Or you could walk down the beach and introduce yourself. She's usually out on her deck in the mornings, drinking coffee and watching the ocean. Kind of like someone else I know."

I could see Harry grinned at me in the half darkness.

"Just promise me something," I said.

"What's that?"

"This really is just a conversation. I'm telling you right now. There is no way on earth I'm getting dragged back into the divorce business."

"Just a conversation," Harry nodded.

He raised his right hand with his first two fingers extended in a V.

"Scout's honor," he said.

"Were you ever actually a Boy Scout, Harry?"

Harry grinned, but I noticed he didn't answer me.

3

After Harry left, I wandered into the kitchen and consulted with my refrigerator about dinner.

My refrigerator informed me that I needed to get my butt up to the Safeway before I starved to death. Staring at me in accusatory silence were a lonely block of cheese with some white stuff growing on one side, three cans of Budweiser, a jar of mustard, and what might once have been a head of lettuce.

I grabbed my keys and headed for the garage.

The Mustang sat there under the overhead lights, all that cherry-red paint and chrome gleaming like a promise. It was my one big splurge with the money my mother had left me, a 1969 convertible with a rebuilt engine and more personality than most of the attorneys I had worked with back in Virginia. Something about the rumble of its big V8 and the way it held the curves of the Pacific Coast Highway as it snaked along the coast made me feel like I'd bought a better life along with it.

I dropped the top and backed out into the evening air. The

PCH stretched north toward our local shopping area, two lanes of blacktop threading between the ocean and the mountains.

The Mustang settled into the curves with the confidence of a car that knew exactly what it was built for.

If there is any better feeling in this life than running the PCH in a vintage Mustang with the top down, listening to the surf crashing on the beach, and smelling the salt in the air, I have no idea what it is.

You've heard Randy Newman sing *I Love LA,* haven't you?

Roll down the window, put down the top
Crank up the Beach Boys, baby
Don't let the music stop
We're gonna ride it till we just can't ride it
no more

Yeah, it's *exactly* like that.

The Safeway occupied one corner of the small shopping center that served the local community's basic needs. Nothing fancy, just a grocery store, a dry cleaner, a pharmacy, and a few other shops that kept the wheels of daily life turning. I parked near the front and made my way inside.

I wasn't much of a cook. Food had just never been a big enough deal with me to bother to learn. I made sandwiches mostly, or nuked frozen food, or occasionally poured pasta sauce out of a jar. I could also scramble eggs and microwave bacon, after a fashion, but I saved those skills for really special occasions.

Twenty minutes later, I emerged with enough provisions that I figured I could last out the rest of the week. Nothing elaborate, just the basics that would keep me fed without requiring too much effort. Some cold cuts, a box of generic raisin bran, milk, a loaf of decent bread, lots of coffee, and enough beer to maintain my reputation as a Budweiser kind of guy.

I was loading the bags into the Mustang when I noticed a small bookstore tucked between the dry cleaner and a place that sold vitamins. Warm light spilled out through the big front window, and I could see shelves packed with books stretching back into the interior. A hand-painted sign above the door said Malibu Books in simple black letters.

I had never noticed it before. Had I just not been paying attention, or was it new? I was a little surprised the place was still open. Most of the other shops had already closed for the evening, and it was getting close to eight o'clock. But I could see someone moving around inside, and the door was propped open to let the evening breezes off the ocean circulate through the store.

Nobody was waiting for me at home, the groceries would keep, and I hadn't been in a real bookstore in months. Back in Virginia, I'd been a regular at a place called Politics & Prose in Washington, but that felt like a lifetime ago now. I locked the Mustang, crossed the parking lot, and walked inside.

The store was smaller than it looked from the street, but every available inch of wall space was lined with shelves. Books were stacked on tables, piled on the floor near the register, and arranged in neat displays throughout the narrow aisles. The air smelled like paper and ink with a faint residue of coffee coming from somewhere.

"We're still open," a woman's voice called from somewhere behind the poetry section. "Just barely, but still open."

She had a warm, throaty voice, but with a slightly risqué finish. She sounded like someone's mother reading aloud from the collected novels of Henry Miller. I immediately imagined her as a tall, sturdy woman with a long, striking face. Then she emerged from between two tall shelves, carrying an armload of paperbacks, and I saw how wrong I had been.

The woman was very small, barely over five feet, and very slim. She had a kind of Annie Hall vibe about her. She was wearing a man's blue-striped shirt with the sleeves rolled up, a pair of baggy khaki trousers, and an unbuttoned brown tweed man's suit vest. An oversized pair of black eyeglasses sat on the end of her nose. I would have guessed her age at about thirty, but who knows with women? Certainly not me.

She set the stack of books she was carrying on the counter and looked me over.

"You're either a customer or a very polite burglar."

"Customer," I said. "I think."

She smiled.

"Good. Burglars never buy anything."

I had just wandered in out of curiosity without any actual intention of buying a book, but you can't just walk into a small bookstore, chat with someone who is probably the owner, and then walk out empty-handed. That would violate some fundamental law of human decency.

I offered another smile that I hoped made me look non-threatening and wandered off into the stacks to browse, leaving the woman to do whatever she was doing with those paperbacks. The collection struck me immediately. This wasn't like the chain bookstores I was used to with their displays of best-sellers and celebrity memoirs stacked up like cordwood. These books felt personal somehow. It was more like looking through someone's private library than browsing a commercial bookstore.

The poetry section was better stocked than most university bookstores. Even the travel books seemed chosen by someone who had actually been to the places they described. The fiction section ran heavy toward literary novels and classic mysteries. I found an entire shelf devoted to Ross Macdonald and another to Mickey Spillane. There was also a section with what looked like every Raymond Chandler book ever published.

I pulled a copy of *The Maltese Falcon* from the shelf and flipped through it. Someone had made notes in the margins, observations about Hammett's style written in a neat and careful script. A used book? I glanced at the title page and saw it was a first edition.

I couldn't imagine what a first edition of *The Maltese Falcon* was worth, and I wasn't sure I wanted to know. I slid it back into place, very gently, and kept browsing.

The mystery section called me back. I had always been partial to crime fiction, maybe because it dealt with the same fundamental human failings that powered my divorce practice. People behaving badly toward each other. People lying, cheating, and generally making a mess of their lives and the lives of everyone around them. People eventually getting what they deserved. Or not.

"I don't want to rush you," the woman called from the front of the store, "but it's closing time, and I need to get home to feed my cat."

Her voice carried that tone people use when they're trying to be polite about hurrying you along. I looked at my watch. Eight-fifteen. I'd been browsing for nearly twenty minutes.

"Just another minute," I called back.

But now I was under pressure. I had to choose something, and somehow it seemed important to make a good impression. This woman had stayed open late, been pleasant about my wandering in at closing time, and now she was waiting patiently while I decided. I couldn't just grab any random book.

I scanned the shelves again, looking for something that

would mark me as a man of taste when it came to the books I read. Something that would suggest I was worth the extra few minutes she had invested in keeping the store open.

My eyes fell on a collection of Raymond Chandler short stories. *The Simple Art of Murder*. Perfect. Chandler was safe territory. Classic American crime fiction. Reading Chandler suggested I had literary sensibility without being a snob about it.

I pulled it from the shelf and headed back to the counter where I found the woman reorganizing a display of local interest books.

"Good choice," she said, glancing at the cover. "Chandler understood Los Angeles better than almost anyone who's ever written about it."

"I figured I should learn something about the place where I'm living."

She rang up the purchase on an old mechanical register that looked like it belonged in a museum. The keys made a satisfying clicking sound when she punched in the price.

"You're new to Malibu?"

"Almost a year now, but it still feels new."

"Where did you come from?"

"Washington, DC. Well ... Arlington, Virginia. Just across the river. But I usually say Washington, DC, because most people have never heard of Arlington, Virginia."

Schmuck, shut up. You're talking too much. Be cool.

"I've heard of Arlington, Virginia."

"What have you heard?"

"That it's a long way from the beach," she laughed.

She handed me the book in a small brown paper bag.

"What brought you out here?" she asked.

I thought about how to answer that. The truth was complicated, of course, far too complicated to blurt out a few words to a stranger. Where would I even start? A divorce practice that had nearly killed my faith in humanity? A mother's unexpected death and inheritance? A friend's generous offer of a house by the ocean?

"Change of scenery," I said.

Close enough for government work.

"Sometimes you just need to reinvent yourself somewhere new," she nodded.

"I'm Charlie Trust," I said, offering my hand.

She paused a beat before she took it, and I wondered if I had overstepped, but I could see a bit of a twinkle in her eyes and I decided that I hadn't.

We shook hands.

"I'm Pele Bouchier," she said.

"Seriously? Your name is Pele? Your real name?"

She nodded, but she didn't say anything else.

"Well," I said, "I'm absolutely certain this is the first time I've ever met a woman who was named after a Brazilian soccer player."

"I'll have you know, Pele is a figure from Hawaiian mythology. She's the goddess of volcanoes and fire who created the Hawaiian Islands."

"Actually, I think I liked you better when you were a Brazilian soccer player."

Pele laughed, and it was a laugh that I thought was quite attractive. Not a polite, ladylike titter, but a genuine, full-throated guffaw that seemed to roll up from somewhere deep inside her.

She walked around the counter and started turning off lights. The store took on a different character in the dimmer light, more intimate somehow.

"What made you open a bookstore?" I asked just to keep the conversation going a bit longer.

"Temporary insanity." She grinned. "I inherited a little money from my grandmother and decided to do something completely impractical with it. My family thinks I've lost my mind."

"Have you?"

"Probably."

We walked toward the front door together. She flipped the sign from *Open* to *Closed*, pulled the door shut behind us, and locked it. The evening air carried the scent of jasmine from somewhere.

"Thanks for staying open," I said.

"Thanks for buying something. Every sale counts when you own a bookstore in Malibu."

"Do you really have a cat?"

She laughed again with the same rumbling guffaw I had enjoyed so much before.

"I don't even have a houseplant, Charlie."

Most men are unreasonably pleased with themselves when they manage to raise a laugh in an attractive woman. I was certainly no exception to that genetic rule, but I tried not to preen excessively. It would have been embarrassing if she had caught me at it. We men are such simple creatures, aren't we?

I walked toward the Mustang, the book tucked under my arm. When I reached the car, I turned back and saw Pele walking toward a little yellow Volkswagen Bug parked behind the store. She raised her hand in a brief wave before disappearing around the corner.

I got in and started the engine. The V8 rumbled to life with its familiar growl, and I pulled out onto the PCH. The ocean was invisible now in the darkness, but even without sight of it, you could feel its huge, brooding presence out there.

It had been a strange evening. Harry's unexpected visit, his talk about feeling washed up, his mention of this Emma Scott woman who wanted to talk to someone about her divorce. And now this bookstore where a woman had decided to sell books in a place I'd be willing to bet few people read anything more demanding than the *LA Times*.

I thought about what the bookstore woman had said about reinventing yourself somewhere new.

People never reinvent themselves in the place where they already are, do they? They always take themselves away to somewhere new, a place where they expect to find a different reality in an unfamiliar context, and they do their reinventing there. It was like some kind of rule of life, wasn't it?

I guess reinventing was a fair characterization of what I was doing here in Malibu, though I wasn't at all sure what I was reinventing myself into. A year ago, I had been a divorce lawyer in Virginia. Now I was a freshly licensed California attorney with no office, no clients, no practice, and no clear idea what to do next.

But now I had a collection of Raymond Chandler short stories to help me figure out this strange and enigmatic place I had taken myself away to, and that seemed like it might be one hell of a good start on something.

4

The next morning, about ten, I settled down on the deck with my third cup of coffee and my Raymond Chandler short stories.

A fine day was unfolding under a cloudless blue sky. There was a light breeze off the ocean, and the tide was out. Low swells rolled in without the usual soundtrack of booming surf slamming into the sand in an endless series of little explosions.

Today was the reason people lived in Malibu. Exactly today. I might just be borrowing this life for a little while, but I was damn well going to enjoy it while I could.

Then the telephone rang.

Of course, it did.

I put down my coffee and my book, and I went inside to answer it.

"Is this Charlie Trust?"

A woman's voice. Light, pleasant, with a bit of a lilt in it. Irish? Maybe.

"One and the same," I said, and immediately felt a little dumb for sounding so flip.

"This is Emma Scott. Harry Wells said he talked to you about me."

I glanced at my watch. Ten-fifteen. Gosh, she was keen, wasn't she?

"He did. When would you like to come by and talk?"

"Well, that's the thing. How about right now?"

"Right now?"

"I'm parked in your driveway. I'm calling you from my car."

I walked to the front window and looked out. On the other side of the fence, I could just see the top of a black car parked by the front gate. She really *was* keen.

I wasn't sure I was ready for this. I guess I had been assuming this woman would call and make an appointment for a day or two in the future, and I would have a little time to psyche myself up for talking to her about her divorce case, but now I was just going to be dropped straight into the mud with no mental preparation.

I sighed to myself, and went out to open the gate.

When I pulled it open, a woman stepped out of the black Mercedes sedan parked in the driveway.

I would have guessed Emma Scott to be in her early forties, but with Hollywood folk, particularly female Hollywood folk, you could never tell for sure.

She was tall and lean, with dark hair pulled back in a ponytail. She wore oversized sunglasses that covered half her face, white jeans that looked like they had never been dirty, and a pale blue silk blouse that probably cost about the same amount I budgeted for groceries every month. She moved like a woman who was comfortable with her place in the world, and she walked toward me with her hand extended.

"Charlie? Thank you for agreeing to see me. Harry speaks very highly of you."

"I'm sure you must know that Harry is extremely prone to overstatement."

She chuckled.

Emma Scott's handshake was firm, businesslike. Up close, I could see she was even prettier than I had first thought, but there were lines around her eyes that looked deeper than they should have been at her age. Maybe that spoke of recent stress, or maybe it was just a sign of the general wear and tear that doubtless comes along with being married to a big-time Hollywood power broker for however many years.

"Come on in," I said. "Can I get you some coffee?"

"That would be wonderful."

I led her through the house and pointed her out toward the back deck while I went into the kitchen and filled an insulated carafe with coffee.

She moved through the living room like someone who was used to nice homes. She didn't gawk at the view or comment on the furnishings. This was just another beach house to her, and I'd guess it was probably smaller and far less impressive than the one she was living in.

When I stepped out onto the deck carrying the carafe and an empty mug for her, I found her leaning on the railing and looking out at the ocean.

"Harry always claimed he had the best view of Carbon Beach," she said. "I can see he was right."

I set the carafe and mug on the table where I had left my own cup.

"Milk? Sugar?" I asked.

She shook her head. "Black is fine."

I poured her coffee and topped up my cup at the same time.

"Harry didn't tell me you were so young," she said, looking me over.

I wasn't sure how to respond to that.

Young? I didn't really think of myself as young or old, or anything for that matter. First, the kids in the bar prep course had treated me like I was the old man, and now this woman I didn't even know was standing on my borrowed deck making me sound like a kid. What was it with these California people and their obsession with age?

"I'm thirty-five," I said, and immediately felt foolish. I had meant that only as a statement of fact, but somehow it had come out sounding prickly and defensive.

"There's nothing wrong with being thirty-five. I guess it's just that Harry made you sound more seasoned."

"I spent nearly ten years in Virginia doing nothing but trying divorce cases. That's not only as seasoned as I'd like to be, I think it's as seasoned as anybody should ever be."

"Yes, Harry told me you specialized in divorce cases before."

"Specialized is a generous way to put it. I was the guy who got stuck with doing the firm's divorce cases because nobody else wanted to do them."

"And now you're out here trying to escape all that."

"Yes, something like that."

I handed her the mug of black coffee and tried to shake off my irritation. She hadn't meant to insult me. I knew that. She had just been making conversation, but something about her comment had hit me wrong. It made me feel like I was still the junior associate getting the divorce cases because nobody else was willing to handle them.

She accepted the mug without comment, settled herself into the same chair where Harry sat yesterday when he had asked me to talk to her, and adjusted her sunglasses.

"Raymond Chandler," she said, noticing the book I had left on the table. "Good choice for a lawyer living in LA."

"You think so? I picked it up last night at that little bookstore up in the shopping center. The owner seemed to think Chandler understood LA better than most writers."

Emma Scott hesitated and looked at me carefully.

"You know Pele?"

"Not really. I just met her last night when I bought this book."

Emma nodded slowly as if she were weighing the truthfulness of my answer, and I wondered why. But after a moment, she let the subject of my connection to Pele go.

"Chandler's version of LA is getting a little dated now, don't you think?" she asked.

I leaned back in my chair and considered that. Chandler's Los Angeles was all rain-slicked streets and corrupt cops, femme fatales in dark bars, and rich men with ugly secrets. A black and white world where the good guys wore fedoras and the bad guys got what was coming to them.

"I'm not sure the fundamentals have really changed that much."

"You think modern LA is still full of Philip Marlowe types wandering around solving crimes?"

"No, but I think it's still full of people lying to each other about money and sex and power. The clothing and the cars might be different, but the basic human motivations are about the same."

Emma took a sip of her coffee and gazed out at the ocean. A gull skimmed the surface of the water right in front of us, wings barely moving, then unleashed a loud *caaaaaaw* as it glided off down the beach.

Emma shifted in her chair, pulling her sunglasses down slightly to look at me over the top of them.

"What I like about Chandler's LA is that it wasn't just about corruption and crime. It was romantic, too. All that noir atmosphere. The city of broken dreams."

"In a place where people come to reinvent themselves, broken dreams come with the territory."

"Is that what you're doing here? Reinventing yourself?"

"I'm trying to figure out what comes next," I said. "Maybe that's pretty much the same thing as reinventing myself, but I like to think putting it that way elevates me at least a bit above the status of a pop psychology cliché."

Emma smiled. It was the first genuine smile I'd seen from her since she arrived.

"At least Chandler's characters always knew what they were doing. Even when everything was falling apart, Marlowe never seemed to doubt himself."

"That's because Marlowe was fiction. Real people doubt themselves all the time."

"Do you think that's what makes his stories feel dated? All that moral certainty?"

I thought about it while I watched another set of waves roll in toward the beach.

"Maybe," I said. "Or maybe it's just that LA has gotten more complicated since then. Chandler's LA was mostly white, mostly male, and mostly middle-aged. The version we're living in now is a lot more difficult to get your arms around."

She nodded, but perhaps she had grown bored with our conversation because she said nothing else.

Okay, so much for the small talk part of the program. Time to get down to business.

. . .

"Before we start talking about your case, Mrs. Scott," I said as I set my coffee cup down, "I should probably remind you that I don't do divorce work anymore."

"Please, call me Emma."

"All right, Emma. And I'm just Charlie."

That brought the second smile of the morning, and I thought it was a very nice smile indeed.

"The thing is, Emma, right now I don't do any kind of work anymore. I don't have any clients. I don't have an office. I'm basically just a guy sitting on Harry's deck watching the ocean and reading Raymond Chandler."

Emma nodded and took another sip of her coffee.

"That's exactly why I trust you," she said. "Your independence. That and Harry's insistence that you're a good man."

She pulled her sunglasses off and set them on the table. Her eyes were blue, and I could see the fatigue in them clearly now.

"All the big firm lawyers in town are in my husband's pocket, Charlie. Either they've worked for him, or they want to work for him. I heard what a wonderful job you did for Harry when his wife was bleeding him dry in Virginia."

I felt the familiar catch in my chest that I got whenever anyone started talking about divorce work as if it were something worthy.

"That's why I need someone like you to represent me," she finished quickly.

"Whoa," I said, holding up my hand. "I told Harry I would talk to you and try to point you in the right direction, but I'm just doing this as a favor to him. I'm not taking on any cases."

Emma's face fell slightly. "But that means whatever I tell you won't be privileged, doesn't it? You're not actually my lawyer."

I understood her concern. The attorney-client privilege was sacred in the legal world. Without it, clients couldn't speak freely to their lawyers, and lawyers couldn't properly represent them. Without a formal attorney-client relationship, there was generally no privilege, but there was one exception to that rule.

"This is considered a case interview," I said. "Even if I don't take your case, what you tell me today would still be protected by privilege. That's how the law works."

Emma relaxed slightly, but I could see she was still uneasy. She kept glancing toward the house as if she expected someone to emerge from the sliding glass door.

"Are you sure about that?"

"Absolutely. The privilege attaches as soon as you seek legal advice from a lawyer, even if that lawyer doesn't end up representing you."

She nodded, but her hands were fidgeting with her coffee mug.

"It's just that I've never done anything like this before. I've never had to talk to lawyers about my personal life. Frankly, it bothers me."

"How long have you been married?"

"Ah ... twelve years. We separated eight months ago."

Emma stared out at the ocean for a long moment and watched a seagull glide past.

"I keep thinking this is all a bad dream and that I'm going to wake up one day and everything will just go back to normal. But it won't, will it?"

I said nothing. I didn't know enough to guess whether it would or wouldn't.

"Zac's lawyers have already filed papers. They're claiming I committed adultery, so they say I should get nothing. Not the house, not alimony, nothing."

"Did you?"

The question came out more bluntly than I had intended, but divorce work had taught me that there was no point in dancing around the hard questions. If she wanted advice, I needed to know what I was dealing with.

Emma's cheeks flushed, but she met my eyes directly.

"I had dinner with someone. A few times. But nothing happened. Nothing physical."

In my experience, when people used the phrase *nothing happened*, something usually had. But I wasn't her lawyer, and it wasn't my job to cross-examine her about anything.

"Do they have any evidence?"

"Photographs of us having dinner. Zac had private investigators following me around, and they took them. But that's all they have because that's all there was."

Emma stood up and walked to the railing. She gripped it with both hands and stared out at the horizon.

"This whole thing is humiliating. Having strangers pawing through your life looking for dirt."

I watched her struggle with her emotions. This was the part of divorce work that had nearly destroyed me back in Virginia. I hated seeing people realizing their lives were being dissected in public and their most private moments were being reduced to ammunition for a legal war.

"Emma," I said, "even if what you're telling me is true, you need to understand that it probably doesn't matter. California is a no-fault divorce state. Adultery isn't supposed to affect property division or alimony."

She turned back to me. "Then why are his lawyers making such a big deal about it?"

"It's just a strategy. They want leverage. They want you scared and embarrassed enough that you'll be willing take whatever they offer you just to make all this go away."

Emma walked back to her chair and sat down heavily.

"Then their strategy's working."

5

"You know who my husband is, don't you, Charlie?"

I nodded. "Zachariah Scott."

"No, I meant, do you know who he *is*?"

"Only what they say in the *LA Times*."

"Well..." She hesitated. "He's all that and more. And he thinks I know things I'm not supposed to know."

I nodded. "And do you?"

"Do I what?"

"Know things you're not supposed to know."

"Oh, do I ever, Charlie. Do I ever know things I'm not supposed to know."

Emma gripped her coffee mug with both hands and stared into it as if some of those things might be floating in the dark liquid.

"It's about money, of course. This is Hollywood. Everything is about money, but this is about *lots* of money. Money that's supposed to be going to writers and actors and production companies, but isn't."

She glanced up at me, then looked back down at her coffee.

"Zac's been moving millions of dollars overseas. Payments to people who don't exist. Companies in places like the Cayman Islands and Switzerland."

I kept my face empty, but I wasn't happy to hear any of that. We weren't just talking about a messy divorce anymore. We had leapfrogged right over that, and now we were apparently talking about large-scale financial fraud. The conversation was only five minutes along, and already I was fighting a major case of whiplash.

"How do you know this?"

"Because I used to help him with the paperwork for his production companies. Years back. Well before we separated. Zac's always been hopeless with paperwork, so I kept the files for the financial side of his companies for a while."

Emma stood up and walked back over to the railing again. The sun was getting stronger, and it sparkled on the foam of the incoming surf like diamonds scattered over the water.

"At first, I thought maybe it was just sloppy bookkeeping. Writers getting paid under different names for tax reasons, that sort of thing. It happens in this business."

"But?"

"But then I started paying closer attention. There was a writer named Marcus Holloway, for example. He was supposedly getting a hundred thousand dollars a month for script rewrites on one of Zac's series. Except Marcus Holloway is a ghost. I've tried to find him, but his social security number belongs to someone else. Marcus Holloway doesn't exist."

She turned back and faced me.

"And he's not the only one. There's a production company in Dublin that got huge payments for location scouting. Another one in Geneva that supposedly handled some European distribution rights. Neither of them is real."

I absorbed this without comment. In my divorce practice

back in Virginia, I'd seen plenty of spouses hiding assets. Offshore bank accounts, shell companies, even cash buried in the backyard. But this sounded much bigger and far more sophisticated.

"Do you have documentation?"

"Boxes of it. Bank statements, wire transfer records, invoices. I've been keeping copies of everything for years."

"Why?"

Emma sat back down and put her sunglasses on even though the deck overhang was keeping us in the shade.

"Because I knew this day was coming. I could see Zac pulling away from me, and I could see what he was doing with the money. I thought maybe if I had evidence of financial irregularities, it might protect me in a divorce."

I tried to keep my expression neutral, but inside I was calculating the legal implications. If Emma was right about what her husband was doing, she might be sitting on evidence of tax evasion, wire fraud, possibly even money laundering. Those were federal crimes, the kind that attracted the attention of the FBI and the IRS.

"Emma, you need to understand how serious this could be."

She nodded slowly. "I know. That's why I can't tell any of the lawyers here about it. They'll sell me out in a minute."

"I already told you, Emma, that I can't—"

"I just need help putting it all together, Charlie. Making sense of it. Seeing what I can prove and what I can't. Harry said you could do that for me."

"Oh, he did, did he?"

I let my eyes stray to the beach. A couple was walking their dog. A sleek golden retriever was running back and forth between them along the water's edge. They looked like they were simply enjoying a carefree moment in their lives, and I thought about how much I wished I could say the same thing.

"Emma, this is way beyond what I can help you with. Even if I were willing to take on a divorce case, which I'm not, this sounds like something that will require a team of investigators and forensic accountants."

"But you understand how these things work, don't you? You've dealt with hidden assets before."

"Not on the scale you're describing. And not when federal crimes were potentially involved."

I shook my head

"You need to find someone who specializes in complex financial fraud. Someone who has experience with federal investigations. Someone who can work with the FBI if it comes to that. I'm just a country lawyer from Virginia, Emma. I'm not up for something like that."

Emma's shoulders slumped.

"But that's the problem, Charlie. Any lawyer with that kind of experience in this town either works for people like Zac or wants to work for people like Zac. How do I find someone I can trust?"

I understood her dilemma. Of course, I did. Los Angeles was a company town, and the company was the entertainment industry. The big law firms that handled complex financial cases all had entertainment clients. They all moved in the same circles as Zac Scott.

"There have to be lawyers in LA who don't work in entertainment."

"Maybe. But there aren't any who don't want to."

I poured myself more coffee and tried to think.

"What about lawyers from outside LA? Someone from San Francisco or New York?"

"I've thought about that, but Zac has connections everywhere. And bringing in an outsider might tip him off that I'm onto what he's been doing."

Emma stood up and started pacing the small deck.

"Besides, I don't even know for sure that I'm right about all this. Maybe there are legitimate explanations for all these payments. Maybe I'm just a paranoid wife looking for a weapon to use against a husband who's through with her."

"Do you believe that?"

She stopped pacing and looked at me.

"No. I know Zac. I've been married to him for twelve years. I know when he's lying, and I know when he's scared. And right now, he's both lying *and* scared. That's why now *I'm* scared."

Emma leaned toward me and lowered her voice as if she were afraid of being overheard.

"Charlie, you could represent me if you wanted to, couldn't you? I mean officially. As my lawyer."

"Emma, I already told you—"

"Zac has the entire LA legal community locked up. Every lawyer who's anyone here either owes him favors or wants to work for him. I can't trust any of them."

She bounced up and began pacing again, her movements sharp and agitated.

"I tried calling three different law firms last week. Big firms with fine reputations for handling complex divorces. You know what happened? Within two hours of each call, Zac's lawyers contacted me and told me they had instructed the lawyers I called not to see me. Two hours, Charlie. Someone at those firms was feeding information directly to Zac."

I watched her pace and felt the familiar weight of other people's problems settling on my shoulders. This was exactly what I had come to California to get away from.

"Emma, I understand your predicament, but you don't know me. For all you know, I could be just as untrustworthy as anyone else."

She stopped pacing and looked at me directly.

"I know Harry. If you were his guy, then you're my guy, too."

"That isn't how it works. You can't just—"

"Harry told me what you did for him in Virginia. How you fought his wife's lawyers even when they had more money and more resources. How you never backed down even when the case got ugly."

I remembered Harry's case all too well. His wife was represented by a Northern Virginia firm with a well-earned reputation for ruthlessness. They had tried to claim half of the royalty residuals coming in from shows where Harry had done the music decades before he and his wife had married. And they refused to back down even when they realized they were wrong about her being entitled to a piece of those residuals. It had led to a nasty fight.

"That was different," I said. "Harry was getting screwed over by people who were trying to rewrite the law to suit themselves."

"And I'm getting screwed over by people who are trying to use their power and connections to get rid of me and keep me quiet."

Emma walked back and sat down again. She seemed calmer now, at least a little.

"Look, Charlie, I'm not asking you to move mountains. I just need someone who knows how financial schemes like this work. Someone who can help me understand what I have and figure out what it proves."

"Emma, you need someone with experience in white-collar criminal cases, not a guy who used to handle divorces in Virginia."

"But you understand how to trace hidden assets, don't you? You know how to follow money trails?"

I did know. Divorce work in Virginia had required me to become something of an expert at finding assets spouses tried to hide. Offshore accounts, shell companies, creative bookkeeping. I'd seen most of it.

"That's really beside the point. I've already told you, I don't practice law anymore."

"But you're a member of the California Bar now. Harry told me. You're licensed to practice here."

"Having a license doesn't mean I want to use it."

Emma was quiet for a moment, studying my face. When she spoke again, her voice was softer, more vulnerable.

"Charlie, I'm frightened. Zac has so much power in this town that he could make me disappear if he wants to. Or he could just decide to ruin my life with a few telephone calls."

What could I say to that? Maybe it was the part of me that had always been drawn to underdogs, or maybe it was just basic human decency, but I felt myself wavering.

"Even if I wanted to help you, Emma, I can't. I don't have an office, and I don't have a staff. I simply don't have the infrastructure to handle a case like this."

"I don't need an office. I need someone I can trust. Someone who won't sell me out to my husband."

She reached across and squeezed my arm.

"At least go through the stuff I've collected, Charlie. The documents. The bank records. Help me understand what I'm looking at. If you tell me I'm wrong, if you tell me there's nothing there, I'll drop it and just take whatever Zac is offering."

I stared out at the ocean, watching another set of waves roll in. I knew it would be a mistake to say I'd look at it. If I did that, I'd be stepping right back into the same swamp I had come to California to get out of. But I also knew I owed Harry Wells more than I could ever repay, and sending a friend of his away in the state Emma was in now seemed unthinkable.

"Just look at the documents I have," Emma prodded. "Nothing more."

"Just look at the documents?"

She nodded.

"And if I tell you to walk away from this after I look at them, you'll listen?"

"I'll listen."

I sighed and felt the last bits of my resistance crumbling.

"All right. I'll look at what you have, and I'll tell you what I think. But then that will be that."

Emma's face lit up with relief.

"Thank you, Charlie. Really. Thank you."

"Where are these documents?"

"At my house. Down on La Costa Beach. Give me a day or so to make sure I have everything organized for you. Can you come down, say the day after tomorrow?"

"I can do that."

"Perfect. I'll have everything organized for you by then. Make it about noon, and I'll get some lunch together for us."

Emma stood up and pushed her sunglasses back into place.

"Thank you, Charlie. You won't regret this, I promise you."

I walked her back through the house to the front door, but I knew perfectly well she was wrong about that. I regretted it already.

But Harry had given me a house on the most famous beach in America to live in for almost a year, and he had asked nothing of me in return. The least I could do was spend a few hours looking at some financial records for a friend of his and try to help her feel more prepared for the onslaught she was facing.

And then that would be that, wouldn't it?
What could possibly go wrong?

6

My second telephone call of the day came at a little after seven that evening. That officially made it a really busy day for me.

"Hello?"

"Charlie? It's Harry."

"Hey, man. What's up?"

"Did you talk to Emma today?"

"I did."

"What did she say?"

I hesitated. It suddenly occurred to me I was in a bit of an awkward position here.

Yes, Harry had asked me to talk to Emma, and I had talked to her as a favor to him, but I had also assured Emma that we were treating the conversation we were having as an initial client interview subject to lawyer-client privilege. That meant everything she said to me was privileged and confidential. Confidential from her husband. Confidential from any court. And confidential from everyone else, too. Including Harry.

"Uh ... Harry, that's a problem. She can tell you what she

said if she wants to, but *I* can't tell you. Emma asked for my assurance that the conversation was protected by lawyer-client privilege, and I gave it to her."

"So you've decided you'll be her lawyer? I'm flabbergasted. I thought you hated divorce cases."

"I do hate divorce cases, and no, I'm not going to be her lawyer. But our conversation is still considered an initial client interview, and it's fully protected by privilege even when I don't end up taking the case."

"You're getting kind of technical on me, aren't you, Charlie?"

"I'm a lawyer, Harry. Technical is what we do. Technical is who we are."

Harry grunted, but he let it go.

"Look," he said instead, "have you eaten dinner yet?"

"I was just thinking about it."

"Well, stop thinking, get in your car, and come down here and join me."

"Here?"

"The Polo Lounge. I'm buying."

The Polo Lounge at the Beverly Hills Hotel is legendary. If there is anywhere on the planet where all the glamor and magic conjured up by the word Hollywood is brought together in one place, it's got to be the Polo Lounge.

I'd never been there, never had any reason to go there really, so there was only one possible way to respond to Harry's invitation.

"I'm on my way," I said.

The Beverly Hills Hotel is the heart of Beverly Hills, both figuratively and literally. It's on Sunset Boulevard between North Crescent Drive and Hartford Way, and as with

Hollywood itself, the history of the Beverly Hills Hotel is a twentieth-century tale of glamor, riches, and romance.

The hotel was built in 1912, before there was even a city called Beverly Hills. Hoping to ignite a land rush, the Rodeo Land and Water Company bought land once owned by the Mexican government in the foothills of the Santa Monica Mountains and built a sprawling hotel in mission revival style on twelve acres. It had a white stucco exterior and terracotta-colored roof tiles, and they named it after Beverly Farms, the company president's home in Massachusetts. It cost them $500,000, which was a staggering sum in 1912.

When Beverly Hills was incorporated as a city in 1914, the hotel became its unofficial headquarters. Movie stars began checking in during the 1920s, and by the 1940s, the hotel had become head office for the Hollywood elite.

I turned off Sunset into the long circular driveway that curved gracefully past a fountain and pulled the Mustang up to the valet stand. Expensive cars were lined up there like jewels in Tiffany's window. Bentleys, Mercedes, Rolls-Royces, even a Ferrari and an Aston-Martin. My Mustang looked embarrassed to be left in that kind of company, but the valet took my keys with the same practiced smile he doubtless gave everyone.

The building sprawls across its landscaped grounds like a pink and green fever dream of old California. The color scheme sounds garish, but somehow it isn't. The signature pink stucco walls glow softly in the early evening light, and palm trees tower over manicured gardens where every flower looks like it has been individually selected and placed by someone with perfect taste. The whole place radiates such glamor that it's both inviting and intimidating at the same time.

The hotel's main entry is up a long, red-carpeted walkway that runs between pink stucco pillars supporting a green and white striped canopy. In the lobby, the furniture is all in shades of cream and gold that somehow manages to look warm instead of cold. Marble floors reflect the light from crystal chandeliers, and fresh flowers are displayed in massive arrangements that probably cost more than I made in a week back in Virginia.

The lobby buzzes with the energy of serious money moving through serious deals, and the staff moves with the well-choreographed efficiency that comes from years of catering to people who expect perfection as a matter of course. Men in thousand-dollar suits speak to each other in hushed tones while women who look like they had just stepped off some magazine cover glide past in designer dresses.

I felt like an intruder in my khakis and polo shirt, but nobody seemed to notice. Or if they did, they were too polite to let me see it.

The Polo Lounge itself occupies a corner of the hotel separated from the lobby by etched glass doors opening into a world of green leather banquettes, mahogany paneling, and the soft murmur of Hollywood's power elite conducting business over cocktails and dinner.

When I walked in, I saw Harry standing at a corner booth talking to the couple sitting in it. They looked vaguely familiar, and as I got closer, I saw why. I had watched them both on television at least a hundred times.

Robert Wagner and Stephanie Powers had starred in the television series *Hart to Hart* which had been a fixture on American television about ten years back. It was about a wealthy, glamorous couple who solved a crime every week when they weren't otherwise occupied with being wealthy and glamorous. Thinking back now, the show really didn't make a lot of sense, but at the time that hadn't really seemed important. Maybe we demanded less of our entertainment ten years ago.

Harry seemed to feel me approaching, and he glanced back over his shoulder and pointed me toward another one of the green leather booths that was in the opposite corner. He didn't seem inclined to make introductions.

Shortly after I sat down, Harry ended his conversation with Robert Wagner and Stephanie Powers, and he came over and slid into the booth across from me with a stony look on his face.

"Little prick," he grunted.

"What?"

"Not you, Charlie. Wagner. I did the music for the first season of *Hart to Hart*, and then that little prick fired me to bring in some asshole buddy of his."

"From the look of you standing there talking to them, I would have thought you were old pals."

"That's the way Hollywood works, Charlie. No permanent enemies, and no permanent friends. The guy you're pissing on today may have your future in his hands tomorrow, so we all just go on year after year, hating each other's guts and pretending we don't. What a way to live, huh?"

A waiter materialized at our table as if he had been right there all evening preparing for the precise moment when we would need him.

"Good evening, gentlemen. Can I start you with something to drink?"

Harry ordered a Macallan single malt, neat. I asked for a beer. I figured that a beer went well with being underdressed in these exalted surroundings.

"What kind of beer would you like, sir?"

I hesitated, and my eyes involuntarily shifted toward Harry. He laughed.

"If you order a Budweiser, Charlie, I'm leaving."

Nothing else came immediately to mind, so I sought shelter behind the waiter.

"What kind of beer do you—"

"Bring him an Anchor Steam," Harry interrupted.

"Yes, sir. One Macallan neat and one Anchor Steam coming up."

I had no idea what an Anchor Steam was, but I supposed I would find out soon enough, and besides, I wasn't about to admit to Harry that I didn't know. He might already think I was a bit of a rube, but I didn't want to hand over hard evidence he was absolutely right about that.

Harry made showbiz small talk until the waiter returned and served our drinks, and I just tried to nod and grunt in all the right places. Harry's scotch came in a heavy crystal glass that caught the light from the table's small lamp. The fancy beer that Harry had insisted on for me arrived with a frosted mug that looked like it had never seen anything so common as a Budweiser.

While the waiter was pouring my beer with considerably more ceremony than I thought it merited, I watched another waiter sweep up to the booth next to us carrying a telephone on a long cord. He plugged it into an outlet at the base of the booth, set it in the middle of the table, and slipped away. One of the two men in the booth, a swarthy guy in a shiny black suit who was wearing sunglasses inside at night, immediately grabbed it and began murmuring into it in a low voice.

Harry saw me staring and glanced back over his shoulder to see what I was looking at.

"Those phones are part of the legend around here," he said. "When someone calls for a phone at their table, it may look like they're just playing with themselves, but at least sometimes those people actually are as important as they're pretending to be. You can't imagine how many people have been made or destroyed through the years over the telephones in the Polo Lounge."

The waiter discreetly slipped away, and Harry took a hit of his whisky.

"Richard Nixon was even taken down over a Polo Lounge telephone."

I chuckled. "I never heard that."

"The high command of Nixon's reelection committee was staying here in 1972 during a west coast fundraising trip, and they were having a breakfast meeting right here in the Polo Lounge when one of the Watergate burglars, Gordon Liddy, call Jeb Magruder, who was vice-chairman of the committee. A telephone was duly brought to Magruder, and he took the call in one of these booths right here, maybe even the one we're sitting in now."

I could imagine that easily enough. The Polo Lounge still felt like 1972, and it certainly felt like a place where Nixon could still be president.

"They talked for a while, then Magruder went upstairs to one of the hotel's suites and met Attorney General John Mitchell and his special assistant Fred LaRue to pass on what Liddy had told him about the Watergate burglary. The hotel's records of the calls made from that suite on the morning after the burglary became the basis of the evidence which convicted each of those men of conspiracy and obstruction of justice, and eventually that was what forced Nixon to resign."

"That's a great story," I said. "I figured the phones were mostly just props."

"Sometimes they are," Harry nodded, "but those phones have made people and broken them, too. John Mitchell and Jed Magruder go on the broken list."

Harry knocked back the rest of his whisky and waved at the waiter. When he came over to the table, Harry pointed at his empty glass and then raised his eyebrows at me in a silent question. I shook my head, and the waiter scurried away.

"Anyway," Harry said, "it won't be long now before the Polo Lounge's famous phones are nothing but nostalgia."

He reached into his jacket pocket, pulled out some sort of device, and dumped it on the table between us. It was black and about six inches long. It looked like a thick candy bar.

"This is the future, Charlie. You don't need to plug a phone into the wall anymore. In another decade, everybody on earth will have one of these things in their pocket."

I knew portable telephones existed, of course, but the only one I'd actually seen before was one a client had back in Virginia. It had been about the size of a World War II walkie-talkie, and the guy carried it around in a briefcase. Harry's phone was a lot different. You really could carry it in your pocket.

"It's made by some European company," Harry told me before I could ask. "I don't really understand the technology, but they call them cellular phones because there are towers out there somewhere that create communication cells that these phones can reach. Then the signal somehow gets passed around among different cells until you reach whoever you want to talk to."

I picked up the phone and examined it. At the bottom, embossed into the plastic of the case, was the word *Nokia*, which I gathered was probably the name of the manufacturer. One side was covered by a numerical keypad and some other buttons I couldn't identify. At the top was a little window of some kind that I assumed displayed the number you were calling, or maybe the number that was calling you, or for all I knew, both. At the very top was a stubby little projection that I thought was likely an antenna.

Harry waved over a waiter and asked for a piece of paper and a pen. The waiter ripped a sheet off the pad he was carrying and handed it to Harry along with one of the ballpoint pens clipped in his breast pocket. Harry scribbled something on the sheet of paper and pushed it across the table to me.

"There you go," he said. "That's the number for my phone. You can dial that number from anywhere in the world and reach me no matter where I am."

"Don't I have to dial some kind of code first?"

"No code. Just the area code and number that are permanently assigned to this phone no matter where it is. It's like calling any telephone anywhere."

I picked up the piece of paper, folded it, and put it in my shirt pocket.

"How much does a phone like this cost?" I asked.

Now, I wasn't in the habit of asking people how much they paid for their toys, but Harry had brought the subject up, and it seemed a reasonable thing to ask.

"That one cost me a little over $2500."

My mouth slowly opened.

"Seriously? $2500? For a *telephone*?"

"It's not just a telephone, Charlie. It's a new way of life. Now you can reach me whenever you want and wherever I am. You don't even need to know where that is, and you don't care. You just dial my cellular phone, and there I am."

"You're telling me you paid $2500 for a telephone, and now anybody in the entire world who wants to talk to you can reach you anytime they want?"

Harry nodded.

"Gosh," I said, "it would be worth $2500 to me for people *not* to reach me anytime they felt like it."

Harry chuckled.

"You just watch, my young friend," he said. "These things may go for a silly price now, but in ten years that price will be down to almost nothing. Everybody will have one. Hell, I'll bet the day is coming when you can walk into a drugstore, buy a phone for $10, call anywhere in the world, then throw it away when you're done. You're looking at the future right here, Charlie."

I wasn't nearly so sure of that.

The price would always be a problem for most people, of course. I couldn't imagine how something that sold for $2500 now could sell for $10 in a few years.

On top of that, I wondered how many people really wanted to be reachable anytime and anyplace. I suddenly had a vision of a long row of men standing at urinals in a men's room somewhere, each of them directing a stream of urine with one hand and holding a little telephone against their ear with the other.

Surely not, I thought.

The world would never come to that, would it?

7

Harry waved the waiter back for his third drink. I was still nursing my first beer, so I shook my head again. I thought Harry was going a little fast, but it certainly wasn't my place to say so.

The waiter glided away, and Harry returned his little telephone to his jacket pocket.

"So tell me about Emma," he said.

"I can't tell you what she said, Harry. I already explained that."

"I'm not asking what she said. I'm asking what you think of her."

I considered that. What *did* I think of Emma Scott?

She was clearly intelligent, clearly anxious, and probably in over her head. She thought she was sitting on evidence of serious financial crimes her husband had committed, and assuming she was right about what her husband had been doing, she thought she could use that evidence to protect herself in the divorce action he had filed. Maybe she could. I didn't know nearly enough to decide yet.

So I measured out a careful answer for Harry. True, just careful.

"She seems like someone who's gotten caught up in something much bigger than she intended."

Harry nodded.

"That sounds about right. Emma's always been a straight shooter. Not naïve, exactly, but not the kind of person who looks for trouble either."

The waiter returned with Harry's drink, served it, and whisked away his empty glass.

"How well do you know her husband?" I asked.

Harry's expression darkened.

"Well enough to know you need to be careful, Charlie. Zachariah Scott is not someone you want to cross."

I waited without comment for the rest, which I knew from the look on Harry's face would be forthcoming in a moment.

"Hollywood is bastard feudalism, Charlie. There are half a dozen feudal baronies on our little magic island, and each one has its own army of nobles, knights, and peasants. Zachariah Scott is one of the barons. Actually, he's one of the most powerful ones. And there are stories about what happens to people who get in his way."

Harry took a sip of his scotch and stared into the amber liquid.

"What kind of stories?"

"The kind that don't get printed in the trades. Career-ending stories. People who suddenly can't get work anymore. Projects that mysteriously fall apart. Financing that disappears overnight. There are even some stories about ... oh, never mind."

I absorbed all that without comment. It wasn't exactly surprising. Hollywood ran on a web of power and connections.

Even I knew that. And people like Zac Scott sat at the very center of that web.

"Has he ever threatened Emma over this divorce?"

"If he has, she's never mentioned it to me. But he doesn't need to threaten her. Just being married to him for twelve years would be threat enough. That would have given her a very clear picture of what he's capable of."

"You don't think he might harm her physically, do you?"

Harry lifted his eyes to mine, and I saw a disquiet in them I had never before associated with Harry.

"Zac would never do his own dirty work. There are plenty of people around to do it for him."

"What are you talking about?"

"Look, Charlie, money is the fuel that keeps Hollywood running, and to keep a huge production operation like Zac's ticking over, a *lot* of money is required. There are always stories around that some of the money flowing through Hollywood might not come from the most respectable of sources."

Harry hesitated, and I waited.

"I'll just say that I've heard more stories like that about Zachariah Scott than any of the other players in this town," Harry finished quickly.

"Are you telling me that some of Scott's financing is dirty?"

"Worse."

"Worse? What's worse?"

Harry bobbed his head around in a gesture that could have meant anything, or nothing, but he fell silent.

My thoughts went immediately to the stories Emma had told me about her husband making questionable overseas payments to people and companies that might not even exist, payments for which she claimed to have documentation.

That's pretty much Money Laundering 101, isn't it? Take in capital from questionable sources, pay it out to fake companies in foreign tax havens for non-existent services, and suddenly that dirty money is all nice and clean. Well, almost. I knew it was a little more complicated than that. But not much.

I pressed Harry a bit.

"Why would someone as prominent as Zachariah Scott take the risk of dealing with dirty money? I don't see it."

"Never underestimate greed as a motivation, Charlie."

"I don't, but I still don't see—"

"And there's something else even more important than greed. It's arrogance, the arrogance that comes from having power. There are people in our business here who accumulate power to a point at which no one will ever tell them no again. A point after which they can't even *imagine* anyone ever telling them no again. They start to believe they can do anything they want without consequences."

I thought again about all that Emma had told me about Zachariah Scott's business operations. A picture was starting to come into focus here, and it wasn't one I particularly liked.

"Harry, are you telling me you've heard that Zachariah Scott is laundering money for criminals?"

"Worse."

"Worse *again*? What's worse? Organized crime? The fucking mafia?"

Harry took a hit on his drink, but he wouldn't look me in the eye. He fell silent, and I let him.

After a bit, Harry leaned back in the booth, and I caught his eyes moving around the room. He looked almost as if he were examining each part of it and carefully memorizing the way it looked right then.

"You know they're closing it at the end of this year," he suddenly said.

Harry clearly wanted to change the subject. He was a nice man, and it wasn't my place to interrogate him over the gossip he may have heard about Zachariah Scott, so I didn't make a fuss about it. I could always come back to the stories he almost told me another time. If I needed to. Which I really hoped I wouldn't.

"Closing what?" I asked.

"This place."

"They're closing the Polo Lounge?"

"They're closing the whole damn hotel. Not permanently, they say, but to remodel and..."

Harry lifted his hands and put little air quotes around the rest of his sentence.

"... *update* it."

"It looks fine to me."

"To me, too. They'll fuck up the whole place, of course. They'll change everything this hotel has meant to us for nearly a century, and they'll replace it with shit they'll call *updated* ...

He added another pair of air quotes.

"... shit no one wants, and absolutely no one likes."

"I hope not."

"You know what the real problem is, Charlie? Nobody respects tradition anymore. Whether they're remodeling a hotel or the whole damn television business, nobody respects the people who have built what we have now."

I thought I could work out pretty easily where Harry was going with this, but I just nodded and said nothing.

"This business is eating itself alive," he carried on. "Used to be, people like Zac had to at least pretend to care about the creative side of things. Now it's all about the deal. The money. The power. The entertainment business used to be about people. Now it's all corporate."

Harry's voice was getting louder, and I noticed a couple at the next table glancing in our direction.

"I've been working in this town for thirty years, and I've watched it change. Used to be about making good television, good movies. Now it's about making money. Nothing else."

I made what I hoped were appropriate sympathetic noises, but Harry wasn't really talking to me anymore. He was talking to himself, working through his anger and frustration.

"Take my meeting today. You know what they told me? They said my music was too sophisticated for modern audiences. Too sophisticated! Can you believe that? They want everything simple now. Dumbed down. They're looking for music that sounds like it was composed by a computer because the only thing these people ever hear now is stuff that *was* composed by a computer."

Harry finished his third scotch and waved at the waiter for another.

"Harry," I said as gently as I could, "maybe you should slow down a little."

"Why? Because I might embarrass myself at the Polo Lounge? Because I might say something inappropriate in front of all these very important people?"

His voice carried a bitter edge that made me uncomfortable. The couple at the next table weren't even pretending not to listen anymore.

"I'm not embarrassed, Charlie. I'm just a has-been composer who doesn't matter anymore. Nobody cares what I say or do."

The next drink arrived. Harry stared at it for a moment before picking it up.

"You know what the worst part is? They're probably right about me. Probably I am washed up. Probably the world has moved on without me, and I'm just too stubborn to admit it."

"That's not true, Harry."

"Isn't it? When was the last time you heard my music on television? When was the last time anyone under forty heard my music anywhere?"

Harry took another drink, larger than the previous ones.

"A man has got to matter, Charlie. He's got to contribute something to the world, or he's nothing. He's just taking up space."

There was something raw and desperate in Harry's voice, and it made my stomach roll. This wasn't just professional disappointment. This was existential fear, the terror of irrelevance that haunted everyone in a business where yesterday's success meant nothing at all.

"You matter to me, Harry. You gave me a place to live when I needed it most. You helped me get out of a situation that was killing me."

Harry looked at me, but the alcohol had made his eyes glassy and unfocused.

"That's just real estate, Charlie. Letting someone live in a house you're not using anyway doesn't contribute anything meaningful to the world."

I wanted to argue with him, to tell him it was sure as hell meaningful to *me*, but I could hear the rot in his voice. It was the decay of a man who had built his identity around his work and now felt that work slipping away from him. Arguing with him would have injured whatever dignity he had left.

So I tried to make a joke of it.

"Well, if you're going to be maudlin about it," I said.

But Harry didn't see the joke, and he didn't laugh. He just stared into his scotch and shook his head.

"Maudlin. Yeah, that's me. A maudlin old man feeling sorry for himself."

He picked up his drink and swirled it around, watching the amber liquid flash even in the low light.

"Ah, fuck it," he said after a moment. "I don't want to get drunk already. Let's order some dinner, and *then* we can get drunk."

Harry was pretty far gone when I managed to extract myself a couple of hours later. Maybe he was entitled to be. Who was I to judge?

Robert Wagner and Stephanie Powers had left sometime while we were eating. I noticed they hadn't come over to say goodbye to Harry.

Walking out of the Polo Lounge and through the lobby of the Beverly Hills Hotel gave me a bittersweet feeling. If Harry was right that they were closing the whole hotel at the end of the year to remodel it, I'd probably never see it like this again.

I could feel the weight of its history all around me. Some of that history was important, most of it was trivial, but whatever it was, it was still part of where we had come from.

Everyone from Richard Nixon's henchmen to Marilyn Monroe, Jimmy Stewart, and Burt Lancaster had walked through this lobby. If the gossip Harry tossed out about Zachariah Scott had any truth in it, maybe there had been a parade of organized crime figures through here, too. Probably had been.

Heroes or villains, it was all part of the history of this place. I wondered if I'd still be able to feel that history after the owners did whatever they were going to do to update the hotel. Probably not. It never really worked out that way, did it?

Harry was right. They'd fuck it up. People were always taking down old things and replacing them with what they described as updated versions. They never were, of course.

They never were anything really, except new, and the things they had replaced were gone forever.

I walked out to the valet stand and gave the kid the ticket for my car. He scampered away, and another man came out and gave his ticket to another of the valets. He was standing just at my right shoulder as we both waited for our cars, and I turned my head to nod politely.

But then I froze, and my mouth dropped open.

Right there in front of me, not two feet away, was Robert Redford.

I didn't manage the nod I had intended. I just stood there and stared. Of course, I did.

Redford grinned at me. "How you doing?" he asked.

"Sorry," I muttered, looking away in embarrassment. "You must get sick of that."

"It goes with the territory," Redford shrugged. "Nobody's forcing me to be Robert Redford."

It was a surreal moment. The valets were all off fetching cars, and there I was all alone with Robert Redford on the red carpet under the famous green and white striped canopy at the entrance to the Beverly Hills Hotel. We might have been just two old pals leaving the hotel after a pleasant dinner together.

I felt like I ought to say something else, but I had no idea what it could be, so I was deeply relieved to hear the rumble of the Mustang's big V8 coming up from the garage to rescue me. The valet pulled it to the curb and hopped out, holding open the driver's door.

"Yours?" Redford asked, inclining his head toward my restored Mustang. It sat there, top down, its candy-apple red paint job glittering in the light spilling out from the lobby of the hotel. It looked like the opening frame of a television series that incorporated Mom, apple pie, and better times.

"Yes, sir," I said. "It is."

"Wow, man, that's a beauty. That's America right there, isn't it?"

I bobbed my head in acknowledgment, but not a single sensible word from which I might compose a suitable response came to me. Finally, I blurted out the only three coherent words I could come up with.

"Good night, sir."

Then I tipped the valet, got into the Mustang, and drove off down the circular drive between the rows of towering palm trees.

When I got to Sunset Boulevard, I glanced up at my rearview mirror and looked back at Robert Redford. He was still there at the entrance to the Beverly Hills Hotel, and now he was still standing all by himself just looking off into the darkness.

Yeah, completely surreal.

I turned right on Sunset and began the long drive back to Malibu.

8

Two days later, I drove down to La Costa Beach to meet Emma Scott. The directions she had given me to get to her house took me to a gated driveway at a property that made Harry's place look like a beach shack

The house was a sprawling architectural statement in glass and steel that sat perched on a bluff overlooking the ocean. The structure seemed to defy gravity. Soaring walls of windows were cantilevered out over the edge of the slope as if the thing were preparing to launch itself off into the Pacific. The whole place was landscaped with native grasses and succulents arranged in beds of white gravel that made the property look like it had been built to be photographed for Architectural Digest. Which it probably had been.

This was the kind of house that spoke of serious money, the sort of money that hired architects whose names you were supposed to recognize and who charged fees that could fund a small college endowment. Even the gate looked expensive, all brushed stainless steel and glass panels.

Emma met me at the front door wearing the same kind of

expensively casual clothes she had worn to our first meeting. But there was something different about her today. She appeared to me to be slightly nervous for some reason.

"Charlie, thank you for coming. I hope this wasn't too much trouble."

"Not at all," I said. "Nice place."

What a lame thing to say, I thought. It made me sound like a rube. Maybe I *was* a rube.

Emma led me into the magazine-layout-perfect living room. Floor-to-ceiling windows offered a panoramic view of the Pacific, and the furniture had been arranged with the sort of deliberation that announced a professional decorator had positioned every last piece of it.

"I've organized some lunch for us. Perhaps we can eat while you go through the documents."

"That's fine."

"Can I get you something to drink now? Coffee? Water?"

"Coffee would be great."

She disappeared into what I assumed was the kitchen, leaving me alone with the view. From here, I could see the beach stretching north through Malibu, including the section where Harry's house sat. I suddenly realized how exposed these beachfront properties were. Anyone with a decent pair of binoculars could sit in a hundred different places and watch the comings and goings of every last one of us.

Emma returned with two mugs of coffee and gestured toward a seating area near the windows.

"Before we start, I need to ask you something again," she said as we sat down. "I can trust you, can't I? You're not one of those lawyers who say one thing and do another?"

The question stung a little. Hadn't she believed me the first time we talked about this? I took a breath and absorbed the insult.

"You can trust me, Emma," I said, and left it at that.

"I'm sorry. I didn't mean that the way it probably sounded. It's just that I've never been in a situation like this before, and I'm scared of making the wrong move."

She set her coffee mug down and looked at me directly.

"I need you to represent me, Charlie. Not just look at documents. Actually become my lawyer and represent me."

"Emma, we've been through this. I told you I would look at what you have and give you some advice, but that's all."

"But you see what I'm up against. Every lawyer in this town is compromised when it comes to my husband. You're the only one I can trust."

She leaned forward, her voice taking on an urgent quality.

"Please. I know you don't really want to practice divorce law anymore, but I'm desperate here. I need someone who won't sell me out."

I knew that was my cue to repeat my refusal one more time, and every instinct I had was screaming at me to walk away from this as quickly as I could. But the desperation in Emma's voice was real, and it gave me pause. I felt myself waver.

"Let me at least see what you have first," I said after a moment. "Then we can talk about next steps."

Emma seemed to relax slightly, but she wasn't finished pressing.

"But everything we discuss today is covered by attorney-client privilege, right? Whether you represent me or not?"

"This is an extension of our initial client interview," I said. "So yes, it would be covered."

I marked the look on her face as relief.

"Good. I just need to know that what I'm about to show you can't be used against me somehow."

I hoped I was right about the privilege issue. The truth was, the finer points of California law on the issue weren't as clear to me as I would have liked. But Emma needed reassurance, and right then, giving it to her seemed more important than my uncertainty.

"Show me what you have," I said.

Emma stood up and walked to a cabinet built into the wall near the windows. She opened it and dragged three bankers boxes out onto the floor. What everyone called bankers boxes were actually just heavy cardboard cartons specifically made for the secure storage of large numbers of documents. Each of these particular boxes was cream-colored with dark brown stripes running down both sides. They were all identical in size. About three feet long, maybe eighteen inches wide, and another eighteen inches deep. And they all had reinforced sides, removable lids, and handhold cut-outs on both ends to make them easier to lift.

If these three boxes were all filled with paper, I was already in trouble. When Emma told me she had some documents she wanted me to look at, I suppose I pictured in my mind a small stack of paper. Maybe a couple of files. Now I found myself looking at what could have been the overflow from the National Archives.

"And this is just the beginning," she said.

I was nearly slack-jawed.

"Holy shit," I said. "You're telling me you have even *more* stuff than this?"

"I have five more boxes out in the garage exactly like these three."

"Where did you get all this stuff?"

"I copied everything I saw for years and just stored it away."

I was completely flummoxed, and I'm sure it showed on my face. It would take weeks just to sort through this much paper, let alone read it and try to understand it.

"Let me get our lunch organized," Emma announced, "while you make a start."

I pulled the first box over to the couch and sat down.

The coffee table was large enough to use to spread things out, so I started pulling stuff from the box more or less at random and sorting what I found into rough piles by type. Little clouds of dust drifted into the air and floated away in the sunlight every time I took something out.

There were manila file folders that seemed well-organized with documents that had been hole-punched and clipped into them using metal tabs mounted at the top, but there were other folders that just had loose papers jammed into them. There were even piles of papers stuck between files that weren't collected into anything.

Nothing seemed to be in any kind of order. Not by type of record, and certainly not chronological. I found bank statements mixed in with wire transfer orders, and financial statements for companies I'd never heard of jumbled together with service contracts of various kinds. I even found documents written in a language I thought I recognized as Japanese, but I really didn't know for sure. Maybe it was actually Chinese or Korean.

One thing I could see clearly was that all the documents Emma had were photocopies. Some of them were crooked and blurred, as if they had been hastily made when no one was looking.

After one dive into the box, I looked down at the stack of papers in my hand and saw a wire transfer order for $850,000 to something called Emerald Isle Productions in Dublin. The next document in the stack was a contract for location scouting services with the same company, but the contract was dated three months after the wire transfer. That seemed backwards.

I found invoices from a company called Alpine Media Services in Geneva amounting to over two million dollars for something described as *European distribution consulting*. The invoices were professionally printed, but something about them felt off. The letterhead looked too clean, too generic.

Emma returned carrying a tray with two Chinese chicken salads that she had obviously had delivered and two glasses of iced tea.

Okay, I thought, she's *not a cook*.

Emma set the tray down on a round table by the windows.

"Bring whatever you're looking at over here and let's have lunch."

"Where are the originals of all these?" I asked, holding up copies of several bank statements.

"Zac had everything picked up when he moved out."

"Remind me when that was."

"A little less than a year ago."

I stopped sorting and looked at her.

"So there's nothing here more recent than that."

"No, nothing." She hesitated. "Is that a problem?"

It was, and it wasn't. Financial fraud cases were built on patterns, on showing a consistent scheme running over time. If all Emma had were documents from years back, it would weaken her position. Of course, I guess that depended on what her position actually turned out to be. She was just trying to develop some leverage to protect herself in her husband's divorce filing. She wasn't the United States Attorney preparing to try a criminal case.

I scooped up one of the piles of documents, took it over to the table where Emma had set out lunch, and plunked it down. Picking up my fork, I began nibbling at the salad while I skimmed the paper on top. It was a wire transfer authorization for $500,000 to Marcus Holloway, the writer Emma had mentioned, the one she said didn't exist. The transfer was dated eighteen months ago. According to the attached invoice, Holloway had been paid for *script revisions and story development* on something called *Metro Squad*.

"What's *Metro Squad*?" I asked.

"One of Zac's cop shows. It ran for six seasons and made him a fortune."

I set that document aside and picked up another one. This was a contract with a company called Pacific Rim Productions for *Asian market development*. The fee was three million dollars, paid two years ago.

"Ever heard of Pacific Rim Productions?"

Emma shook her head. "Never."

I was already starting to see the pattern. Legitimate-sounding company names, professional-looking contracts, and massive payments for vague services. It was sophisticated enough to pass casual inspection, but sloppy enough that someone who knew what to look for would quickly spot the red flags.

The wire transfers all went to banks in countries with strict banking secrecy laws. The Cayman Islands, Switzerland, Ireland, Singapore. Classic money laundering destinations.

The gossip Harry had repeated to me while we were drinking in the Polo Lounge immediately came back to me, but I pushed it away. The documents said what they said. Gossip didn't change that.

I pushed the Chinese salad around on my plate and tried to calculate what I was looking at. At a glance, it appeared Emma really did have the goods. Zac Scott had clearly sent many millions of dollars offshore over the past few years, most of it labeled as payments that were questionable at best. But proving that would require more than photocopied bank statements. It would require access to the actual bank records and cooperation from foreign financial institutions. Maybe even a federal task force.

"Emma," I said, "this is way beyond what any divorce lawyer can handle. This is federal prosecutor territory."

She set down her fork and looked at me.

"I know, Charlie. But I'm not trying to get Zac charged with a crime. I'm just trying to protect myself in a divorce case. If Zac understands the damage I can do, maybe he'll back off, and we can settle all this as if we were actually civilized people."

It was a thought, but in my experience, things like this seldom worked out like that. When you threaten people, they don't necessarily back down. They're more likely to come straight at you.

"What exactly do you want me to do with all this?" I asked.

"Help me organize it. Figure out what it proves and what it doesn't prove. Find me enough ammunition in it that Zac's lawyers will have to take me seriously."

I looked down at the scattered documents. Bank statements, wire transfers, contracts, invoices. Pieces of what might be a massive financial crime, or might just be sloppy record-keeping by a busy television producer.

"This is going to take time, Emma. Weeks, maybe months to go through it all properly."

"I have time. Do you?"

I didn't know what to say to that, so I said nothing at all.

We finished our lunch largely in silence. For her part, Emma just didn't seem to have much to say, and for mine, I had been intimidated into near speechlessness by discovering the enormity of the task I had so casually agreed to undertake.

But what was I going to do now other than my best to make

some sense out of all this? I could hardly tell Emma that I'd changed my mind about helping her now that I had discovered what it involved. And I certainly couldn't tell Harry I was taking back the favor he had asked of me. I had dug this hole for myself, and there was nothing left for me to do but keep digging until I found a way out the other side of it.

I took a couple of more bites of salad just out of politeness, then I put my fork down and pushed the plate away.

"Now that I see what's involved, Emma, the only thing that makes sense is for me to take all this stuff back to Harry's house and go through it over the weekend. This isn't something I can do in an afternoon. It's going to take a while, and I need to concentrate."

She nodded, but she didn't say anything.

"Can you come down to Harry's place on Monday?" I asked her. "Let's say about two in the afternoon? By then, I ought to have some kind of handle on what you've got here, and we can have a serious conversation about it."

Emma looked fretful about something. I didn't know what it was, but it was impossible to miss.

"What?" I asked.

"This is all I've got, Charlie. If you take it with you, you have to promise me nothing will happen to it."

I didn't blame her for her concern. After all, she didn't really know me, and here I was asking to pack up the things she thought were protecting her from her husband and just walk away with them.

"I'll guard them with my life," I said.

At the time I said that, I thought it really didn't mean much of anything. That was just an expression, right?

Imagine my surprise when I discovered I might actually have to do that.

9

The next morning, I sat on the deck drinking coffee, watching the ocean, and reading the *LA Times*.

The election was over. An obscure governor from Arkansas, Bill Clinton, would be moving into the White House in January, and now everybody was sick of politics, even the *LA Times*. The *Times* had reverted to its traditional strength: the grotesque crime stories that seemed to sprout in LA like weeds after a rainy winter.

Why did so many shocking crimes seem to occur in LA? Didn't places like Iowa and Pennsylvania have criminals, too? If they did, they were certainly no competition for the ones LA produced.

The big story now was Lyle and Erik Menendez, whose trials were supposed to begin in a few months. The brothers had shotgunned their parents to death in their Beverly Hills mansion back in 1989, then spent the insurance money on Rolex watches and tennis lessons before the police caught up with them. The prosecution claimed it was premeditated murder for financial gain. The defense was going with emotional abuse, claiming that years of repeated sexual molestation by their father had driven the boys to snap.

Both sides were gearing up for what promised to be the trial of the decade. The prosecutors had hired additional staff and were building their case around financial records that they thought showed the boys had been planning to kill their parents for months. The defense was hauling in expert witnesses on childhood trauma and post-traumatic stress disorder by the busload.

The media circus was already in full swing. Book deals were being negotiated. Movie rights were being discussed. The whole thing was beginning to feel less like real life than a big-budget Hollywood production, which I supposed was fitting for murders that had occurred in Beverly Hills.

I didn't recognize the names of the lawyers being mentioned as defense counsel for the Menendez brothers, but I found myself feeling sorry for them, whoever they were. Defending clients everyone knew had committed such a brutal crime, and trying to dream up ways to justify what they did, couldn't be much fun. At least in a divorce case, the worst thing that usually happened was that people screamed at each other about money and furniture. Nobody got shotgunned in the family room. Well, not very often anyway.

Maybe there was something worse than trying divorce cases after all, I thought. Maybe representing a couple of vicious, greedy little shits like the Menendez brothers for murdering their parents was worse. A lot worse.

My coffee was getting cold, but I kept reading. There was something mesmerizing about the way so many LA crime stories combined ordinary suburban settings with acts of extraordinary violence. Shopping malls where gang shootings erupted. Quiet residential streets where bodies turned up in dumpsters. Expensive restaurants where drug deals went wrong. Beverly Hills mansions where families slaughtered each other.

This was still Raymond Chandler's Los Angeles updated for the 1990s, wasn't it? Exactly the same fundamental human failings still played out in different ways year after year, all set against the same backdrop of swaying palm trees and glittering swimming pools.

Finally, I folded up the newspaper and dropped it onto the table next to my chair. The waves were rolling in with a steady rhythm that made it easy to lose track of time. Four-foot sets, maybe five, with long intervals between the larger swells. Flocks of seagulls rode the ocean breeze, their honking cries blending with the booming of the surf. It was perfect beach weather today. It was exactly the kind of morning that had made millions of people vow to move to California in the first place.

I finished my coffee and stood up. I had problems of my own to deal with. Five bankers boxes full of problems stuffed into the trunk of the Mustang. Emma had eight boxes in all, of course, but the five she had in the garage were all I could fit into the trunk, so I had left the other three boxes she had inside the house with her. I'd worry about those later. Or maybe not.

Okay, I told myself, time to stop stalling and get on with it.

The Mustang sat in the garage gleaming under the overhead lights like it belonged in a vintage car museum instead of hauling around evidence of possible federal crimes. I popped the trunk and looked down at the boxes Emma had given me.

They were heavy, and I had to lug them into the house one at a time. Back and forth I went until I had all five lined up on the dining room table. Now Harry's house felt less like a borrowed beach house and more like a temporary office. I think I liked it more as a borrowed beach house.

I pulled out a chair and sat down, then I sighed heavily and pulled the first box toward me.

This was going to take a while.

I started pulling papers from the first box and sorting them into rough categories. Bank statements here, wire transfer authorizations there, contracts and invoices in their own piles. The work was tedious, mind-numbing, and exactly the kind of document review that had made me hate practicing law in the first place.

Every few minutes, I found myself asking the same question: *How the hell did I get myself into this?*

And the answer was always the same.

I'd gotten into it the way I always got myself into things. By saying yes when I should have said no. By letting other people's problems become my problems. By thinking I could help someone without getting sucked back into the very swamp I had worked so hard to get myself out of.

I picked up another wire transfer authorization. This one was for $750,000 to something called Celtic Media Partners in Dublin. The attached invoice claimed the money was for *international co-production development,* but the invoice was dated two weeks after the wire transfer went out. Another backwards transaction.

How many fake companies had Zac Scott created? I was already losing count. Emerald Isle Productions, Alpine Media Services, Pacific Rim Productions, Celtic Media Partners. The names all sounded professional and legitimate, but none of the companies appeared to exist anywhere except on these invoices and wire transfer orders.

I set the Celtic Media document aside and reached for another one. This time, it was a bank statement from First

Cayman Bank showing a deposit of two million even into an account belonging to something called Westminster Holdings. The deposit had been made the same day as a wire transfer from Zac's production company to Westminster Holdings for the same amount. At least that transaction made sense chronologically, even if Westminster Holdings was probably as fake as all the rest.

The problem was that sorting through all this properly would require cross-referencing every wire transfer with every invoice, every bank statement with every contract. It would take a team of paralegals weeks to organize it all, and then it would take another team of forensic accountants months to trace where the money actually went.

I just had me. And I'd promised Emma Scott I would make sense of all this by Monday afternoon.

I leaned back in my chair and rubbed my eyes. The California sunshine was streaming through the windows, the ocean was sparkling just outside, and here I was sitting in a dining room, drowning in old financial documents. This certainly wasn't the new life I'd imagined for myself.

But what choice did I have now? I couldn't just dump everything back in the boxes and tell Emma I'd changed my mind. I owed Harry too much for that. And Emma was a decent woman in over her head and counting on me to help her figure out what she was dealing with. I couldn't simply walk away and let her drown.

I stood up and went to the kitchen to make a fresh pot of coffee. Every noteworthy accomplishment on earth begins with a fresh pot of coffee, doesn't it?

While the coffeemaker bubbled, I watched Ryan O'Neal next door working out on his deck, pounding away at the heavy bag he had hung out there. He was hitting the bag with his gloves so hard that the rhythmic *thump-thump-thump* carried through the closed windows and into Harry's kitchen. At least somebody was having a productive morning, even if it involved nothing more complicated than pounding the stuffing out of a leather-covered bag.

When I came back with my coffee, I stood and stared for a moment at the five boxes lined up on the dining table. Thousands, probably tens of thousands of documents to sort through. Financial records that might prove Zac Scott was laundering millions of dollars, or might just prove he was sloppy with his bookkeeping.

I sat back down and pulled another handful of papers from the box, but when I began to sort them into the piles I had created, I stopped and stared. There were maybe a dozen more documents written in the same language I had noticed when I first poked through one of the boxes at Emma's house. Was it really Japanese? I thought it probably was, but I couldn't be sure without asking somebody.

On top of everything else, did I now need to find a translator to figure out what I was looking at here? That wasn't going to happen by Monday. Probably not at all, but quite certainly not by Monday. I made a mental note to ask Emma if she had any idea why these documents were here and if, as I suspected, they were indeed written in Japanese. After all, she had made the copies. Maybe she had some idea what they were.

I told myself to stop muttering and get back to work, but as I pulled out the next pile of documents, the same thought echoed over and over in my head.

This was exactly what I came to California to get away from. And now here I was, right back in the middle of it.

Two hours later, I'd had enough. My eyes were burning from staring at photocopied documents, my back ached from hunching over the table, and I was developing a serious case of cabin fever. The beautiful Malibu day was slipping away while I sat inside sorting through other people's problems.

I needed a break. I needed food. I needed to get out of the house and remember why I'd moved to California in the first place.

I grabbed my keys and headed out to fire up the Mustang. The Malibu Country Mart was only a few miles up the Pacific Coast Highway, and they had a decent deli where I could grab a sandwich. Then I could take that sandwich out to a bench in the garden and clear my head by watching the yummy mummies chase their children around the playground while I ate.

The Malibu Country Mart had a carefully cultivated casual elegance that marked it as a place where wealthy people went to pretend they were just regular folks doing regular folk things like buying groceries and eating lunch. The buildings were arranged around a central courtyard like a small Mediterranean village, all weathered wood and climbing vines, with a little children's playground in the middle next to a fountain that gurgled pleasantly in the afternoon sun.

I walked into the deli and grabbed a ham and cheese on rye, then I decided to live dangerously and added a bag of chips and a Diet Coke. The woman behind the counter was probably in her sixties, with sun-weathered skin and a no-nonsense attitude that suggested she had been feeding people for decades without ever developing any particular interest in impressing them.

"You want mustard on that?" she asked.

"Please."

She slapped the sandwich together with practiced efficiency and handed it to me in a white paper bag. I paid for everything and walked back outside, looking for somewhere to sit that would give me a break from Emma Scott's financial documents and the mess I'd gotten myself into.

The garden area behind the main buildings was exactly what I needed. Mature oak trees provided shade over scattered wooden benches, and beyond them lay a playground where a handful of perfectly groomed mothers supervised their equally perfect children. The whole scene looked like something out of a catalog for expensive suburban sportswear.

I found a bench under one of the oaks and unwrapped my sandwich. The ham was probably organic, the cheese was definitely imported, and the bread had that dense, grainy texture that marked it as seriously expensive. Even the simple stuff was complicated here in Malibu.

The playground buzzed with the sort of controlled chaos that happens when small children with boundless energy meet parents with boundless money. The mothers all looked like they had stepped straight out of a fitness magazine. Perfectly styled hair, designer workout clothes, and careful makeup that was supposed to look natural but probably took an hour to apply.

They called to their children in voices that carried just the right mix of authority and affection.

"Madison, don't throw sand at Harper."

"Sebastian, use your words, not your hands."

"Brooklyn, come have some organic apple slices."

The kids, meanwhile, seemed blissfully unaware that they were living a carefully orchestrated fantasy. They ran and climbed and screamed with the same abandon children showed everywhere, their designer clothes getting dirty despite their mothers' best efforts to keep them pristine.

I bit into my sandwich and watched a little girl with blonde pigtails attempt to climb a wooden fort while her mother hovered nearby, ready to catch her if she fell. The mother wore designer yoga pants that probably ran close to four figures and a tank top that advertised some boutique fitness studio in Santa Monica.

"Be careful, Sage," the mother called out. "Remember what we talked about. Use your core muscles."

The kid ignored her completely, of course. She scrambled up the wooden structure like a monkey, her designer sneakers finding purchase on surfaces that would have defeated most adults. When she reached the top, she turned and waved at her mother with the triumphant grin of someone who had just conquered Everest.

Another mother was trying to interest her son in something that, from what I could overhear, was an educational toy designed to teach him about sustainable agriculture. The boy, who couldn't have been more than four, kept wandering away to chase a butterfly that had made the mistake of landing in the playground.

"Preston, come back. We need to practice our sorting skills."

Preston had no interest in sorting skills. He was completely absorbed in his pursuit of the butterfly, running in circles with his arms outstretched like he thought he could catch it if he just tried hard enough.

I finished half of my sandwich and opened the bag of chips. They were some kind of artisanal variety made with sea salt and herbs I couldn't identify. Even the junk food was upscale here.

A woman pushing a stroller walked past my bench talking animatedly to her toddler who was probably sleeping peacefully despite her chatter and the noise from the playground. She gave me the once-over, then nodded pleasantly.

Apparently, I didn't look like a desperate character. Little did she know.

The guilt started creeping in around the time I finished the chips. Here I was, sitting in a pleasant garden watching other people's children play, while five boxes of financial documents sat on Harry's dining room table waiting for me to make sense of them. Emma Scott was counting on me to figure out what her husband had been doing with millions of dollars, and what she ought to do now. She was scared, she was isolated, and she had nowhere else to turn.

And here I was sitting on a bench eating artisanal potato chips and watching perfectly groomed mothers in expensive yoga pants chase after their designer children.

I crumpled up the chip bag and the sandwich wrapper and stood up. The mothers were still calling instructions in their carefully modulated voices. The kids were still ignoring them and having a great time doing it. The fountain was still gurgling, the oak trees were still providing shade, and I was still a guy who had made promises he wasn't sure he could keep.

Time to get back to work and at least try.

I walked to where I had parked the Mustang and fired up the engine. The V8 rumbled to life with its familiar growl, and I rolled slowly across the parking lot toward the Pacific Coast Highway.

The ocean stretched away to the west, blue and endless. It was completely indifferent to all my misgivings and self-doubts today, and it would be equally indifferent to them tomorrow.

Be the ocean, I told myself. *Be the ocean.*

10

I didn't even make it out of the parking lot before I changed my mind about going back to work.

When I drove by Malibu Books, I could see Pele moving among the shelves organizing books. I stopped in front and sat there a moment, debating whether or not I should go inside. It didn't look like there were any customers in the store, so maybe she wouldn't mind a visit.

What the hell? I decided. *All those boxes will still be sitting there waiting for me whenever I get back to Harry's house, won't they?*

The door chimed when I pushed it open, and Pele looked up from behind the counter where she was unpacking a box of books.

"Charlie," she said, and her smile appeared to say that she was genuinely pleased to see me. "Back for more Raymond Chandler?"

"Actually, I came to see if you make coffee as well as you sell books."

She laughed with the same rolling guffaw I remembered from our first meeting.

"I do make coffee. It's terrible coffee, but I make it. Want some?"

"Terrible coffee sounds perfect right about now."

She disappeared into the back of the store, and I heard the sounds of an ancient coffeemaker being coaxed into life. The bookstore felt different in the afternoon light than it had at night, warmer somehow. I wandered over to the mystery section and found myself looking at the same shelves I'd browsed a few nights before.

"So, what brings you back?" Pele called from somewhere behind the poetry section. "Getting tired of the beach life already?"

She emerged carrying two mismatched mugs and handed me one. The coffee was indeed terrible, but it was hot and caffeinated, so it wasn't a complete loss.

"You look like a man with something on his mind," she said, settling onto the stool behind the counter.

I took a sip of the coffee and tried to figure out how to answer that without telling her more than I should.

"I've been asked to help someone with a legal problem. A divorce case, actually. The woman mentioned that she knows you."

Pele's expression shifted slightly, becoming just a little guarded.

"Really? What's her name?"

"Emma Scott."

Pele shook her head slowly.

"I don't think I know anyone named Emma Scott."

Something in the way she said it made me think she wasn't being entirely truthful about that, but I couldn't put my finger on what it was. Maybe it was just the way her eyes didn't quite meet mine when she spoke.

"She lives down on La Costa Beach," I said. "Married to a television producer named Zachariah Scott."

"Sorry. Doesn't ring a bell."

I studied Pele's face, looking for some tell that would confirm my suspicion she was lying. But why would she do that? She just sipped her coffee and looked back at me with what seemed like genuine puzzlement.

"Huh. Maybe I misunderstood what she said."

"So you're a lawyer," Pele said, steering the conversation away from Emma Scott. A teasing note entered her voice. "I should have guessed. You have that lawyer look about you."

"What kind of look is that?"

"Serious. Slightly suspicious of everything. Like you're always waiting for someone to lie to you."

"Maybe that's because someone usually *is* lying to me."

I took another sip of the terrible coffee and realized Pele was studying me through those big black glasses perched at the end of her nose.

"What kind of law do you practice?"

"I don't. I'm retired."

"You look a little young to me to be retired."

"Thank you," I smiled.

"So let me rephrase the question, Counselor. What kind of law *did* you practice before you took early retirement?"

"I did divorce work, mostly. It wasn't my choice. It was what the firm that hired me assigned me to. I hated it."

"Then why are you involved in a divorce case now?"

It was a simple question, but I didn't have a simple answer. Why *was* I doing this, really? Why had I agreed to help Emma Scott when I'd come to California specifically to get away from exactly this kind of work?

"That's a very good question," I said finally. "I wish I had a very good answer."

"Maybe you do it because you're good at it."

"Being good at something you hate isn't much of a recommendation."

"Or maybe you do it because people need help, and you can't bring yourself to turn them away."

That hit closer to home than I was comfortable with. Time to change the subject.

I set my coffee mug down on the counter and looked around. "What made you decide to open a bookstore?" I asked.

"Like I told you before, temporary insanity. Although it's starting to feel like it might be permanent insanity."

"Having second thoughts?"

"Daily. Do you know how hard it is to make money selling books in a place where most people think reading is something you do at red lights?"

I laughed despite myself.

"But you're still here."

"Still here. Though that might just be stubbornness."

Pele stood up and walked over to the window, looking out at the parking lot where my Mustang sat gleaming in the afternoon sun.

"That's a beautiful car," she said.

"Thanks. It's my one big extravagance."

"What's the point of living in California if you don't have a beautiful car?"

"Exactly."

She turned back to me.

"So, this divorce case you're working on. Is it complicated?"

I thought about the five boxes of financial documents sitting on Harry's dining room table and Emma Scott's fears about her husband's power in Hollywood.

"More complicated than I expected when I agreed to help."

Then something occurred to me.

"Say," I asked Pele, "you don't happen to read Japanese, do you?"

"What?"

"Japanese. Do you read Japanese?"

"Seriously? Why would you suddenly ask me that? Do I *look* like someone who reads Japanese?"

"I came across some documents written in Japanese, and I need to find out what they're all about."

Pele made a face. "So you weren't commenting on what you've perceived about my intellectual depth. You were just trolling for a free translator."

"So, I guess that's a no then. You're telling me you don't read Japanese, despite your obvious intellectual depth."

She grinned and shook her head.

"Know anyone around here who does?"

She grinned some more and shook her head again.

"Then I guess I'm shit out of luck. This case is going to eat me alive if I can't figure out some way to get out of it."

"They always do, don't they? Legal cases, I mean. They start simple and then become monsters."

"How do you know that?"

"I read a lot of legal thrillers. Plus, my grandfather was a lawyer."

Something in the way she said that made me pay attention.

"What kind of lawyer?"

"Criminal defense, mostly. A lot of civil liberties work. He was pretty well known back in the day."

"Is he still practicing?"

"Retired. But he still thinks like a lawyer. Still reads the law journals and second-guesses every case he reads about in the newspaper."

I finished my terrible coffee and set the mug down on the counter.

"You want some more?"

I nodded. "Sure."

"No, you don't," Pele laughed.

"I do. Honest."

She gave me a look I couldn't quite put a name to, scooped up my mug, and disappeared among the bookcases to wherever she kept the coffeemaker.

While she was getting the coffee, I wandered behind the counter to look at some of the framed photographs hanging on the wall. They had obviously been taken at book signings and other events at the store. Local authors posing with customers, groups of people holding wine glasses at what looked like literary gatherings, and that sort of thing.

I found myself studying the faces, wondering if I recognized anyone. Most of them were strangers, but there was something familiar about one of the older men in several of the pictures. He was tall and lean with long hair and the kind of commanding presence that suggested he was accustomed to being the most important person in the room.

I knew that face, but I couldn't put a name to it. Then I spotted a photograph in which the same man was standing next to a display of biographies. He was smiling broadly and had his arm draped over the shoulders of a woman who had to be Pele. The nameplate on the bottom of the frame read, "Sandy Bouchier Book Signing - October 1991."

And then it hit me why I had recognized the man's face. Sandy Bouchier was one of the most famous criminal defense lawyers of the past forty years.

Wait. Bouchier? *Sandy Bouchier?*

Pele Bouchier?

The pieces suddenly fell into place with an almost audible click.

"Find something interesting?" Pele asked, returning with my refilled coffee mug.

I turned to face her and pointed at the photograph.

"That's Sandy Bouchier."

She followed my gaze to the wall of pictures and nodded.

"My grandfather."

Of course. How had I missed it? The same last name, her casual mention of a grandfather who was a famous lawyer, and even her obvious comfort discussing legal matters. She was Sandy Bouchier's granddaughter.

"Jesus," I said. "Sandy Bouchier is your grandfather? Really?"

"Guilty as charged, Counselor."

I felt like an idiot for not putting it together sooner. Sandy Bouchier wasn't just any famous lawyer. The man was an outright legend. A former Supreme Court clerk who had built a practice defending everyone from civil rights activists to white collar criminals and the kind of high-profile murder defendants whose cases dominated the evening news.

"I can't believe I didn't make the connection before. When I was in law school, Sandy Bouchier was my idol."

Pele smiled at that, but there was something almost shy about her expression.

"He was *everybody's* idol," I went on when she said nothing. "Everybody I knew at UVA wanted to *be* Sandy Bouchier. He was the gold standard for lawyering."

"He'd be pleased to hear that. He still reads everything written about his famous cases, still argues with the television whenever he sees lawyers being interviewed about their strategies."

"How old is he now? He must be in his seventies."

"A little over eighty, actually, but he's healthy as a horse. Lives in Brentwood with a maid and a driver, reads three newspapers every morning, and acts like he's going to be good for another eighty years."

I shook my head in amazement. Sandy Bouchier. Right here in my neighborhood, or near enough. The man who had defended some of the most important criminal cases of the past four decades, who had argued before the Supreme Court more times than I could count, and who had written law review articles that were regularly cited by courts all over the country.

"Does he miss practicing?"

"Every day. He talks about cases like they happened yesterday instead of twenty years ago. Sometimes I think he stays current with things because he's really waiting for someone to call and ask him to come out of retirement for one more case."

Pele handed me the coffee mug and walked back to the wall of photographs.

"He's actually the one who encouraged me to open this place. Said a bookstore would give me a chance to meet interesting people and have engaging conversations."

"Has it?"

Pele chuckled, but there was a rueful sound to it, and she said nothing.

I studied the photographs again, seeing them differently now.

Sandy Bouchier at book signings and literary events, clearly a regular presence in his granddaughter's store. One of the great legends of the legal profession, spending his retirement years supporting a small independent bookstore.

"Maybe..." I started, then stopped myself.

"What?"

"Nothing. I was just thinking out loud."

But Pele was looking at me from behind those big glasses, and I could tell she knew exactly what I had been about to ask.

"You want to meet him," she said. It wasn't a question.

"The thought crossed my mind."

"About this complicated divorce case you're working on?"

"Oh no, not about that. I wouldn't bother him with something so trivial."

"Then why?"

I shrugged, but I stayed silent. I'd said far too much already.

Pele gave me a long look, and I started feeling slightly embarrassed. Here I was, hitting up a woman I hardly knew for an introduction to her famous grandfather like I was some bumpkin from Virginia. Of course, I *was* some bumpkin from Virginia, but I didn't have to make a career out of it.

"Nah, forget it," I said. "I shouldn't have said anything. I need to get going. Thanks for the coffee."

"Anytime. And Charlie?"

I turned back at the door.

"Be careful with that divorce case. There are a lot of powerful people around here who don't want anyone poking into their business. And powerful people around here have all sorts of ways of getting what they want. Not all of those ways are nice."

Something about the way she said that made me pause, but before I could ask her exactly what she meant by that, two women came into the store. Pele wiggled her fingers at me and turned to wait on the women.

I wiggled my fingers back and walked out to where I had parked the Mustang.

11

I spent most of the rest of the weekend pulling papers out of boxes, trying to read them, stuffing them back in, then pulling out other papers and doing it all over again.

Eventually, I had to admit to myself that I was completely overwhelmed. To catalog all the material Emma had collected and shape it into some coherent narrative would take a dozen paralegals working for months. I was just one guy. What in the world could I hope to accomplish in two days?

Just before sunset on Sunday afternoon, I gave up on the documents and walked down to the beach to clear my head. I needed to figure out what I was going to tell Emma tomorrow when she showed up at two o'clock expecting answers I didn't have.

I unwrapped the rope that held up the stairs and lowered them down to the beach. The sand was still warm from the day's sun, and the waves rolled in with that steady four-count rhythm that had become the soundtrack to my life here. A flock of seagulls worked the shoreline, their sharp cries cutting through the booming of the surf as they stabbed at whatever the receding waves left behind.

I walked north in the direction of Point Dume, my bare feet sinking into the sand with each step. The beach stretched empty in both directions except for a couple walking their dog near the water's edge. Their voices carried on the evening breeze, but the words were lost in the constant boom of waves hitting the packed sand.

Why had I ever told Emma I would have some kind of advice for her by Monday? What sort of arrogance made me think I could sort through years of complex financial records in a weekend and emerge with anything resembling coherence?

A gull landed ten feet in front of me and fixed me with one black eye, as if it were waiting for me to explain what I was going to tell Emma tomorrow. When I didn't, it launched itself back into the air with a disgusted squawk and glided away down the beach.

The smart thing to do was to extract myself from this mess as quickly as possible. I'd have to make Emma understand tomorrow that she needed an entire team of investigators and forensic accountants, not just one former divorce lawyer from Virginia who was living on the beach and trying to avoid the practice of law altogether.

But did I honestly *want* to extract myself? That was the sixty-four dollar question, and I'd been avoiding it all weekend.

I had to admit I was intrigued by what I had seen, even if I wasn't certain what it all meant. The wire transfers to non-existent companies, the contracts dated after payments were made, the millions of dollars flowing to banks in countries with strict secrecy laws. All of that pointed to something much bigger than sloppy bookkeeping, and part of me wanted to find out exactly what that was.

The sun was getting lower, painting the water in shades of

gold and orange. A gull skimmed just above the surface, its wings barely moving as it rode the air currents along the shore. Everything about this place was peaceful and restorative.

So why did I feel like I was standing at the edge of a cliff?

I found a piece of driftwood and sat down, watching the waves and trying to be honest with myself about what I really wanted to do. Emma Scott was clearly a nice woman who needed help, and Harry had asked me to provide that help as a favor to him. How could I abandon them now?

The couple with the dog had disappeared, leaving me alone on the beach with the seagulls and my doubts. The waves kept rolling in, indifferent to my problems, carrying the same rhythm they'd carried for thousands of years before I arrived and would carry for thousands more after I was gone.

Maybe that was the lesson the ocean was trying to teach me. Just keep moving forward, one wave at a time, and let the bigger picture take care of itself.

I stood up and brushed the sand off my jeans. The sun was almost touching the horizon now, and the moon was establishing a pale presence in the darkening sky. Tomorrow, Emma would arrive expecting answers, and I would have to give her the best answers I could with what I had. Those answers wouldn't be much, but they would be something. And maybe something would be enough to keep her afloat until the next wave rolled in.

As it turned out, I need not have worried so much about having those answers ready for her.

Just before two the next day, I put on a fresh pot of coffee and settled down to wait for Emma's arrival.

She didn't turn up.

Around three, I called her house to see where she was.

Maybe there had been a misunderstanding. Maybe she thought I was coming down there.

No answer.

I waited another half hour, but then I got impatient. I got out the Mustang and drove down to Emma's place on La Costa Beach. I pulled up to the gate and killed the engine.

The house was dark and quiet. The whole property had a shut-down feeling to it, like nobody had been there for days instead of just hours. There were no lights visible through any of the massive windows. Just that sleek architectural statement sitting silent on its bluff overlooking the ocean.

I got out and tried the intercom at the gate. Nothing. I pressed the button again, holding it longer this time. Still nothing.

A vague tickle of dread appeared from somewhere and tapped me on the shoulder.

The gate was locked, but I noticed a smaller service gate off to one side that led to what looked like a delivery area. I walked over and tried it. It was also locked, but it was lower than the main gate and looked like something I might be able to climb if I got desperate enough.

I wasn't that desperate yet.

Instead, I walked around the perimeter of the property, following the fence line that ran along the street side. The whole place was sealed up tight, every window closed, every door locked. When I got to the ocean side of the property, I found another gate that opened directly onto the beach.

This one wasn't locked.

I pushed through and found myself on a private beach access path that ran down the bluff toward the sand. From here, I could see the back of the house. The deck that stretched along the ocean side was empty, and the floor-to-ceiling windows were covered by drapes that had been pulled closed.

I pulled myself over the railing onto the deck and tried the sliding glass door. Locked. I cupped my hands against the glass and peered through a gap in the drapes, but I couldn't see much. Just shadows and furniture shapes. I moved along the deck, trying each window, each door. All locked. All covered. The house had been battened down like someone was expecting a hurricane.

Emma wouldn't have gone away without calling me, would she? She had been anxious when I saw her two days ago, of course, but why would she have left without telling me when she was counting on me to help her figure out what to do with all those documents from her husband's business she had collected over the years?climbed

Maybe Harry had heard from her.

I walked back out to the front of the house, got in the Mustang, and drove back to Carbon Beach. When I went inside, I looked up the number for the Beverly Hills Hotel and called Harry. There was no answer in his room. When the operator came back on, I left a message.

I pulled out my wallet and found the piece of paper where Harry had written down the number for his very expensive portable telephone. I dialed it, half expecting nothing at all to happen, but I could hear a ringing on the other end just like I had dialed a real telephone. Maybe I had. But whether I had or not, Harry didn't answer.

Just for the hell of it, I called Harry's New York apartment, too. When his answering machine picked up, I left a message asking him to call me urgently. Maybe he could check his machine remotely, and I supposed it was at least possible he would do that before he got the message I had left at the hotel.

What the hell was I supposed to do now? Call the cops? And tell them ... what? That a woman I barely knew had missed an appointment with me? That her house was dark? They would just laugh and hang up on me.

I paced Harry's deck for twenty minutes, trying to decide what to do. The sun was getting lower, painting the ocean in shades that should have been beautiful but were beginning to look ominous to me. My imagination was running wild.

So, I got back in the Mustang and drove down to Emma's house again.

This time, I didn't bother with the front gate. I went straight to the beach access gate and walked up to the deck. The drapes were still pulled. Everything still looked shut down and abandoned.

I examined the sliding glass door. The lock was a standard residential model, nothing fancy despite the expensive house it was supposed to be protecting. Back in Virginia, I'd had clients who had gotten locked out of their own homes when vindictive spouses changed the locks, and I had learned a thing or two about getting past standard residential door locks.

I walked back down to the beach and found a piece of driftwood about the size of a baseball bat. Then I climbed back up to the deck and positioned myself in front of the sliding glass door. I stopped and looked around. The houses on either side were far enough away that nobody would see me unless they were specifically watching, and the beach below was empty except for a couple walking together probably a quarter mile down.

Hefting the piece of driftwood in one hand, I slammed it down hard on the door handle. The impact made a sound like a gunshot, but the handle shattered. I pulled away the broken pieces and reached through the hole they left in the door to work the lock mechanism. The door slid open.

That was what I had learned back in Virginia about getting past standard residential door locks. Finesse was swell, but in a pinch, nothing worked better than raw physical violence.

I stepped inside.

"Hello?" I called out. "Emma? Are you here?"

No answer.

Something was obviously wrong. I could easily see that the house had been searched. Not trashed exactly, but definitely gone through. Books pulled slightly forward on the shelves. Couch cushions not quite aligned properly. Cabinet doors not completely closed.

The air had an electric feeling to it, the kind that reminds you that you're someplace you're not supposed to be.

I walked through the living room and into the kitchen. Drawers looked like they had been opened and carelessly closed again. The pantry door stood ajar. Someone had been looking for something. No doubt about that.

I moved deeper into the house. In the master bedroom door the bed was made, but the closet doors stood open, and I could see clothes on hangers pushed to one side like someone had been rifling through them.

I checked the garage. Emma's car was still there. A black Mercedes sedan, the one she had driven to Harry's house the day we met.

The car might be here, but Emma obviously wasn't. Who left Malibu without their car? Nobody. Not unless they left with somebody else, of course. Whether that leaving was entirely voluntarily or not was an entirely different question.

I walked back through the house, looking now for anything that might tell me what had happened here. There were no obvious signs of violence. Certainly no blood or anything like that. Just the indications that Emma's house had been systematically searched. I checked the cabinet from which Emma had dragged out the first three bankers boxes of documents she had shown me.

It was empty. The boxes were gone.

I stood in the middle of the living room and tried to think. Emma had eight boxes of financial documents. I had taken the five she had in the garage. The other three, the three she put back into the cabinet, were no longer here. Did that mean whoever had searched her house had taken them, or had Emma just moved them somewhere else for safekeeping?

What the hell had happened to those boxes?

But, much more important than that, what the hell had happened to Emma?

When I got back to Harry's house, I started dialing again. The Beverly Hills Hotel. The number Harry had given me for his new toy telephone. Harry's apartment in New York.

Nothing.

Who else could I call who might know where Emma was?

The answer to that question was nobody. My only contact with Emma had been through Harry, and the only other person I knew of to whom she was connected was her husband. Calling him obviously wasn't on the menu, and that left nobody.

I thought again about filing a missing person's report with the police, but I discarded that idea almost as quickly as it came to me. What was I going to tell the cops? That a woman who wasn't actually my client had failed to turn up for a client conference? That hardly made her a missing person. The cops would just laugh at me, and I really didn't need that.

Yes, Emma's house had been searched, which was suspicious to say the least, and three bankers boxes of documents were missing, but I could hardly tell the cops I had discovered that because I'd broken in myself, could I? Maybe if I could somehow get the cops to check her house, they would find the broken the lock on the sliding door at the back and that would get them moving. But how was I going to get them out there to discover that?

I eyed the five bankers boxes I had taken away from Emma's house that were now lined up on my dining room table. If those documents were what somebody was looking for when they searched Emma's house, and they had found the three boxes I left there, did they know that there were more boxes that weren't there? And more to the point, did they know where those other boxes were right now?

Leaving those boxes just sitting on my dining table in plain sight suddenly seemed very foolish, but I had no idea what else to do with them. Maybe I should rent a storage locker somewhere and get them out of the house in case anyone came looking for them.

Get a grip, Charlie. How could anyone know you have this stuff?

They couldn't, of course. Emma and I were the only two people who knew I had these five boxes. I sure as hell hadn't told anybody, and I couldn't believe that Emma had either.

Still, the storage locker might be a good idea, just to be on the safe side. I found Harry's yellow pages telephone directory and looked up Self Storage. Sure enough, there were several self-storage companies listed in Malibu, two of which had addresses not far away, and half a dozen more just over the hills in the San Fernando Valley. I guess even rich people need a little extra storage room sometimes.

So, should I get a storage locker for the boxes or not?

If it turned out that Emma had just forgotten about our

meeting and gone shopping, I'd feel like a right mug for panicking and hiding the boxes somewhere inconvenient.

The more I thought about it, the more certain I became that I was jumping the gun. On the other hand, I didn't much like the idea of just leaving the boxes sitting on my dining room table either, so I decided to split the difference. One by one, I lugged all the boxes out to the garage. Then I rooted around in Harry's stuff until I found a roll of heavy packing tape, taped all five of the boxes closed, and tucked them away in the trunk of my Mustang.

Now the boxes weren't on my dining table any longer, but they weren't in a storage facility either. They were pretty much halfway in between both.

Genius, huh? Lawyer-like thinking at its very finest.

The sensible thing to do now, I knew, was to settle down and just wait rather than kick up a fuss simply because Emma had missed an appointment. I wasn't Emma's keeper. I was just the temporary, and entirely accidental custodian of a bunch of documents that belonged to her.

She would turn up sometime soon, surely, or she would call, and then we could talk about what I had found in the boxes. Besides, what alternative did I have? I hardly knew Emma, and I knew only one other person in the entire world who knew her.

That was Harry.

And I couldn't find him either.

12

Two days passed. Slowly. I walked on the beach, drank a little beer, and read Raymond Chandler.

I called Emma's house repeatedly, but got no answer. I left more messages at the Beverly Hills Hotel for Harry and on the machine at his New York apartment, but I didn't hear from Harry either. I even called the number I had for Harry's toy phone a few times, but it just rang without being answered instead of going to a message machine. Was that even a real telephone number? I had absolutely no idea.

The waiting was eating at me. Every time the phone rang, I jumped. Every time I heard a car door slam somewhere, I looked out the window to see if it could be Emma. But the calls were junk, and the car doors belonged to neighbors I didn't know, people who were just going about their normal lives.

I tried to lose myself in *The Simple Art of Murder*, but even Chandler didn't hold my attention. His detective stories felt too real now, too much like what I was living through myself. People disappearing without explanation. Powerful men with ugly secrets. Money changing hands in the shadows.

By the third day, I was starting to wonder if something had happened to Harry, too. I insisted the operator at the Beverly Hills Hotel check to see if he had picked up my messages, but when she came back, she told me Harry Wells had checked out the day before. Maybe his business meetings had fallen through and he had decided to cut his trip short, but would he have gone back to New York without telling me? I honestly didn't know.

It was close to the end of the third day, and I was just wondering if it was too early for a beer, when the door buzzer sounded. The sound shot through me like electricity. It had to be Emma, I knew immediately, and I rushed out to open the gate.

But it wasn't Emma.

Standing at my gate was a middle-aged guy in a Dodgers cap and board shorts holding what looked like a small stack of documents. He was maybe forty-five, with the kind of deep tan that came from spending serious time outdoors and the slightly weathered look of someone who worked with his hands. His shorts were faded, and his T-shirt had seen better days, but there was something about the way he held himself that suggested he was comfortable with whatever he was doing here.

"Are you Charles Trust?" he asked.

His voice had that flat, professional tone that people use when they're working. Probably a courier of some kind then. Something from Emma that would explain just what the hell was going on here.

"I am."

The man held out the papers, and I took them immediately. Maybe Emma was in some kind of trouble and couldn't call me directly. Maybe these were instructions about what I should do with the documents I had.

But suddenly the man took a step back and lifted a cheap camera. He snapped two quick pictures of me holding the papers.

"You've been served," he said.

Then he turned and trotted away down the driveway toward the PCH.

"What the hell?" I asked right out loud.

But nobody answered my question.

I carried the papers the guy had handed me out to the back deck and settled into one of the chairs. When I unfolded the document, I saw printed across the top of the first page in bold capitals the words **SUBPOENA DUCES TECUM**.

Not a message from Emma then. Not instructions about what to do next.

A subpoena.

A *subpoena duces tecum* is a court order requiring someone to appear in court and bring specific documents with them. The *duces tecum* part is Latin for *bring with you*, and it means the court wants to examine whatever documents are listed in the subpoena. It's a powerful legal tool, one that carries the full weight of judicial authority behind it.

I read through the document with growing astonishment. The subpoena asked for *any and all documents, records, files, correspondence, or other materials provided to Charles Trust by Emma Scott, including but not limited to financial records, bank statements, wire transfer authorizations, contracts, invoices, or any other business records allegedly belonging to or concerning Zachariah Scott or any business entity controlled by him.*

The subpoena alleged that these documents constituted *stolen business records unlawfully obtained from Scott Productions, Inc*, and it demanded I produce them for examination at ten o'clock Friday morning, in room 111 of the Santa Monica Courthouse, at 1725 Main Street in Santa Monica.

The subpoena was signed by Judge Edith McClanahan, presiding judge of Department E of the Superior Court, West District, Family Law Division.

For the second time in the last five minutes, I asked exactly the same question right out loud.

What the hell?

And for the second time in five minutes, nobody answered me.

I read through the subpoena again, more carefully this time. I looked for a long while at the name of the lawyer who had requested the subpoena, but it meant nothing to me.

Brian Hurter. Johnson, Brobeck, and Hurter. The firm had an address in Century City where all the big dogs hung out, but then they would, wouldn't they?

Hurter had convinced this judge that Emma had stolen business records from her husband's company and given them to me. Not only did he somehow know about the boxes of documents that were now sitting in my car trunk, he also seemed to know exactly what was in them. But how could that be?

Emma and I were the only people who knew I had taken those documents home from her house to study them. Had Emma told someone I had them? Or had someone been watching us and seen me take them? Surely that couldn't be, could it?

I looked out at the ocean, but the endless blue expanse offered no answers. A seagull circled overhead, riding the thermal currents, probably wondering why I was sitting motionless in my chair instead of throwing it something to eat.

The implications of the subpoena I was looking at were

starting to sink in. If I didn't show up in court Friday morning with my five bankers boxes of documents, I could be held in contempt of court and arrested, and that was no joke. I knew I wouldn't be the first member of the California Bar ever to be arrested, but I was pretty sure I'd be the only member ever to be arrested during his first week of bar membership. That was a distinction I could well live without.

The legal system doesn't mess around when it comes to obeying a direct order from a judge. I had seen enough stubborn clients back in Virginia learn that lesson the hard way when they tried to get cute with documents they had that constituted evidence in their divorce cases. If I didn't turn over Emma's documents to Judge McClanahan, I could be facing fines that would drain what little remained of my mother's inheritance, or worse yet, I could even be left cooling my heels in a county jail cell until I decided to cooperate.

But that left me with a problem. A really big problem.

None of the documents in those five boxes were mine to turn over to Judge Edith McClanahan or to anyone else. They were all Emma's documents, regardless of how she had gotten them. She had given them to me only to examine them and offer her legal advice about their contents. That meant they were protected under attorney-client privilege, and I was legally and ethically bound not to give them to anyone else or reveal their contents to anyone without Emma's permission.

Which I didn't have, and which I couldn't get.

Because Emma was missing.

This judge wouldn't really put me in jail if I refused to turn over Emma's documents, would she?

She probably would since I was nobody, and a judge can't let a nobody walk all over her.

Surely there was a solution that didn't end up with me either in jail or giving up Emma's documents. There had to be. I needed advice from a California lawyer who was experienced in dealing with the courts and maybe had a little personal clout. There was only one problem there. I didn't know any.

Then all at once it occurred to me that I *did* know one. And he was exactly the man I needed now.

Sandy Bouchier, Pele's grandfather

Well, I didn't know him really, but I knew *of* him, and applying the *Six Degrees of Separation* rule, I was only one degree of separation away from him.

Would Pele be willing to introduce me? There was only one way to find out.

I timed my arrival at Malibu Books for just a few minutes before closing. When I pushed in through the door, Pele gave me a big smile. I hoped that smile just might be a good omen.

"I'm on my way to the Baja Cantina for a margarita or two," I announced, "and I'm looking for a little company. Know anybody who might be interested?"

Pele looked down at the counter, straightened some bookmarks that didn't need straightening, then glanced back up at me.

"Give me five minutes to lock up."

She flipped the sign in the window to Closed and started turning off lights. I waited by the door, watching her move through the store with the efficiency of someone who had done the same thing a thousand times before. She grabbed a small canvas bag from behind the counter, checked the cash register one more time, and joined me at the entrance.

"Lead the way, Counselor."

The Baja Cantina was just up the street from the shopping center. It was a low-slung, faux-stucco building painted in faded turquoise with a neon sign that promised Best Margaritas in Malibu. Whether that was true or not, I had no idea, but it was one of the better places in the area to drop into for a drink or two in the evening, and it seemed to draw a steady crowd of locals, including the usual sprinkling of Hollywood celebrities.

Inside, the décor ran heavy to California kitsch, meaning surfboards on the walls and nets draped from the ceiling. The bar stretched along the right side of the room, and the bottles lined up behind it on glass shelves glinted in the light from the strings of colored bulbs overhead. Most of the tables were empty tonight, but the bar had a decent crowd.

At the far end, taking up the last five stools, I spotted Larry Hagman and his regular posse. Hagman and his gang were here a lot. J.R. Ewing himself holding court, a rocks glass in one hand and gesturing expansively with the other. We had never actually spoken, but after my first few times there at the bar, he started recognizing me when I came in, and I remember fondly the night he had raised his glass to me in a silent greeting. That marked the first time I thought I might just find a niche for myself in this strange little world after all.

When Hagman saw us walk in, he slid off his stool and advanced on us with his arms spread wide.

"Pele!" he boomed,."Where have you been? I haven't seen you in weeks."

Hagman pulled Pele into a hug that lifted her off the ground and left me feeling like a third wheel.

"Running a bookstore, Larry. Some of us have to work for a living."

Hagman laughed, a big theatrical sound that filled the room.

"Work? That's what I pay other people to do, darlin'. You should try it sometime."

He set her down and turned his attention to me, his eyes sharp despite the drink in his hand.

"I've seen your friend here quite a few times, but we've never been introduced."

"This is Charlie Trust. Charlie, meet Larry Hagman."

I shook his hand, trying not to feel like a star-struck kid.

"It's a pleasure to meet you, sir."

"*Sir?* Okay, now I officially feel older than shit."

"Charlie's a lawyer, sort of," Pele said. "He moved here from Virginia a few months ago."

"A sort of lawyer?" Hagman grinned. "Well, welcome to California, Charlie. You'll fit right in. Half the people I know are sort of lawyers, and the other half sort of need lawyers."

His posse laughed on cue, and Hagman clapped me on the shoulder.

"Don't let me keep you kids from your evening. Pele, come by the house soon. We'll make dinner."

"Will do, Larry."

Pele led me to the opposite end of the bar, where we took two stools far enough from Hagman's group to have a conversation without shouting. The bartender appeared, a woman in her forties with bleached blonde hair and the kind of weathered prettiness that suggested she had already spent too many years in the California sun.

"Margarita," Pele told her. "No salt."

"Same," I said.

The bartender nodded and disappeared. I glanced down the bar at Hagman, who was telling some story that had his group hanging on every word.

"You know Larry Hagman?" I asked her.

"Everyone in Malibu knows Larry. He's been coming into

the bookstore since I opened. Buys mysteries mostly. Loves private detective novels."

"Does he always travel with an entourage like this?"

"Pretty much. Larry doesn't do anything alone if he can help it."

The margaritas arrived in oversized glasses, bright green and sporting lime wedges pushed onto the rims. I took a sip. Good stuff. The sign outside hadn't been lying.

Pele and I talked for a while about nothing in particular. The bookstore business, the Malibu community, the difference between East Coast and West Coast living. She was easy to talk to, with a quick wit and that wonderful rumbling laugh I'd heard before.

But after maybe twenty minutes, she set down her glass and gave me a look.

"Okay, Charlie. You seem uneasy. Do I make you nervous?"

The question caught me off guard.

"No, of course not."

Although I had to admit to myself that maybe she did, at least a little. With Pele, I always felt slightly off balance, like I was one step behind in a conversation I didn't even know we were having.

"Then what is it? Because you're acting like a man with something on his mind besides my sparkling company."

I took another sip of my margarita, stalling. How was I supposed to ask this now without sounding like the reason I had asked her for a drink was to get her to do something for me? Which I suppose wasn't entirely untrue.

"I need to ask you a favor, and I don't quite know how to do it."

Pele leaned back on her stool and crossed her arms.

"Uh-oh. Suddenly, it sounds like I'm about to get the bill for this drink. Okay, let's have it."

"Would you be willing to introduce me to your grandfather?"

Pele didn't respond right away. She just let the question hang in the air. But I could see her expression shifting from curiosity to something cautious and guarded.

"Why?"

I chose my words carefully.

"A man who did a huge favor for me asked for one in return. He asked me to review some documents and give my thoughts from a legal standpoint about what they meant. But now that I've agreed, I suddenly see I have a serious ethical problem."

"What kind of ethical problem?"

"I can't tell you, but it is serious. If I don't handle it right, I could go to jail."

"*Jail?*" Pele said a little louder than she really needed to, and I saw one of Hagman's posse turn his head in our direction.

I bent toward her.

"I'm not looking for legal advice here, Pele. What I need is guidance on how to fulfill my ethical obligations as a lawyer without causing difficulties for anyone else, and I can't think of a better man to put that question to than your grandfather."

Pele studied my face for a long moment, and I tried to keep it as empty as possible. When she finally spoke, her voice had an edge to it.

"So this invitation from you was because you needed something from me. The margaritas and the friendly conversation were just to grease the way for you to ask me to introduce you to Sandy."

Her words stung because they were partly true. I had come here tonight with an agenda, and now she knew what it was.

"Not *just* because of that," I said, "but I was served with a subpoena today, and I'm in a real bind here. If I weren't, I would never have asked."

Pele just looked at me and said nothing.

"I'm sorry," I mumbled, shifting my eyes away from Pele. "I'm making a real mess out of this. I do want your company, but yes, I also need your help. And I was hoping I could have both tonight."

Pele drained the rest of her margarita in one long pull, set the glass down hard enough to make the bartender look over, and stood up.

"I need to get going."

"Pele, wait."

"Don't say anything else, Charlie, please. I'll think about it. Maybe I'll call you tomorrow. Maybe I won't."

She pushed a cocktail napkin and a pen across the bar toward me.

"Write down your number."

I scribbled the number for Harry's beach house on the napkin and slid it back. Pele grabbed it, stuffed it in her bag, and headed for the door without looking back. I watched her go, then turned back to what was left of my margarita.

"Nice going, Charlie," I muttered to myself. "You've really got the magic touch with women, don't you?"

Down at the other end of the bar, Larry Hagman's crew began to chortle again. Suddenly I felt like everybody in the whole place had just watched me crash and burn, and now they were having a good laugh about it.

I could hardly blame them.

13

I was wearing my slightly ratty dressing gown and carrying my first cup of coffee of the day out to the deck when the telephone rang a little after seven-thirty the next morning.

"Hello?"

"Sandy is expecting you at eleven," Pele said, not bothering with the normal courtesy of a greeting. "His address is 362 North Rockingham. That's in Brentwood."

I hesitated. I was still in the grip of my usual pre-coffee fog, and working out the right thing to say in response to Pele was going to take me a moment, so I didn't respond quickly enough for her.

"Did you get that?" she snapped, the impatience obvious in her voice.

"362 North Rockingham in Brentwood. Eleven o'clock."

"Yes," Pele said, and then she hung up without another word.

I took a quick hit on my coffee, then went out to the garage and got my dog-eared copy of the Thomas Guide out of the glove box of the Mustang.

The Thomas guide is a survival tool in LA. It's a spiral-bound map book that indexes the whole massive city into a few hundred pages of detailed maps marked out in grids. Its index could quickly pinpoint any street in the whole LA area for you. The Thomas Guide is so commonly used as a navigation tool by everyone in LA that sometimes you see advertisements in the newspaper that include an address with a notation like *Thomas Guide, page 63, grid C4*. If you have driven a car in LA for more than a couple of days, you know exactly what that means, and you're grateful for the help.

Back out on the deck, I looked up North Rockingham in my Thomas guide. It was just north of Sunset on the edge of the foothills of the Santa Monica Mountains. That was a really nice neighborhood. Of course, it was. Where else would I expect to find Sandy Bouchier living out his retirement but in a really nice neighborhood?

It was just a short drive for me, at least it was by LA standards. Twenty or thirty minutes. Maybe a bit more if I got lost, which I probably would. That gave me plenty of time to load up on coffee and think about the best way to approach Sandy Bouchier to get the sort of guidance from him that I needed.

I dropped the Thomas Guide on the little table next to me and sat there on the deck cradling my coffee mug in both hands. I watched the ocean. I did that a lot. It seemed benign today. None of the huge breakers that usually battered the beach into submission. Just gentle swells rolling in under a soft gray sky that looked like the sun couldn't decide whether it wanted to make an appearance or not.

Half a dozen seagulls strolled along the high tide line, picking through debris the ocean had left behind during the night. They moved with purpose, heads bobbing, keeping their formation together like cops working a crime scene.

I wondered if they were all friends. If seagulls even had friends. Maybe they met up every morning at the same stretch of beach and caught up on whatever passed for seagull gossip.

Then I wondered if they had gotten tired of flying and decided to try walking for a change. Switch things up a little. Maybe one of them had pitched the idea earlier this morning. "Hey guys, let's skip the whole swooping and diving routine today. My wings are killing me."

The coffee was getting cold in my hand.

I was stalling.

I really needed to think about how to approach Sandy Bouchier. What exactly was I going to say to a man who had worked with Supreme Court justices to decide major cases and spent decades defending the kind of clients who made national headlines? A man who had probably forgotten more about criminal law and legal ethics than I had ever learned. I had to come up with exactly the right approach.

But I just kept on watching the seagulls.

One of them found something interesting, and the others converged. There was a brief scuffle, wings flapping, a bit of aggressive squawking. So much for friendship. Then they settled back into their formation and kept moving down the beach like nothing had happened.

The sun broke through the clouds for a moment, turning the wet sand silver.

I drained the last of my cold coffee. I had about two hours to figure out how to convince Sandy Bouchier that I was worth his time, and I had better use it well. I went inside to shower and find something to wear that wouldn't make me look like a washed-up divorce lawyer from Virginia who was in way over his head and desperately needed help from a legend.

It had been a nice morning so far. I hope it stayed that way.

I put the top down on the Mustang, backed out of the driveway onto the Pacific Coast Highway, and turned south.

The morning had gone bright and clear, the clouds burned off by a sun that was making up for lost time. The ocean kept me company as I drove. A few surfers bobbed in the water off Topanga Beach, waiting for waves that looked too small to me for them to bother with.

At Sunset, I turned east. The road wound through neighborhoods where people who had made it in this town came to roost. Pacific Palisades gave way to Brentwood, the houses getting larger and farther apart, tucked behind walls and gates and hedges that said money without having to shout about it.

I passed the entrance to the Riviera Country Club where, according to Harry, half of Hollywood made deals over eighteen holes and martinis. Joggers in expensive athletic wear ran along the sidewalks. Gardeners worked on lawns that looked like they belonged on golf courses. A woman walked three small dogs that probably ate more expensive food than I did.

This was old money mixing with new money, moguls and producers and lawyers who billed by the quarter hour. The kind of people who probably once had Sandy Bouchier on speed dial for when they needed someone who could make problems disappear.

North Rockingham was the first left past Mandeville Canyon Road. The street climbed into the foothills, and the houses got more impressive with each block. I checked addresses on mailboxes and gates until I found 362.

I had expected it to be a nice house, of course, but it was way beyond nice. It sat on what had to be at least two acres of prime Brentwood, maybe more. A circular driveway that swept up from the street was lined with sycamore trees that sheltered it under a natural canopy.

The house itself was what I think is called Spanish Colonial. It was all white stucco with a red tile roof, arched windows, and a portico supported by thick columns. Bougainvillea in deep purple and magenta climbed the walls. The landscaping looked like it probably required a whole team of gardeners working full time to keep it up.

The gate looked formidable, constructed of closely spaced black iron bars that rose about eight feet high, topped with decorative spikes that managed to look elegant and unwelcoming at the same time. I pulled into the driveway and stopped next to an intercom box mounted on an iron stalk. I reached out to push the talk button, but before I could say anything, the gate rumbled to life and began to slide open.

I took my foot off the brake, and the Mustang rolled through.

The front door opened as I walked toward it, and I was pretty sure the man I saw standing there couldn't possibly be Sandy Bouchier.

For one thing, he was too young. For another, he looked Chinese, or maybe Korean. I wasn't very good at identifying the ethnicity of Asians just by their appearance. Most Americans weren't. So I wasn't sure.

The man wore an expensive-looking dark suit with an open-necked white shirt. It appeared to be custom tailored and probably cost more than my entire wardrobe.

He was on the short side, about five-seven or five-eight, but he was broad through the shoulders and chest, and he looked hard and solid. His black hair was swept back and perfectly in place, not a strand out of order. No gray anywhere. Smooth skin, unlined face. He could have been thirty. He could have been sixty. It was impossible to tell.

He said nothing at all and simply stepped aside for me to enter. When I did, I found myself in a foyer that was bigger than most people's living rooms. The floor was white marble. A chandelier hung overhead, all crystal and brass. There were oil paintings on two of the walls that looked like I should know the names of the painters. I didn't.

The man closed the door behind me with barely a sound. His movements were precise and economical. Nothing wasted. He held himself perfectly balanced on the balls of his feet as if he were prepared to move any direction in an instant. He had the bearing of someone who had spent time in the military or law enforcement, or maybe he was just a martial arts nut.

"This way, please," he said.

His voice was quiet with no trace of an accent. American as apple pie. Probably grew up in California, maybe second or third generation.

He led me through the house. I tried not to be a rube and gawk at the artwork and furniture. It shouted old money and good taste, of course. The kind of taste that didn't need to prove anything to anyone.

The man's shoes made no sound on the hardwood floors. Mine did. They squeaked as I walked. I felt like the proverbial bull in a china shop, all noise and awkwardness as I trudged along behind my silent guide.

We reached a set of double doors, and he opened one of them and stepped inside. I noticed he hadn't bothered to knock.

I followed him through the doors and stepped past him. Behind me, I heard the doors close with a barely there click. When I glanced back, the man had disappeared. I wouldn't have been in the least surprised to see a puff of smoke floating in the air where he had been, but of course, there wasn't one.

The room was all wood paneling and floor-to-ceiling bookshelves that were crammed full of books that looked both well read and well loved. A massive wooden desk that could have been carved from a single enormous block of mahogany sat in front of the windows. Beyond it, I could see what looked like an acre of manicured lawns.

And behind the desk sat Sandy Bouchier.

My first thought was that Sandy Bouchier looked like Abraham Lincoln without the beard. Or at least he looked like an actor playing Abraham Lincoln without the beard.

Even sitting down, I could tell that he was very tall. He was gaunt with thin shoulders and a narrow chest to the point of looking downright cadaverous, and he had a long, thin face that was deeply lined and sagged precariously toward the floor. His face looked as if it fought a daily battle with gravity not to slide off his head altogether.

But the thing that grabbed most of my attention was what I was sure grabbed most of everyone's attention about Sandy Bouchier. His eyes. They were fighter-pilot eyes, cold and clear. And green. So green they looked like two chips from an old Coke bottle.

He waved me toward a mahogany straight chair in front of his desk that had a dark red cushion on the seat. It looked uncomfortable, and when I sat down in it, I found out it was even more uncomfortable than it looked.

"Thank you for seeing me, Mr. Bouchier."

He didn't reply immediately, but he simply sat there silently and studied me. I would have expected nothing less, so

I waited him out in matching silence. It almost felt like a test, and I was pretty sure that was the correct response.

Eventually, of course, he rumbled to life.

"You know my granddaughter, I understand."

"I'd characterize us as acquaintances, sir. I can't really say that I know her very well."

"You apparently know her well enough for her to tell you she's my granddaughter."

"I only found that out because I saw you in a picture taken at a book signing that she has hanging in her bookstore."

"You could pick me out of that crowd?"

"I could pick you out of any crowd, sir. You were my hero in law school. When I graduated, I wanted to *be* Sandy Bouchier. Hell, *everybody* I knew wanted to be Sandy Bouchier."

"I would have thought you could come up with a higher ambition than that."

"I don't see how, sir. You were part of some of the most important civil liberties cases going back then. You were famous for standing with people against the weight of the government. You made the law seem like a noble calling. You were doing what we all wanted to do. Or at least what we believed then that we wanted to do."

He looked at me in silence for a minute or two after that. I imagine he was trying to decide if I was serious or just trying to soft-soap him.

Then he held out a hand.

"Give me your card."

"I don't have one, sir."

He got a strange look on his face.

"You don't have a business card?"

"No, sir."

"I thought my granddaughter told me you were a lawyer."

"Yes, sir. I am."

"You're a lawyer, and you don't have any business cards?"

"No, sir."

"There's no such thing as a lawyer without business cards."

"I guess I just never got around to having any printed."

Sandy Bouchier chuckled.

"Well, they say if you live long enough, you'll see everything. And now I guess I have."

He leaned back in his chair and folded his arms.

"Okay, then tell me your story and why you're here sitting in front of me, Charlie Trust. A lawyer who never bothered to get any business cards printed deserves to be heard."

So, I told him all of it.

Well, most of it, at least.

"Did you bring the subpoena with you?" he asked when I finished.

I pulled it out of my pocket and unfolded it. Then I leaned forward and put it on the desk in front of him. He picked it up and read it. I could see from the way that his eyes moved over it that he really *did* read it, not just scan quickly through it.

He looked up when he was done.

"And you have no idea where your client is?" he asked me.

"No, sir, but I should remind you that she's not exactly my client. I agreed only to review the documents she had as part of the initial client interview process. I haven't actually decided yet whether I will represent her or not."

He smiled at that.

"Very artfully put, my young friend without any business cards."

His eyes dropped back to the subpoena, and he flipped to the last page.

"I don't know the judge," he said after a moment, "but I

wouldn't. I don't think I know any judges in the Family Law Division, thank Christ."

I waited. I could tell something more was coming.

"But I do recognize the name of the attorney who applied for the subpoena. Brian Hurter is tough, smart, and mean as a snake. Johnson, Brobeck, and Hurter has a reputation for going to the wall for their clients. That's not a bad thing, of course, but it matters to me exactly what wall it is you're going to, and the word on them is that they're not too choosey about that."

That wasn't exactly what I had wanted to hear.

"If you're going up against Brian Hurter," he added, "I'd suggest you take along a baseball bat. You'll probably need it."

That *certainly* wasn't what I wanted to hear.

"Do you think I could actually be held in contempt if I don't turn over these documents?"

"Probably."

"But the judge isn't really likely to jail me, is she?"

"You're not afraid of some pissant local family law judge, are you, young man?"

"Well—"

"I've been threatened by the biggest there is. I've had two Chief Justices of the United States, Warren Burger and Bill Rehnquist, threaten to lock my ass up, and I never served a day."

"Then you don't think she would really jail me for contempt?"

"Oh, she probably would. She can see that you don't have any real standing here and wouldn't want anyone to see you getting away with defying her. But it would be mostly for show. I doubt she would hold you for very long."

"Any idea how—"

"Three or four months tops would be my guess."

That *really* wasn't what I wanted to hear, but when I looked at him, he was grinning.

Suddenly, he shot to his feet and slapped the desk with one hand.

"Here's what we're going to do," he said. "You're going to take me to lunch, and we'll talk about how to handle this judge."

"Lunch, sir?"

"Damn right. I used to get two thousand dollars an hour for the kind of advice you're asking me for. You're getting off light."

He came around the desk and strode toward the door with surprising grace and agility for a man of eighty.

"Come on, young man," he said, flinging open the door. "You're driving."

14

Sandy walked around the Mustang twice before he got in, running his hand over the fenders like he was examining the conformation of a thoroughbred.

"I love American cars," he said. "Best in the world."

That surprised me, coming from a man who probably could have afforded anything on wheels. A Ferrari. A Rolls. An Aston Martin. Whatever the hell rich people drove these days.

"It's beautiful restoration work," he added, peering at the chrome. "This is a sixty-nine, right?"

"Yes, sir."

"V8?"

"Three-ninety."

"Perfect."

He opened the passenger door and lowered himself into the seat with the cautious movements of a man who knew his body wouldn't forgive him if he wasn't careful with it.

"Put the top up, would you?"

I looked at him. It was a gorgeous day. Clear sky, sun

pouring down, temperature in the mid-seventies. Exactly the kind of day you put the top down for.

"Sir?"

"The top. Put it up."

"Yes, sir."

My Mustang didn't have the power top option, so I had to get out and wrestle with the canvas top, pulling it forward and locking it into place. I climbed back in behind the wheel. The Mustang felt smaller with the top up, the interior suddenly intimate and close. Maybe too close.

"Where to, sir?"

"Just turn right out of the gate, go up to Sunset, and turn left. I'll direct you from there."

I started the engine. The V8 rumbled to life with that deep growl that never got old. I rolled toward the gate, which opened automatically when we approached.

As soon as we cleared it, Sandy pulled a cigar and a box of wooden matches out of his jacket pocket.

Now I understood why he wanted the top up.

"You don't mind if I smoke, do you?"

Without waiting for me to answer, he struck a match and brought it to the end of the cigar. The smell of sulfur briefly filled the car, then gave way to something sweeter and more organic as he puffed the cigar to life. He leaned back in the seat and took a long, slow pull.

"That is *so* good," he said, exhaling a cloud of blue smoke that filled the interior.

The smell was strong, but not unpleasant. Rich tobacco, earthy and complex. Nothing like the stale cigarette smoke that used to fill the offices back at Pritchard, Wells & Monroe.

"Turn left up here at the light."

I followed his directions east on Sunset and deeper into Brentwood, and we headed in the general direction of the San

Diego Freeway and Beverly Hills. I hoped I wouldn't find myself too badly underdressed for whatever celebrated restaurant we were heading for.

Sandy rolled his window down about halfway, letting some of the smoke escape while keeping the car mostly closed. He seemed completely at ease, one arm draped through the window, the other with the cigar held loosely in his hand.

Sunset was a twisty drive, but a lovely one, too. The Mustang handled the curves easily, the rebuilt suspension tight and responsive. We passed under the 405, and it wasn't until we were somewhere north of UCLA and almost to the Bel-Air Country Club that Sandy spoke again.

"You know what the biggest problem with being eighty years old is?" he asked.

"No, sir."

"Everybody treats you like you're already dead. They talk to you in hushed voices. They ask if you need help with every goddamn thing. They act like you're made of glass."

He took another pull on the cigar.

"But this," he gestured with the cigar toward the windshield, the road ahead, the world in general, "this is what it feels like to be alive. Smoking a good cigar while riding in a classic American muscle car with a young man who needs help and doesn't know how to ask for it properly. This sure beats the hell out of sitting in that house waiting for the Grim Reaper to knock on my door."

He shot me a look.

"You can't say a word to Pele about me smoking. You hear me?"

I nodded slowly, but I said nothing.

"She doesn't allow it," he went on after a moment. "Here's some advice for you, and I won't charge you two thousand dollars an hour for it. Watch your ass around Pele. She's a tyrant, man."

I remained silent, which Sandy apparently took to suggest the possibility of dissent on my part.

"You don't think so? She tells Mr. Wu to keep me from smoking. She really does. She even tells him to take away any cigars he finds."

Sandy glanced over at me and winked. He patted his jacket pocket.

"But he doesn't know about these."

I was rapidly losing track of the narrative here.

"Mr. Wu?"

"You met him. He brought you into my study."

Oh, that Mr. Wu.

"He's my driver, mostly, but he's Pele's enforcer, too. Not only does Pele insist Mr. Wu stop me from smoking, she's also given him a list of restaurants where he's not allowed to take me."

Sandy puffed mightily on his cigar and grinned.

"That's why *you're* driving us to lunch."

We stayed on Sunset all the way through Beverly Hills, then Sandy told me to turn right on Doheny. At Beverly Blvd, he suddenly called out, "*Left!*"

I jumped into the left-turn lane just in time to beat the light. We were a bit north of Cedars-Sinai Medical Center and coming up fast on the Beverly Center when I figured out where we might be going.

"Tail O' the Pup?" I asked Sandy.

"You got it," he said.

"I gather it's on Mr. Wu's forbidden list?"

"You're two for two. Pele says the food is bad for me. Of course, it is. That's why I like it."

Tail O' the Pup is a hot dog stand, but the Tail O' the Pup is a hot dog stand in the same sense you can say a Bentley is a car. It is, of course, but that's barely the beginning of the story.

The appearance of Tail O' the Pup alone is enough to make it an LA icon. It's one of those pop art monuments that makes LA seem so endlessly cool to people who don't actually have to live here. The business end of the stand, the place where you put in your order, is designed to look like a giant, brightly painted hot dog. Brown buns top and bottom, red dog in the middle, and smears of yellow mustard on both sides.

There's no dining room. The giant hot dog is parked on a large wooden deck that looks as if it could have been hijacked out of somebody's backyard. It offers a selection of aluminum tables scattered both in front of the giant hot dog and down along both sides.

There's a big rectangular window in the middle of the giant stucco hot dog where you order. The regulars never speak a word. They just hold up fingers to indicate how many dogs they're ordering. There's not much chance of confusion since there's very little else on the menu.

We got our dogs and a couple of Cokes. I had two with just mustard and relish, but Sandy went for three loaded with chili and onions. We found a table down one side that was far enough away from everybody else to allow for quiet conversation, but we skipped the conversation and gave the dogs our complete attention until they were finished.

They're great hot dogs, of course, but it occurred to me that maybe Pele wasn't all wrong. I had no idea what was in them, and I knew enough not to ask.

When we were both finished, Sandy wiped his mouth with

a paper napkin, gave out a polite little belch, and got down to business.

"How many documents did this woman give you?"

"Five bankers boxes. All full."

"And you say there were three more bankers boxes you didn't take?"

"Yes. But they were gone when I discovered Emma's house had been searched and she had disappeared."

Sandy nodded, wiped his mouth again, and thought about that.

"Did you go through the documents in the boxes you took?"

I nodded.

"I'm not going to ask you what was in them, but did they leave you with any general impressions?"

I nodded again.

"It's bad," I said. "Not for her. For her husband. Really bad."

"So he wouldn't want whatever is in those boxes to see the light of day."

"Would he ever not."

Sandy thought some more.

"Where are those five boxes now?"

"I had them sitting on my dining room table, but after the other three boxes disappeared, they seemed a bit conspicuous there, so I moved them."

"Where did you take them?"

I inclined my head toward where we had left the Mustang in the little parking lot on the other side of the giant hot dog.

"I don't understand," Sandy said.

"They're in the trunk of my car. I didn't know where else to put them."

Sandy laughed.

"When we get back to Rockingham, I'll ask Mr. Wu to collect them and take them somewhere safe."

"Where do you have in mind?"

"Don't take offense, young man, but I think it's better if you don't know. That way, when the judge demands you tell her where they are, you can just say your co-counsel is studying them, and you don't know."

"You're my co-counsel?"

"Well, if you're not actually this woman's attorney, I can't actually be your co-counsel either, can I?"

He had me there.

"Look, Charlie, you do understand that you can't turn these documents over to the court without your client's permission, don't you?"

"That's the conclusion I came to on my own, but I wanted to check it with you."

"Then tell yourself that you're absolutely right. The whole lot is clearly subject to attorney-client privilege. Showing them to anyone except for your co-counsel, of course, would be a gross violation of legal ethics and subject you to disciplinary action and all sorts of unpleasant legal penalties."

"Even under subpoena?"

"Even under subpoena."

I cleared my throat and considered that.

"What if the judge threatens to fine me, or even jail me if I don't turn them over?"

"Come on, Charlie. Man up! Don't be a pussy. This is just some local family law judge, not the Chief Justice of the United States Supreme Court. Did I ever tell you about the time—"

"Yeah, you told me. I just don't see how that helps me. This judge does have the power to charge me with contempt of court and do all sorts of things to me if I don't produce the documents, doesn't she?"

Sandy nodded.

"Swell," I said. "A member of the California Bar for one week and I might be headed for jail for contempt."

Sandy looked horrified.

"You've been a lawyer for one week?"

"I've been a member of the California Bar for one week, but I've been a member of the Virginia and DC bars for nearly ten years."

"You had me worried there for a minute," Sandy said. "I'm not sure I can work with a co-counsel who only has a week's experience."

"I thought you were only pretending to be my co-counsel for purposes of storing the documents somewhere, so why would it matter?"

"Oh yeah," he said. "Right."

"So what do I do if this judge really does threaten to jail me for contempt?"

"You stand tall and politely say that you are bound by attorney-client privilege and, as much as you would like to, you are ethically barred from surrendering the documents to her without permission from your client."

"Then she'll ask me if I've asked my client, who is not yet my client, for permission to surrender them."

"And you will say no with a pure heart because you haven't."

"And the judge will ask me why I haven't."

"And you will tell her that you don't know where your client is."

"And the judge will get really pissed off and tell the bailiff to take me straight back to the lockup."

Sandy's head bobbed around as if it had momentarily become detached from his body.

"Quite possibly," he conceded.

"So what do I do then?"

"Oh, stop being an old woman," Sandy said. "We'll think of something."

"Look, Sandy, that's easy for you to say, but it's my ass—"

"I've got to get back to Rockingham," he interrupted, "but maybe I'll have one more dog before we go. You want another one? This time I'm buying."

I shook my head.

"You sure?"

"I'm sure," I said and started wondering what they served for lunch in county jail.

15

I drove Sandy back to Rockingham, weighted down by my rapidly accumulating misgivings.

But the sun was bright, and the Mustang was purring like the proverbial contented cat, and that helped a lot. Maybe I was staring down the barrel of a contempt citation that could land me in jail before the week was out. Maybe I wasn't. I'd worry about that later.

When I pulled into his circular driveway, Sandy shifted in his seat.

"Pop the trunk," he said.

I pulled the release and heard the trunk lid click open. Before I could get out, Mr. Wu materialized from somewhere. One moment, the driveway was empty, and the next moment, Mr. Wu was standing at the rear of the car like he had been waiting right there for us all along.

Sandy climbed out with more effort than he had used to get in, gripping the door frame to steady himself. He walked back to where Mr. Wu stood looking down at the five banker's boxes.

"Mr. Wu, I need you to take these boxes somewhere safe. Somewhere nobody will think to look for them."

Mr. Wu nodded once, a sharp dip of his chin that conveyed understanding without requiring words. He reached into the trunk and lifted the first box out with an ease that suggested he was even stronger than he looked.

I stood there and watched him carry that box away. Part of me wanted to ask where he was taking it, but Sandy had already told me why it wasn't a good idea for me to know that, and I realized he was probably right. Still, watching documents for which I had assumed both moral and legal responsibility disappear into the hands of a man I had met barely three hours ago made me uneasy.

Mr. Wu returned for the second box. Then the third. Each time, he moved with that same economic efficiency. No expression on his face, no wasted motion.

"How well do you know Mr. Wu?" I asked Sandy.

"He's been with me fifteen years. Former military. Army Ranger, I believe, though he doesn't talk about it much. Came to work for me after he left the service." Sandy paused. "He's the most reliable man I've ever known. If he says he'll do something, it gets done. If he says he'll keep something safe, it stays safe."

Mr. Wu carried the fourth box away.

"You're worried," Sandy observed.

"These documents are supposed to be in my custody. I'm the one responsible for them."

"And now they're in the custody of your co-counsel. Perfectly legitimate." Sandy's eyes held mine. "Charlie, if you walk into that courtroom Friday morning with those boxes sitting in your car trunk, what do you think will happen?"

"The judge will probably order me to surrender them."

"And when you refuse?"

"She's likely to hold me in contempt."

"And then?"

I didn't answer. I saw where this was going.

"If she detains you long enough, eventually somebody is likely to locate your car and search it," Sandy said. "Then they'll have all Emma's documents anyway, and you will have gone to jail for nothing."

Mr. Wu returned for the fifth and final box. I watched him lift it and saw the slight adjustment he made in his grip to balance the weight. Then he disappeared around the corner of the house, taking with him any illusion I had of being in control of this situation.

Sandy clapped me on the shoulder.

"I've decided I like you, Charlie. And I'm guessing you're a pretty damn good lawyer."

"You don't know that."

"Yeah," Sandy said, "I do."

The words should have felt reassuring. Instead, they made me feel like a kid getting ready to receive a participation trophy.

"I still don't know what I'm going to tell that judge on Friday," I said.

"You're going to tell her the truth. That you don't have the documents in your possession and don't know where they are. Both of which will be entirely accurate."

"She's not going to accept that."

"Probably not. But don't cross that bridge until you come to it."

Sandy turned toward his house, then stopped and looked back at me.

"One more thing. If Emma has gone to ground, there's a reason for it. Let her stay there until she's ready to surface."

"And if she never does?"

"Then you've got bigger problems than a family law court judge who wants to throw her weight around."

He walked toward his front door, moving with the careful gait of a man who knew his body was betraying him bit by bit but refused to acknowledge it.

That left me alone in the circular driveway, staring at my empty trunk. The boxes were gone. Emma was gone. Harry wasn't answering his phone.

And in two days, I had to stand in front of Judge Edith McClanahan and explain why I couldn't produce documents that a duly issued subpoena demanded I produce.

I closed the trunk, climbed back into the Mustang, and fired up the engine. The V8 rumbled reassuringly beneath the hood, but I couldn't stop wondering if I'd just made a terrible mistake.

On the way home, I drove into Santa Monica and found a copy shop on Wilshire with exactly the sign in the window I was looking for.

Business Cards Printed
While You Wait

I had seen a lot of signs like that around LA. Quickie business cards were apparently a booming industry here. It seemed to me half the people in town were busily working to convince the other half that they were somebody worth knowing.

I parked the Mustang and walked inside. The place smelled like toner and hot plastic. A kid who couldn't have been much more than twenty stood behind the counter, his nose pierced, his hair dyed an alarming shade of blue.

"Help you?" he asked without looking up from whatever magazine he was reading.

"I need some business cards."

He closed the magazine and gave me a once-over, probably trying to figure out what kind of business I was in. The khakis and polo shirt I were wearing wouldn't help him much.

"Standard size? Raised lettering?"

"Just basic. Nothing fancy."

He pulled out a form and slid it across the counter along with a pen.

"Fill this out. Put down whatever you want on them. Name, title, address, phone number. Like that."

I stared at the form. What did I want to put on the cards? I suppose the obvious, right?

CHARLES TRUST
ATTORNEY AT LAW

That looked painfully sparse now that I saw it written out there on the form. No firm name. No partners. Just ... well, me.

And what about the address and telephone number? The only address I had was Harry's house, and using that felt wrong somehow. Like I was borrowing Harry's legitimacy along with his real estate. But I didn't have an office, so I didn't have anything else to put on them. The phone number would have to be Harry's landline, too.

The kid took the form and studied it.

"That's it? No firm name? No specialties?"

"That's it."

He shrugged and punched some keys on a computer keyboard.

"We can have them for you in about twenty minutes," he

said. "Twenty-seven fifty for five hundred cards on standard stock."

I had no idea what standard stock meant, and I had no intention of asking.

"That works."

I paid the kid and wandered around the shop while he fed the information into whatever machine cranked out business cards. Killing time, I leafed through a sample book that showed different fonts and layouts I could have ordered, plus a bunch of fancy options with embossing and gold foil that probably cost several times what I had paid. I was okay with the plain cards I had ordered. Plain was good. I was a plain kind of guy.

Through the front window, I could see the Mustang sitting at the curb, which made me think again about the five bankers boxes worth of empty space now available in the trunk. Mr. Wu probably had those boxes tucked away somewhere so secure that even the CIA couldn't find them.

A machine behind the counter started humming, then it began clicking in a steady rhythm. I listened to the sound of the machine and smelled the faint odor of chemicals and ink. I thought about Emma. I thought some more about those documents I no longer had. I thought about standing in front of Judge Edith McClanahan in two days and telling her I had nothing to give her.

The clicking stopped. A few minutes later, the kid came over to the counter carrying a small white box.

"All set."

I took the box and looked at it. It was surprisingly light for something that now represented my entire professional infrastructure.

"Thanks."

"Good luck with the lawyer thing," the kid said, already returning to his magazine.

I walked back out into the California sunshine and got in the Mustang. Before I started the engine, I opened the box and pulled out one of the cards.

The printing was clean, and the lettering was sharp. My name was in bold at the top with **ATTORNEY AT LAW** printed underneath. Harry's address and phone number were in smaller type at the bottom.

I had to admit the cards looked pretty legitimate. Genuinely professional. Holding them made me feel like I was actually a real lawyer again. Which I guess I was. Sort of. I just hoped I would have the chance to use a few of the cards before I got thrown in jail for contempt of court and possibly disbarred.

It would be a shame to waste them.

Now that I was an official lawyer again, it occurred to me I probably ought to figure out where the courthouse was.

I grabbed my Thomas Guide from the glove box and looked up courthouses in the index. There were a lot of them. At least thirty or forty. The Superior Court of Los Angeles County had courthouses scattered across the entire county, most of them in places that meant nothing to me.

Downtown LA housed the main courthouse, of course. Major criminal cases were mostly tried there, as far as I knew. Then out here on the west side of town, there was the West Los Angeles courthouse, and the LAX courthouse near the airport. Beverly Hills had a courthouse, too, though I'd heard somewhere it was only being used for limited purposes now. Malibu used to have a courthouse, but I was pretty sure that one had been closed.

And then there was Santa Monica.

I had heard somewhere that the Santa Monica Courthouse

got confused with the West LA Courthouse all the time. Lawyers and litigants spent half their time whizzing around LA trying to figure out which courthouse they were supposed to be in. Sometimes cases got filed in one location and then transferred to another for reasons nobody could quite explain. You might start at Santa Monica, get bounced to LAX, and then end up in Van Nuys if you were particularly unlucky.

The whole system seemed designed to make sure nobody ever showed up at the right place at the right time. It was perfectly organized for that, just like the rest of Los Angeles was.

I needed to figure out where I was supposed to be Friday morning when Judge Edith McClanahan was going to decide whether to throw me in jail or not, and since I was in Santa Monica now, locating the building and figuring out how the parking thing worked seemed a wise move. Maybe that would reduce my stress levels a little on Friday. Yeah, fat chance, huh?

I spotted a pay phone on the wall at the end of the little strip of shops on Wilshire in front of which I was parked, and I got out and fed a quarter into it. I got the number of the Superior Court information line, and a woman with a bored voice answered on the fourth ring.

"I need to find out which courthouse handles family law cases," I said.

"Which district?"

"I'm not sure. Is there something called the West District? The subpoena just says Superior Court of Los Angeles, Department E, West District, Family Law Division."

"Yeah, there's a West District."

"So that would be at the West LA Courthouse?"

"No. Family Law Department E, West District, would be Santa Monica."

"The Santa Monica Courthouse?"

"Yes."

"The West District is at the Santa Monica Courthouse, not at the West LA Courthouse?"

"Right."

Of course, it was.

"Can you give me the exact address?" I asked just to make absolutely sure I had this right.

She sighed as if I'd just asked her to explain quantum physics.

"1725 Main Street in Santa Monica. You want directions?"

"No, I can find it. Thanks."

I hung up and walked back to the Mustang. I tossed the Thomas Guide in the glove box and started the engine. At least now I could drive over and make sure I was all organized for Friday morning, so I wouldn't be one of those idiots showing up at the wrong courthouse.

Or probably I wouldn't be.

LA being LA, few things ever turned out to be quite that simple.

It was only a short drive from Wilshire over to Main Street, but when I got to where the courthouse was supposed to be, I wasn't absolutely sure at first that I was in the right place.

The building was set well back from the street behind a neatly trimmed lawn. It was low-slung, rambling, and white, and it was built in the general style that LA real estate agents insisted on calling *mid-century*, but I'd never understood whether that was an actual school of architecture or just something a bunch of real estate agents had made up so ordinary old buildings would sound more interesting.

The building didn't really look like any courthouse I had

ever seen before. There were palm trees in front of it, for God's sake. *Palm trees?* Welcome to California, huh?

Most courthouses I had been in back in Virginia and the District of Columbia were a little shabby and run down while trying to look like they were really solemn and stately. The Santa Monica Courthouse didn't look like that. It looked more like a small-town elementary school. I half expected to hear a school bell ring and see a mob of kids come running out for recess.

I drove around a few blocks and marked the location of two garages where I could park, and now I felt properly prepared for Friday morning. I had the address where I was supposed to be, I knew where that address was, and I had found some places where I could park my car when I got there.

And in LA, that put me way ahead of the game already.

16

I got to the Santa Monica Courthouse early that Friday morning, made my way through a perfunctory security check, and went looking for room 111. It was on the second floor. Go figure, huh?

The subpoena was for 10:00am, but I was there a little after nine. I hadn't been in a courtroom in a long time, and I had never been in a courtroom in California at all, so I figured I ought to give myself some time to get the lay of the land. Or maybe I just didn't want to be late for my own hanging.

Courtrooms inspire phrases like the *majesty of the law* a lot, and television has raised our expectations as to what a real courtroom looks like to something that stops just short of the Sistine Chapel. I can say with some certainty that no one who uses that phrase or has an expectation like that has ever been inside the Santa Monica Courthouse. A rival to the Sistine Chapel, it isn't.

Room 111 looked more like a meeting room for an insignificant suburban Home Owners Association than it did anything that most Americans would recognize as a courtroom, but for better or worse, it was still the home of Department E, Superior Court, West District, Family Law Division.

The space looked like it had been designed by a committee that couldn't decide between institutional efficiency and beach town informality. So they split the difference and achieved neither.

The walls were paneled in some kind of blond wood veneer that was probably supposed to look basic and modest, but ended up just looking cheap. The judge's bench sat at the front of the room, raised maybe two feet off the floor. Not the imposing height you would expect from television, but just high enough to make the point. A dozen or so wooden chairs the same color as the paneling lined the low wooden railing that divided the front of the courtroom from a small spectator section in the rear. They looked like the kind of chairs you might find in a DMV waiting room.

Two tables for opposing legal counsel faced the bench just inside the railing, separated by an aisle barely wide enough for the very wide, brown-uniformed bailiff to waddle through. The bailiff was a Hispanic guy in his fifties with a heavily pock-marked face who looked like he was taking a nap even when he was standing up.

The ceiling tiles showed water stains in one corner. A clock on the wall ticked loudly enough to hear when nobody was talking. There was no jury box, of course. This was Family Law Division. There were no juries here, just judges making decisions about who got what.

There were a few people moving back and forth at the front of the courtroom. Some were conferring with the judge's clerk, who occupied a small table right in front of the bench, while others seemed to be conferring mostly with each other. Two were carrying on a whispered conversation with the judge, who was seated behind the bench.

Most of the people present were scattered around in the spectator seats waiting to be called for their time in the spotlight. Those people largely sat alone, a few feet of space between them and whoever they were divorcing, but there were small groups of three or four as well. Some of the people whispered back and forth with other people who were probably their lawyers. Others clutched folders and papers and looked like they were going to try representing themselves. All of them looked exactly like you would expect people to look in a divorce court on a Friday morning. Angry. Resigned. Tired.

I had chosen a seat about midway back in the spectator section and off to one side. It gave me a good view of the whole courtroom without making me particularly conspicuous.

Judge Edith McClanahan presided from the bench with the air of someone who had seen it all and wasn't impressed by any of it. She was a tiny black woman who looked to be in her sixties. Her gray hair was short and kept in a practical-looking cut that I didn't know the name for. She appeared to wear no makeup, and she mostly kept her eyes focused down on the files and pleadings her clerk shuffled up to the bench for her to read.

When she looked out at the room, it was over the top of rectangular silver reading glasses perched at the end of her nose. The black robe she wore was faded and appeared as if it might have been through a few more dry-cleaning cycles than it should have. The judge made me think of the seagulls I watched on the beach behind my house. There were long periods of stillness that were interrupted by abrupt, jerky movements, then followed by more long periods of stillness.

Judge McClanahan moved her cases along with brisk efficiency, her voice carrying just enough authority to keep order without having to raise it. Either the bailiff or the clerk would call a case, and the parties and their lawyers would shuffle around until they had all gathered in the front of the courtroom. Sometimes the judge would ask somebody a few questions, but mostly she would just consult the papers her clerk piled in front of her, make a ruling of some kind, and move on. Next case.

No drama, no television theatrics. Just the grinding machinery of the family law court doing what it does.

I watched the judge work through maybe half a dozen matters. There was a child custody modification that was unopposed, so it was put through without any fuss. Temporary spousal support was set in two cases. She resolved several discovery disputes that were too boring for me even to try to follow them.

Judge McClanahan seemed like a decent judge. Fair enough. Certainly better than some judges I had been in front of, but maybe not as engaged as others. She showed obvious impatience with lawyers who she didn't think were adequately prepared or otherwise wasted her time, but I could hardly fault her for that.

The clock on the wall read 10:03. Then 10:09. Then 10:16.

Around 10:30, the bailiff called out in a voice that made it plain to everybody that he had done something similar at least ten thousand times before, "Scott versus Scott."

I felt a buzz go through me.

Judge McClanahan looked down at the papers her clerk placed on the bench in front of her.

"The matter before the court today is a *subpoena duces tecum* issued by me on application from the Petitioner to one Mr. Charles Trust for documents allegedly in his possession. I understand the subpoena has been served."

She lifted her head and looked over her reading glasses.

"Is Mr. Trust in the courtroom?"

I stood up and cleared my throat.

"I'm Mr. Trust, Your Honor."

The judge barely glanced at me.

"Is the Petitioner or the Petitioner's counsel here?"

"Yes, Your Honor."

Off on the other side of the spectator section, four men wearing well-cut dark suits came to their feet. One was about my age, one appeared to be a few years older, and the other two were clearly much older. Late fifties, certainly. Maybe even sixties.

My guess was that the two younger guys were associates, bag-carriers really. Law firms like to flood courtrooms with people like that just to remind everyone that they had unlimited manpower on hand to throw into every conflict, no matter how minor, not to mention the increase in billable hours those extra people added. The two older men in the group would be the important players. Zachariah Scott was one of them, and the other would be Brian Hurter, the partner the subpoena had said was Zachariah Scott's attorney of record.

But which man was Scott and which was his attorney?

The judge lifted both hands and gestured us forward.

"Take your places, gentlemen," she said. "Time's a-wasting."

When Team Zachariah Scott reached the swinging gate in the little railing separating the spectator section from the business end of the courtroom, it became obvious who was who. One of the two older men stepped aside and held the gate as the other walked through, which pretty much sealed the deal.

The attorney stood aside for the client, not the other way around. However highly we thought of ourselves, we were just the servants around here, the hired hands, and we knew it all too well.

I hung back and studied the man who walked through the

gate first. He had to be Zachariah Scott. Not only was he probably the oldest in the group, he had the best suit.

Scott looked like a man doing a Cary Grant shtick. He was well over six feet tall, and very slim, and he carried himself with the same loose-limbed, boyish nonchalance that had made Grant such a huge star. His suit was a soft-looking dark blue cashmere and wool that draped his body so perfectly that I would bet it had cost him more than I paid for my Mustang. The light of glamor illuminated the man as if a spotlight were following him everywhere he went.

"We're on the record in the matter of Scott versus Scott," the judge said as the four men took their places at one of the counsel tables, and the court reporter seated facing the judge's clerk began clicking away at her machine.

I pushed through the little gate right behind Scott's entourage. I walked as confidently as possible to the other counsel table and sat down. Always act like you know what you're doing, right?

I could feel Scott's eyes on me as I sat. Well, fair enough. He was probably as curious about me as I was about him. But I kept my eyes forward. I wasn't going to give him the satisfaction of knowing that I had noticed.

The judge peered at me over her reading glasses, and I had a moment of panic. Was I sitting in the wrong place? That wouldn't be a good start, would it?

"Mr ..."

She glanced down at the papers on her bench again to remind her who I was, but she said nothing about where I was sitting so I figured I was okay.

"Mr. Trust. Please give the clerk your card so that she can enter your appearance for the Respondent."

I got to my feet and cleared my throat again.

"I'm not appearing for the Respondent, Your Honor. I am

here purely in response to the *subpoena duces tecum* issued by you."

"But I've been told you represent the Respondent. Do you not, Mr. Trust?"

"No, ma'am. I do not."

The judge looked at me.

"You do not?"

"I do not."

She shifted her eyes to Mr. Hurter and his entourage.

"Was I misinformed, Mr. Hurter? When you applied for the subpoena, you represented that Mr. Trust was appearing for Mrs. Scott in this matter."

Hurter rose to his feet, and I smiled. Hurter was the guy who had stood back and held open the gate just as I thought he was. He took a moment to smooth out his suit jacket. Maybe he was stalling, or maybe very expensive suits simply required smoothing out every time you stood up. I really didn't know.

"That was the information we had, Your Honor," Hurter finally allowed. "I had no reason to doubt it at the time I applied to you for the subpoena. Nor, quite honestly, do I doubt it now."

Hurter slowly rotated his head and gave me a look that made me think of a barracuda sizing up its next meal.

The judge's eyes flicked to me, back to Hurter, and then back to me again.

"But Mr. Trust just told me he does not represent Mrs. Scott, Mr. Hurter. Surely, you're not suggesting he was being less than candid about that."

I was getting a little sick of standing there listening to people talk about me, so I figured it might be time to grab this particular bull by its horns.

"Your Honor, may I be heard?" I asked.

"For what purpose?"

"For the purpose of explaining the misunderstanding that seems to have occurred here."

"Then by all means, Mr. Trust." The judge waved one hand in the air, leaned back, and folded her arms. "The floor is yours."

Judge McClanahan stared down at me and waited, and I could sense Hurter, Scott, and their entourage giving me a similar look from off to my right.

I cleared my throat.

"Your honor, a friend asked me to meet with Mrs. Scott and listen to what she had to say. In the course of our conversation, she provided me with a number of documents, which she said would help me understand her position. I am still in the process of reviewing and digesting those documents, and it is my belief that the materials she has provided to me for review are clearly subject to attorney-client privilege and therefore not subject to production under the *subpoena duces tecum* issued by you."

"That's ridiculous, Your Honor," Hurter spoke up. "He just said that he doesn't represent Mrs. Scott, and then in the next breath he asserts attorney-client privilege. He can't have it both ways."

"Actually, Your Honor," I pointed out. "In this instance, I think I can."

"This I've got to hear," the judge said.

"I have conducted an initial client interview with Mrs. Scott, and I am still in the process of reviewing and digesting the materials she provided to me in connection with that interview."

The judge waited. Hurter waited. I was going to have to do better than that.

"It is well settled that an initial client interview is subject to attorney-client privilege," I continued, hoping that was true.

"The materials I am reviewing are part of that initial interview and obviously covered by that privilege."

"It's not obvious to me at all, Your Honor," Hurter started up again, "particularly not if the materials referred to are stolen."

"Your Honor, I see nothing in the subpoena to support Mr. Hurter's claim that these are stolen documents. Surely something more than his bare assertion that they are stolen should be required before he can advance that claim to support the subpoena."

"I'm sure it's obvious to the court that there is no other way—"

"That's enough for now, Mr. Hurter."

Now it was Judge McClanahan's turn to stop and clear her throat.

"Let me see if I can cut through this, Mr. Trust. Has Mrs. Scott asked you to represent her?"

"Yes, ma'am. She has."

"But you are saying you do not in fact represent her?"

"I'm still reviewing her position and considering whether or not to do so."

"Then you are in possession of the documents addressed by *subpoena duces tecum*. Is that the case?"

I hesitated, and then immediately wondered if anyone had noticed.

"Yes, ma'am."

Close enough for government work.

"Give me an idea what we're talking about here, Mr. Trust. A few sheets of paper? A file or two? A box full of papers?"

"I was given five bankers boxes, and all five of those boxes are filled with files and other documents."

"What sort of files and documents, Mr. Trust?"

That was a tricky question to respond to. I suspected the

judge knew it and was intentionally squeezing me to see how far I would push the privilege claim. I looked away from the judge and then looked back.

"You're putting me in a difficult position, Your Honor. I don't see how I can answer that without violating attorney-client privilege."

"I'm not asking you what the documents say, Mr. Trust. I'm merely asking you what the general subject matter covered by them is."

She wasn't going to make this easy, was she? Well, as the cliché goes, in for a penny, in for a pound.

"I must respectfully give you the same answer I gave you before, Your Honor. The documents themselves, their contents, even their subject matter are all clearly covered by attorney-client privilege."

"It's not at all clear to me, Your Honor," Hurter started up, but the judge waved him into silence again.

"Hush up, Mr. Hurter. I'll handle this."

I searched the judge's face for some indication as to how far she was willing to go. I thought her expression might be more bemused than hostile, but maybe she had just had too much caffeine that morning and was feeling it. I'd hate to bet my life on trying to read her face.

"Did you bring the documents covered by the subpoena duces tecum with you this morning?"

"Uh ... no, ma'am."

"Have you filed a motion to quash the subpoena that hasn't yet come to my attention?"

"Uh ... no, ma'am.

"Then you see my dilemma, Mr. Trust. On the one hand, you admit you are able to comply with the subpoena, but are simply refusing to do so. On the other hand, you haven't asked me to quash the subpoena either. You do realize I can now find you in contempt of court and either fine you or even detain you until you comply with the subpoena, don't you?"

"Respectfully, Your Honor, I cannot comply with the subpoena without violating both my legal and ethical duty to Mrs. Scott."

"I admire your principles, Mr. Trust, even if I do not admire your actions."

"Pardon me, Your Honor?"

"If you're so concerned about the issue of attorney-client privilege, why didn't you file a motion to quash the subpoena and put the privilege issue in front of me for a decision? Why did you choose simply to defy the subpoena and make the decision about what is privileged and what is not entirely on your own?"

I had to admit that was a pretty damn good question, and I figured I had about ten seconds to come up with an equally good answer before the judge lost patience and told the bailiff to take me into custody.

"I'm waiting, Mr. Trust."

Five seconds left now.

That was when a gravelly voice boomed out from the spectator area behind me.

"May I be heard, Your Honor?"

I didn't dare turn around, but then I didn't really need to turn around.

I had no doubt at all exactly who it was.

17

"Who are you, sir?" Judge McClanahan asked.

"I am Mr. Trust's co-counsel. I am assisting him in undertaking the evaluation of Mrs. Scott's position that has brought him here today, Judge. My name is Sandy Bouchier."

The judge's mouth actually opened.

"*The* Sandy Bouchier?"

"I'm the only one I know, ma'am."

I've always thought the expression *the room went silent* was mostly a poetic exaggeration. But it's not. Because, right then, this one did.

The silence was so complete that I could hear Sandy's shoes squeak as he walked up the aisle behind me and passed through the gate that divided the front of the courtroom from the spectator section. He positioned himself at my right elbow and gave me a slight hip check. It was plain he expected me to move down the counsel table and make room for him in the prime position closest to the judge.

As I moved, I examined him out of the corner of my eye

without turning my head. He was wearing a deep blue double-breasted suit with a wide chalk stripe that made him look like an old-fashioned mouthpiece out of a fifties movie, a guy who had spent his whole life in courtrooms representing unpopular causes and even less popular people. Which made sense, because that was pretty much what Sandy was.

Sandy seemed to feel me looking at him, because his Coke-bottle green fighter pilot eyes suddenly flicked toward me. They met mine for just an instant, and then they were gone.

"I apologize for not recognizing you, sir," Judge McClanahan said. "I had no idea you were still practicing. I assumed you had settled into a well-deserved retirement long ago, Mr. Bouchier."

"Age comes for us all, Your Honor, but I find I still have a little life left in me yet."

"I must say then, Mr. Bouchier, you are most welcome in my court. You were an idol of mine back when I was a young lawyer with the ACLU. I am honored to have you here today."

"The honor is all mine, Judge."

"I doubt that, but I will accept it as the gesture of gallantry it so obviously was."

All that was missing in this little love-fest was the judge jumping down off the bench, running over, and planting a big, sloppy kiss on Sandy's cheek, and it was starting to sound to me like that might be coming any moment.

Apparently, it was starting to sound like that to Mr. Hurter, too.

"Your Honor, I know we all have the greatest respect for Mr. Bouchier's accomplishments in the past," he spoke up, "but what does any of that have to do with—"

"Didn't I ask you to hush up, Mr. Hurter? You know, I could always arrange for you to join Mr. Trust in one of our holding cells."

Oops.

I was just starting to think that the Judge's professional infatuation with Sandy might shoulder aside the issue of me producing Emma Scott's documents, but apparently it wasn't going to be nearly that easy. Holding me in contempt still appeared to be very much on the table.

That was when Sandy made his move to take it off the table.

"Your Honor, may I address your question about why no motion to quash was filed?"

"You may."

Sandy placed both hands flat on the counsel table and leaned forward slightly.

"The fault lies entirely with me."

Judge McClanahan tilted her head.

"How so, Mr. Bouchier?"

"I committed to Mr. Trust that I would prepare and file a motion to quash the subpoena with an appropriate brief detailing the cases supporting that position. Unfortunately, I forgot to do so."

The judge's eyebrows went up.

"You forgot?"

"I'm afraid so, Your Honor. I'm eighty years old, and my memory isn't what it used to be. I take full responsibility for the oversight."

I kept my face blank, but inside I was scrambling to see where Sandy was going with this. The man had argued before the Supreme Court. He didn't just forget to file motions.

Judge McClanahan studied Sandy for a long moment.

"Mr. Trust, is this accurate? You asked Mr. Bouchier to file a motion to quash, and he failed to do so?"

Before I could answer, Sandy spoke up again.

"I must interject myself again here, Your Honor. Mr. Trust

is too much of a gentleman to say so, but I believe he refrained from mentioning my failure to you out of misguided loyalty. He was simply trying to protect me from embarrassment."

The judge looked at me.

"Is that true, Mr. Trust?"

I swallowed. Sandy had just handed me a lifeline, but taking it meant lying to a judge. On the other hand, what choice did I have?

"I wouldn't want to put Mr. Bouchier in an awkward position, Your Honor."

Close enough.

"I see," the judge sighed.

Judge McClanahan leaned back in her chair and drummed her fingers on the bench. Down at the other counsel table, Hurter looked like he wanted to say something, but he was smart enough to keep his mouth shut this time.

"Mr. Bouchier, how long would it take you to prepare and file the appropriate motion?"

"I could have it to you within a week, Your Honor. I apologize profusely for the delay and any inconvenience it may have caused the court."

The judge pursed her lips.

"One week, Mr. Bouchier. I want your word that the motion will be on my desk by next Friday."

She pointed one finger at Sandy like a schoolteacher warning a particularly troublesome student.

"You have it, Your Honor."

"Meanwhile, I will hold this matter in abeyance pending review of your motion and the supporting brief."

Hurter shot to his feet.

"Your Honor, I must object. The subpoena was duly issued and properly served. Mr. Trust has admitted he possesses the documents. There's no legal basis for—"

Judge McClanahan turned her gaze on him, and the temperature in the courtroom seemed to drop about twenty degrees. Hurter froze mid-sentence.

"Are you finished, Mr. Hurter?"

"Your Honor, I merely—"

"Because if you're finished, you may sit down. If you're not finished, I may have to consider my options."

Hurter's face went red, and he lowered himself back into his chair without another word.

The judge returned her attention to Sandy.

"One week, Mr. Bouchier. Don't make me regret extending you this courtesy."

"You won't regret it, Your Honor. Thank you."

Judge McClanahan glanced at her clerk.

"Next case."

I started to speak as Sandy and I walked out through the double doors at the front of the courtroom, but he fixed those green eyes on me and gave a small shake of his head.

"Not here," he said quietly. "Wait."

We walked out to the front of the building in silence. The morning had warmed up, and the palm trees cast sharp shadows across the lawn. I could see the ocean a few blocks away, a sliver of blue between two office buildings.

A black Lincoln Town Car sat parked in a no-standing zone directly in front of the courthouse entrance. Mr. Wu stood beside it, hands clasped in front of him, even though I knew Sandy hadn't called him. Maybe he just had a sixth sense about when Sandy would need him.

"I've got my car," I said. "I don't need a ride."

"It's not a ride," Sandy replied. "It's a secure conference room. Get in."

Mr. Wu had already opened the rear passenger door. Sandy climbed in without waiting for me to respond. I stood there on the sidewalk for a moment, then followed him into the car.

The interior smelled like leather and expensive cologne. The seats were soft and deep, the kind you could sink into and disappear. Mr. Wu closed the door behind me with barely a whisper of sound, then got behind the wheel. The engine started, smooth and quiet, and we pulled away from the curb.

I hadn't heard Sandy tell Mr. Wu where to go. I glanced at Sandy, but he was looking out the window, apparently unconcerned with our destination. Maybe they had some kind of telepathic communication system. Or maybe Mr. Wu just knew.

We headed north on Main Street, away from the courthouse.

"I only like talking in places I can control," Sandy said, still looking out the window. "Places that I'm sure are secure."

"Like your car?"

"Like my car."

He turned to face me, those green eyes sharp and focused.

"It gets a full security sweep every week. Mr. Wu sees to it. I can talk to people here without worrying about bugs or recording devices or other surprises. In courthouses, restaurants, offices, or anywhere else in this town, there's always somebody around who might well have an interest in what we're discussing and make the effort to overhear."

I thought about that. About the level of caution Sandy must have learned to have his car swept for bugs every single week, month in and month out. Then I thought about the documents Emma had given me and the kind of people who might want them, and Sandy's caution started to seem downright reasonable.

"Where are we going?" I asked.

"Does it matter?"

"I suppose not."

Mr. Wu turned right on Santa Monica Boulevard, heading north. Traffic was building as we got closer to noon. The Lincoln glided between lanes with the smooth confidence of a shark cutting through waters it owned.

"Can I talk now?" I asked.

Sandy nodded.

"I'm surprised to see you here, of course, but I appreciate it."

Sandy nodded again.

"Thank you for solving my problem," I added.

"I didn't solve your problem," Sandy said. His voice carried the same gravelly quality it had up in Judge McClanahan's courtroom, but now it was quiet, almost conversational. "You just have a different problem now."

I waited for him to explain. Through the window, I could see we were heading away from Santa Monica in the direction of the 405.

"You've just admitted in open court that you have a huge number of records and documents that Emma Scott turned over to you, Charlie. Five bankers boxes worth of material. Judge McClanahan heard it. Mr. Hurter heard it. His two associates heard it. The clerk heard it. The bailiff heard it. Every lawyer sitting in that courtroom waiting for their cases to be called heard it."

Sandy turned those green eyes on me.

"I'm sure Emma Scott's husband already knows what's in those records and documents. And if he knows, then other people know, too. They can't take the risk that you'll leak them to somebody. The press. The IRS. The FBI. The U.S. Attorney."

A cold feeling settled over me.

"So, they'll be coming for them," Sandy added.

"Who's coming for them?" I asked.

"Ah, well," Sandy said. "That's the thing."

He pulled a cigar from his jacket pocket and rolled it between his fingers without lighting it. He was probably contemplating Pele's rules even now.

"I told you that I wasn't going to ask you what was in those documents. I'm still not going to ask. But I've been doing this for a long time. Long enough to know that when a television producer's wife runs away and his lawyers start issuing subpoenas for boxes of financial records, that we're not talking about a garden-variety divorce."

"No," I admitted. "We're not."

"Wire transfers? Offshore accounts? Shell companies?"

I didn't answer. Sandy waved his hand.

"I'm not asking you to confirm. I'm just thinking out loud." He paused. "The kind of people who move large amounts of money through questionable channels aren't the kind of people who react well to exposure. They have resources. Connections. Ways of protecting their interests that don't involve the legal system."

"What are you saying here, Sandy?"

"I'm saying you just put your ass on the line, my young friend, and you did it for a woman you hardly know who isn't even your client."

"I didn't really have any choice. Attorney-client privilege—"

Sandy waved me into silence.

"You don't need to explain. It was the right thing for you to do."

Those green eyes flicked over and pinned me to the seat.

"And doing the right thing even when you don't have to do it is worth a big gold star in my book."

Sandy went back to looking out the window.

I waited for a while, but eventually, of course, my patience wore thin, and I gave him a verbal nudge.

"So, Sandy, what now?"

"You prepare a motion to quash, and write a brief in support of it," he said.

"I thought you told Judge McClanahan you were going to do that."

Sandy gave me a look.

"I'd hardly know where to begin, Sandy. Legal writing was never my strong suit."

Sandy's green eyes fixed on me with the kind of look that made me feel like I was back in law school and being called on by a professor who already knew I hadn't done the reading.

"Naturally, you'll sign my name to both the motion and the brief. But you're the young lawyer here, Charlie. The assignment goes to you."

"I don't think—"

"There's only one good thing about becoming an old lawyer," Sandy interrupted, "and that's having young lawyers do the grunt work for you."

There wasn't much I could say to that, so I didn't say anything. I just nodded.

"You have a week," Sandy continued, brushing aside my protest. "So take a week. Don't file the motion until next Friday at the end of the day. Make it thick. And long. Force the judge to get her clerk to research every case you cite. That will buy us another week or so before that gets done and she can rule on it."

He turned those eyes back out the window, watching LA slide past beyond the tinted glass.

"Maybe that will even buy you enough time for this woman to show up and take you off the hook."

Mr. Wu made a lane change without signaling, which was

so smooth I wouldn't have noticed it at all if I hadn't been looking past Sandy and out the window. He slipped neatly between a Mercedes and a BMW and slid into the left lane like water flowing around rocks.

"What if Emma doesn't show up in those two weeks?" I asked.

"Then you'd better write a really good brief."

"And if the judge denies the motion anyway?"

"Then we'll figure something else out." Sandy turned back to me. "You know what the secret to being a good lawyer is, Charlie?"

I waited.

"Buy time. Always buy time. You can't think clearly when the pressure is on, so buy time any way you can get it."

He gestured with the cigar.

"A motion to quash buys time. Discovery disputes buy time. Continuances buy time. Hell, even showing up late to court buys time if you do it right."

"I'm not sure that's what they taught us in law school."

"That's because law schools are run by people who have never had to save either a client's life or their own. They teach you theory. I'm teaching you survival."

And with that, Sandy turned away. He stared out the window, and said nothing else.

18

Mr. Wu passed under the 405 and continued east toward Beverly Hills. Sandy still hadn't told me where we were going, and not asking him had become a point of pride.

"I'll need help," I said. "With the brief."

"You'll figure it out. Go to a good law library. Do the work."

"I don't even know where there *is* a good law library."

"I used to lecture at UCLA," Sandy said. "I still have library privileges there, so I'll call and tell them you're doing some research for me. They'll put your name on the admission list, and you'll be golden."

Sandy gave me a look.

"You do know where UCLA is, don't you?"

I ignored his question, as he no doubt expected me to, and asked one of my own that felt much more pressing.

"How do you suggest I get started?"

"Find some California law review articles on attorney-client privilege in California. There must be a few. Those ought to point you to the major cases. Find the cases that support your position and read them. Then cite and argue those cases in your brief. String together enough legal reasoning to make your argument look weighty."

"And if my legal reasoning isn't very good?"

"Doesn't matter. What matters is volume. Judges hate reading long briefs, so they hand them off to their clerks. Clerks are usually fresh out of law school and terrified of missing something important, so they find and read every case you cite and they check every citation. That takes time."

Sandy smiled, and I could see the fighter he must have been twenty or thirty years ago.

"Time, Charlie. When you come right down to it, it's the only thing any of us has got that's worth a damn. And whatever you're trying to do, everything usually turns out to depend on it."

We were rapidly sinking into fortune cookie territory, so I pulled us back to another practical consideration that had just occurred to me.

"I'm going to have a problem preparing the final version of the motion and brief for filing."

Sandy gave me a quizzical look.

"I don't have a typewriter," I explained.

"A typewriter?"

Sandy enunciated the word as if he might be unfamiliar with its meaning.

"Don't you have a computer with a word processing program on it?" he asked.

I shook my head.

"Good Lord," Sandy muttered, "and I thought *I* was old."

"I guess I could rent—"

"I bought Pele a new PC for her bookstore just a few months ago. I'll call her and tell her you need to use it. Probably working there is a good idea for you, anyway. Less chance of an unwelcome interruption."

"Uh ... I'm not so sure about that."

Sandy cocked his head and gave me a look.

"Young love running rough?"

"There's no young love to it, Sandy. I've already told you that."

"Yeah, you've already told me that. I just don't believe you."

I shook my head and looked away.

"So then what's the problem?" Sandy nudged.

"When I asked Pele to arrange for me to meet you, she decided that I was leveraging our acquaintanceship to get to you through her. She wasn't very happy about it."

"Oh, come on, Trust. Man up! You're not going to let a young woman who runs a bookstore intimidate a member in good standing of the California Bar, are you?"

"Well, maybe I could take the PC and sneak out to my car to write the brief. Kind of like you sneaking out to my car to smoke a cigar because you didn't want Pele to catch you doing it."

Sandy nodded slowly.

"Okay," he said, "you got me there."

I smiled, but I left it at that.

"Anyway," he went on, "don't worry about it. I'll talk to Pele and smooth it out. I'm sure there won't be any problems. Just take her some flowers or something, and everything will be fine."

"Take her some flowers?" I laughed. "My God, Sandy, you really *are* eighty years old, aren't you?"

Sandy just kept looking out the window and said nothing. But I was almost certain I could hear Mr. Wu chuckling quietly under his breath up front behind the wheel.

. . .

Just past the Beverly Hills City Hall, Mr. Wu turned on Melrose and headed east. We were on the other side of La Cienega before Sandy said anything else. When he did, he finally told me where we were going.

"There's a guy I want you to meet," he said. "You need to hear some things he can tell you."

It was a start, but then Sandy fell silent again.

"Who is this guy?" I prodded after it became apparent that was all I was going to get.

"His name is Max Furman. He's a PI. Well, he used to be. Now he's just a retired old fart like me."

The name seemed vaguely familiar, but I had no idea why it should be. I'd used investigators occasionally back in Virginia when they were needed in some of the messier divorce cases that landed on my desk, but as an occupational category, PIs were a long way from my favorite people. Besides, I didn't know any PIs in California. Not a one.

Sandy turned his head toward me and offered a little half-smile.

"You're asking yourself why his name sounds so familiar when you don't know any PIs in California, aren't you?"

Damn. How does he do that?

"Max got a lot of publicity back in the mid-80s when he was brought into the McMartin Preschool mess. You remember that?"

"Vaguely."

"Several people who ran a large preschool here in LA were accused of molesting children at the school, hundreds of them. That resulted in the longest and most expensive criminal trial in American history, but nobody was ever convicted of anything."

"What did Max have to do with it all?"

"He was hired by a group of parents who thought the

LAPD was dogging the investigation. Max was already pretty well regarded then as a Hollywood PI who knew where the dirt was, but what really made him famous was a piece *Sixty Minutes* did on him after he quit the McMartin investigation. He said that the LAPD wasn't trying to solve the case. Instead, they were actively working to prevent the truth from coming out."

"*Sixty Minutes*? You mean that television show?"

Sandy gave me a look.

"You do know what television is, don't you, kid?"

"Yes, Sandy, I know what television is. I just don't watch very much of it. And I'm pretty sure I've never watched *Sixty Minutes*."

"It was the way *Sixty Minutes* described Max that stuck, not what they said about the McMartin investigation. They said he was Raymond Chandler's real-life model for Philip Marlowe."

I laughed. "Well, I can certainly understand how any PI could dine out on a description like that for a very long time, no matter how ridiculous it might be."

"Oh, it's not ridiculous," Sandy said. "It's absolutely true."

"Come on, Sandy. Raymond Chandler wrote the Philip Marlowe books more than fifty years ago."

"Chandler was writing *The Big Sleep* when Max met him. Max was just a young man then, but Chandler must have seen something in him, and he became Chandler's model for Philip Marlowe."

"My God, how old is Max now? He'd have to be—"

"Yeah," Sandy interrupted, "he's even older than I am."

I was pretty sure Sandy was pulling my leg and just waiting to see if I'd fall for it, so I kept quiet. Of course, I supposed it was just possible that there was at least some truth in the story.

This was Hollywood, after all. The unbelievable was part of the air you breathed.

"So we're going to see Philip Marlowe," I finally said.

Sandy nodded, but he said nothing else.

Mr. Wu continued east on Melrose into the hipster precincts where funky little shoe stores sold tennis shoes that started at $1000, and sushi joints offered up tiny globs of rice with even tinier pieces of fish on them for $100 a pop. It was a terminally trendy neighborhood of older buildings, stylish coffee shops, and people who didn't have much to do in the mornings.

When we passed the front gate of Paramount and crossed Western, the world abruptly took a turn, and we entered a sketchy, slightly shabby area that was a few blocks and a million miles away from what everyone thought of when they thought of Hollywood.

Maybe gentrification had been coming here, too, but if it had been, somebody had mugged it along the way.

This stretch of Melrose was all littered sidewalks, old men camped out in doorways, and a dreary array of worn-down commercial buildings decorated with banners, signs, graffiti, peeling paint, and a thick crust of grime. All sorts of small shops lined the sidewalks. They claimed to sell clothes, jewelry, mattresses, furniture, toys, shoes, and electronics. Some claimed to sell all of them at the same time. In this Hollywood, there was no room for romance, no nights filled with possibilities, and no one tapped for stardom. Life here was not an adventure. Life here was workaday, and ordinary, and a grind.

Just before we got to the 101, Mr. Wu turned right, and I clocked the street sign as he did.

Normandie Ave

That was an all-too-familiar street name now to almost everyone in LA. This crummy urban street of no great importance was now the symbol of something no one wanted symbolized.

"This is where the LA riots started, isn't it?" I asked Sandy.

"Further south," he said. "Through Koreatown, and across on the other side of the 10."

The intersection of Normandie and Florence was where mobs had begun pulling drivers out of cars and trucks and beating them into unconsciousness with their fists and bottles and even a folding chair that had been abandoned on the sidewalk. News helicopters circling like vultures captured the grim images and beamed them out to the entire world. The mayhem at Normandie and Florence was now seared into the memories of millions, maybe hundreds of millions of people, none of whom really wanted to remember it at all.

"Max's office is just down here a few blocks," Sandy said. "He's been in the same place for as long as I've known him. He must be eighty-five now, but he still goes to his office every single day."

Normandie Avenue along here was lined with sad-looking strip malls filled with even sadder looking businesses that seemed to just be hanging on. There were also a few two and three-story apartment complexes that looked as if they had been thrown up in a few days and had a useful life of not much longer than that. The area didn't feel particularly dangerous, but neither did it look like a place where you might want to go for an evening stroll.

It was a neighborhood whose only truly outstanding feature was its dreariness. It was exactly the sort of neighborhood I would have gone to looking for Philip Marlowe.

Mr. Wu turned off Normandie into a small parking lot between two identical buildings. They were finished in stucco that had probably once been tan, but had yellowed in the relentless sunshine and carbon-monoxide fouled air of Central LA.

The building on the left sported a huge billboard on top painted in garish shades of yellow, red, and black.

Psychic and Tarot Readers
Spiritualist to the Stars

The building on the right was dark and quiet and had no signage at all.

"Max has been involved in a number of investigations of the film and television industry over the years," Sandy said. "We're old friends, and he owes me more than one favor. I called him to ask him what he knew about Zachariah Scott and his business operations, and as it happens, he knows a great deal. I've asked him to tell you what he told me, because I don't think you know what you've gotten yourself into here."

That much was undoubtedly true. I had no idea at all what I had gotten myself into here, and I understood that all too well.

But what really bothered me was that Sandy was in whatever it was up to his neck now, too. First, he bailed me out when Judge McClanahan looked like she was about to start tap dancing on my head, and now here he was calling on his old sources to give me the real skinny on Zachariah Scott and his business operations.

I hadn't asked Sandy to get directly involved in any of this, of course, but now he was. And I had to ask myself why that was. Had Sandy gotten curious and started poking around in Emma's document stash?

"Sandy, I know you told me you wouldn't look at those documents you arranged to store for me, but—"

"And I *haven't* looked at them. I didn't need to look at them. I know what's in them already."

"How could you possibly—"

"Look, Charlie, this is really a small town, and small towns are driven by gossip. I've heard some of the gossip about Zachariah Scott. Max has heard all of it. Let's just go inside and talk to Max, and in an hour or so I promise, you'll be a much smarter man than you are now."

Mr. Wu opened Sandy's door, and Sandy stepped out into the parking lot. I wondered if I just sat there whether Mr. Wu would walk around and open my door, too, but I decided not to push my luck. Mr. Wu seemed to have a limited amount of tolerance for me, and it looked like I was already hanging around somewhere close to his limit.

I scooted across the big back seat and stepped out through Sandy's door before Mr. Wu could close it.

19

I followed Sandy up a rusted metal staircase bolted to the outside of the building on the right. Not the *Spiritualist to the Stars* building. The other one.

The staircase had a railing along one side that had once been painted black to match the stairs, but most of the paint had peeled off long ago and now nothing was left but bare metal. The steps themselves were stained and cracked, and cigarette butts were ground into the corners. A faded sign on the wall of the building warned against loitering, but I couldn't imagine why anyone would loiter here. The staircase smelled like rotting garbage, car exhaust, and urine.

At the top, Sandy pulled open a heavy metal door, and we entered a narrow hallway with linoleum floors worn through to the concrete in places. The walls were the same yellowed stucco as the building's exterior. Three unmarked doors lined the right side of the hallway, all with pebbled glass windows so heavily patterned that nothing was visible inside any of them.

Sandy went to the middle door and knocked twice.

"Come in," a man's voice called out from inside.

The voice was rough. It sounded like too many cigarettes and too much bourbon. Sandy pushed the door open, and we trooped inside.

The room was of average size, and square, maybe twenty by twenty feet. A single window looked out over Normandie Avenue. The venetian blinds were half closed against the sun, and the room was striped with bars of light and shadow. Dust motes hung suspended in shafts of sunlight streaming between the blinds.

A battered wooden desk sat on one side of the room, its surface scarred with cigarette burns and water rings from decades of coffee cups. Two mismatched chairs faced the desk. One was a green vinyl thing that looked like it had been stolen from a bus station, and the other was wooden with a cracked brown leather seat. Behind the desk, a dented filing cabinet leaned slightly to the left. On top of it sat an old manual typewriter and a stack of manila folders tied with a string. The wall displayed a calendar from 1987 showing a blonde in a bikini washing a Corvette. Maybe nobody had ever bothered to take it down. Or maybe somebody here thought it was still 1987.

A coat rack in the corner held a tan trench coat that looked like it might have been new back during the Truman administration. Next to it, a small table held a hot plate, a chipped coffee mug, and a bottle of bourbon with maybe two fingers left in it.

A trench coat and a nearly empty bottle of bourbon? Seriously? The only thing the office lacked was Humphrey Bogart with a half-smoked cigarette dangling from his lips.

This couldn't be real. It was a movie set, right? Had to be.

"Max," Sandy said, extending his hand to the man sitting behind the desk. "I see you've still got the trench coat."

"You Brentwood high-society types call that ambiance, don't you, Sandy?" Max replied, taking his hand and shaking it.

They both laughed.

Max Furman had skin the color of an old sheet of copy paper that had been left lying in the sun so long it had turned yellow. He was short and thick, although he wasn't a large man overall, and he had a lined face that would have qualified him to be cast as a minor villain in a made-for-television movie. It made me think of the slightly crooked face of a former boxer.

He was dressed in jeans with a blue sport coat over a black shirt, and his hair, mostly white with streaks of black here and there, was slicked back and held down by something greasy. If Sandy's story about Raymond Chandler using Max as the model for Philip Marlowe were true, he had to be in his mid-eighties, but he looked at least twenty years younger than that. So maybe the story wasn't true. Or maybe it was true, and it was the bourbon that was keeping him young.

Max turned those sharp eyes on me and looked me over in silence until we all sat down.

"So this is the kid who's stepped in it," he said then.

That seemed as good a description of me as any, so I decided to say nothing and await developments.

Sandy cleared his throat.

"He needs to hear what you told me, Max. Don't hold anything back."

Max continued to size me up while he thought about that. He looked as if he were chewing on the inside of his cheek while he did. I would lay odds that Max had once been a smoker, and that what he really wanted to be chewing on right at that moment was a cigarette. I wondered how long ago he had quit.

After a minute or two, Max kind of grunted without taking his eyes off me.

"Ground rules," he said.

He held up one finger.

"Number one. You don't know me. We never met. We never talked."

I said nothing and waited to see what was coming next, but that wasn't good enough for Max.

"I need an answer before I go on," he said. "Yes, or no?"

"Then yes," I nodded. "I understand. We never met."

Max held up two fingers.

"Number two. Nothing I tell you can ever be attributed to me. Nothing."

"Yes to that, too," I said.

Three fingers.

"And number three. You may not use any of the information I give you for any purpose or repeat it to anyone at all unless you can find another credible source for it, and you attribute it fully to that source."

"Again, yes," I said. "I understand."

Max pushed back in his chair and swung his feet up on the desk with surprising agility for a man of his age. No hesitation, no awkwardness. Just stretched out, legs crossed at the ankles, right foot hooked over left ankle.

"Television killed the glory days of Hollywood," Max began. "It killed them stone dead. And not just because people started watching television at home rather than going out to the movies. It was because television changed the way the film business worked."

I nodded and just listened. I had no quarrel with what Max was saying, of course. I couldn't even remember the last time I'd been in a movie theater myself.

"Television killed the movies," Max went on, "but it created in its place an enormous money machine."

He paused and reached for something on the desk. A pack of gum. Juicy Fruit. Yeah, ex-smoker. No doubt about it.

He unwrapped a piece and folded it into his mouth. The wrapper went into an ashtray.

"In the golden age of Hollywood, films were made by studios. And the same studios created the stars. Real movie stars. Charlie Chaplin, Joan Crawford, Marlene Dietrich, Clark Gable, Marilyn Monroe, Fred Astaire, the Marx Brothers, Katharine Hepburn, Jimmy Stewart. Like that."

Max chewed slowly while he talked. The pack of gum sat on the desk between us.

"Those were different times," Sandy said quietly.

"Making movies was pretty much a closed loop then. The studios controlled everything. They owned the writers, they owned the directors, they owned the stars. They decided what movies got made, and by whom. And they paid for them, so they got what they wanted."

Max shifted in his chair. He uncrossed his legs, then he crossed them back again in the opposite direction, left foot hooked over right ankle now.

"The television business really took off in the 70s, and that was when everything changed for good. The studio system fragmented, and small independent producers began popping up everywhere to feed the new demand for programming. Those companies didn't have the capital to finance their own productions like the studios did, so hustling production money became a major Hollywood skill. The biggest independent production houses were built by the guys who hustled money best, not necessarily by the guys who made the best films and television shows. Zachariah Scott was one of those guys."

"Tell him about the source of Zac Scott's funding," Sandy said.

I noticed Max shoot Sandy an annoyed look. He clearly

didn't appreciate coaching on how he should tell this story, whatever this story was going to turn out to be.

"Zachariah Scott developed a specialty in cultivating sources of capital abroad. He was one of the first in Hollywood to see how the international love of American pop culture could be tapped for production money. And he wasn't always discriminating in who he raised his production money from."

"You're telling me Zachariah Scott tapped into some dirty money," I said, trying to nudge Max into getting to the point before I became eligible for Social Security.

"The polite term, Charlie, is black money, and there's an ocean of it out there."

"I know," I began, but Max interrupted me.

"No, you don't. Whatever you know, or think you know, you're not even close. Stolen money, drug money, money from arms smuggling, money from government corruption, money evading taxes. There's a flood tide of black money sloshing around all over the world looking for a safe and legitimate home. Always has been. And finding a safe and legitimate-looking home for it is a massive business."

"You're talking about money laundering?"

"Of course, I am. Zachariah Scott saw the demand and decided to become the supply. He built a television production empire based entirely on laundered money. His list of investors was bland to a fault. Nothing but companies organized in places like the Cayman Islands and Monaco that had names like Westwind Investments and EMT Funds Management.

"It wouldn't have served anyone's best interests for him to mention the names of the men who were ultimately behind those bland names. People like Muammar Gaddafi and Saddam Hussein whose specialty was looting their countries' treasuries. Organizations like the Russian mob and the Colombian cartels, which were just out-and-out criminals. There were financial institutions, too, most of them well-known and respected, that charged their clients big fees to keep their money outside the net of the taxman. Not to mention uncountable villains of other kinds, ranging from the petty to the serious, from all over the world."

"How did the money laundering work?" I asked.

"It was simple in theory," Max said. "Let's suppose the Russian mob needed to wash a hundred million dollars. They would form a shell company in some tax haven jurisdiction like the Cayman Islands and capitalize that company with the hundred million. Then the Cayman Islands company would invest with Zac in one of his television projects. He'd spend some of their investment on a television series or maybe a new pilot, but not nearly as much as his books said he had.

"Most of the invested money was paid back out again to other shell companies, and Zac kept paying it out until it was all gone, naturally taking a cut of the pass-through payments. When Zac eventually delivered the television series, it carried a price tag several times what it really cost to make because of all the pass-through money. The television series was now made, but two-thirds of the money supposedly invested in it was right back where it started, and all of it traceable to a completely legitimate source. One of Zachariah Scott's production companies."

I nodded and waited.

"Anyway," Max went on, "that's how Zachariah Scott became the biggest dog on the porch. He had access to an almost unlimited amount of money. Eventually, the entire production schedule of Zachariah Scott Productions was being financed by black money from overseas."

"Is this all mostly just speculation on your part, Max? Or do you have —?"

"No," Max interrupted, "I could never get documented

proof, but from what Sandy tells me, it sounds to me like now you've fallen right into what I could never find."

"I asked Sandy not to—"

"I already told you," Sandy said, "I never looked at anything in those boxes. I just put what you told me together with what I've heard around LA for years, and here we are."

"There have always been whispers that Zac kept several sets of accounts," Max took over again, "depending on who he needed to show them to. It had always seemed obvious to me that he probably only allowed a few people very close to him to see the real disbursements he was making. Frankly, it never crossed my mind that his wife might be one of those people. She always came across to everybody as a bit of an insignificant airhead, but I'm guessing now that she might have been creating that impression as a form of insulation."

"Then out of the blue you came to me with all this," Sandy cut in. "This story about Zac's wife turning boxes of documents over to you that she thought she could use to back him off in the divorce. I put that together with what I'd heard, and called Max to ask him what he thought."

"I knew immediately what she had given you, Charlie," Max said. "So did Sandy. We didn't need to look at what's in those boxes, although I admit I sure as hell would like to. Hey, what else could it be? Zac's wife must have kept evidence of Zac laundering money through his production companies and put that evidence aside for a rainy day. Now that rainy day is here, and she's given it to you to analyze and find a way she can use it to protect herself in the divorce. Just tell me one thing about what you have, and I'll stop badgering you with questions."

"If I can," I said.

"Did you find documents in those boxes written in a foreign language?"

I tried to keep my face empty, but I failed miserably. My mouth opened slightly in surprise.

"Yes," I said.

"Dollars to donuts, everything you found is in Japanese."

"How could you possibly know that?"

"Because Max knows what Zac's biggest single source of foreign money is," Sandy said.

"A Japanese company?"

"Japanese, yes, but not a company. For the last couple of decades, Zachariah Scott has handled billions of dollars for one major investor. The Japanese Yakuza."

Now my mouth dropped completely open.

"The Yakuza?"

Sandy nodded.

"You're telling me Zac Scott's television empire is built on laundered money from Japanese organized crime?"

Sandy nodded again.

"Then you're also saying—"

"I'm saying that's who wants those documents back that Zac Scott's wife turned over to you, Charlie. Forget about Zac Scott, and forget Judge McClanahan. What you really need to be worrying about right now is the Yakuza."

Oh, shit.

20

The drive back to the Santa Monica Courthouse for me to pick up my car was a straight shot west on Santa Monica Blvd. Driving Santa Monica Blvd from the Hollywood Freeway almost all the way to the ocean was nobody's idea of a good time, but there weren't a lot of other routes that made any sense.

It would take us at least half an hour to get to the garage where I had parked the Mustang, probably longer, but that was okay. Sandy and I had a lot to talk about. Neither of us much wanted to talk about any of it, but we had to, and the security of Sandy's car while Mr. Wu was driving us back to Santa Monica was a good time to do it.

"What do you know about the Yakuza?" I asked Sandy after Mr. Wu had turned left off of Normandie onto Santa Monica Blvd and settled into the flow of traffic heading west.

Sandy didn't answer right away. He looked out the window until we stopped at the red light at Western Avenue. A guy in torn jeans and a filthy sweatshirt worked his way down the line of cars with a squeegee and a spray bottle, washing windshields whether the drivers wanted them washed or not.

"You want the short version or the complete history?" he finally asked,

"Let's start with the short version."

The light changed, and Mr. Wu pulled smoothly through the intersection.

"They're a Japanese criminal organization, of course," Sandy said, "but then you probably know that much already. They're like the Mafia in a way, but older. Much older. They've been around for more than four hundred years in one form or another."

"How do they operate?"

"The Yakuza is organized into families like the American mafia, although the Japanese refer to them as clans. The biggest is the Yamaguchi-gumi. Then, Sumiyoshi-kai. Then, Inagawa-kai. And there are dozens of smaller ones."

Sandy pulled out a cigar. He rolled it between his fingers, but he didn't light it. I wondered how often he actually smoked the things or whether he mostly kept them around to use as props.

"Each clan has an *oyabun*, a boss. Under him are various lieutenants, soldiers and associates. All very hierarchical. Very traditional. Lots of ritual and ceremony."

"And they're active in California?"

"Oh yes. They've been here since the sixties. Probably earlier. They started moving into Hawaii first, then the West Coast. The usual rackets. Smuggling, extortion, prostitution, drugs, gambling. But the Yakuza is more sophisticated than the Mafia ever was, and they've got their fingers in legitimate businesses, too. They're big in real estate and finance. International money laundering is a particular specialty."

"How come you know so much about them?" I asked.

Sandy gave me one of those looks.

"I represented the American *oyabun* of the Yamaguchi-gumi about twenty years ago. The DOJ was trying to deport him back to Japan. We fought them for three years."

"Did you win?"

"Of course not. We lost eventually, but we made them work for it."

Sandy went back to staring out the window. We were passing Fairfax now. The traffic was heavy, but Mr. Wu slipped us through it as if he were threading a needle.

"Do you think Zachariah Scott has really been laundering money for the Yakuza?"

"Max says he has, and that's good enough for me."

I thought about Emma's boxes. Copies of wire transfers to companies in the Cayman Islands and Switzerland. Payments to people who didn't exist. Tens of millions of dollars moving through shell companies with innocuous names. And all those documents I couldn't read that Max said were probably in Japanese.

"So, are these mostly just rumors?" I asked. "Or should I actually be worried about the Yakuza?"

Sandy turned those green eyes on me.

"Oh yes," he said. "You should absolutely be worried."

He paused.

"The Yakuza isn't what it once was, of course. The Japanese government has cracked down over the last thirty or forty years, and that's weakened them. And they're having all the usual internal problems, succession fights, that kind of thing."

Another pause.

"But the real problem for them is that younger people see them as passé, like something from another era, and their membership has fallen off a lot. They're not the force they once were, but then none of us are, are we?"

He looked out the window again.

"They're still dangerous, Charlie. Very dangerous. Especially if they think you have something that belongs to them. Or something that could damage them. They don't forget, and they don't forgive."

He rolled the cigar between his fingers.

"And they don't leave loose ends."

A silence fell after that, and I let it run until we had passed under the 405 and became bogged down in traffic around Bundy.

"You think she's dead, don't you?"

When Sandy turned his head toward me, he looked startled for a moment, as if he had forgotten there was anyone else in the car with him.

"Zachariah Scott's wife? The woman who got you into all this?"

I nodded.

Sandy pursed his lips and appeared to think about my question, although I doubted he really needed to.

"Probably."

Sandy said it in the sort of flat, matter-of-fact voice he might use to tell me the time.

The Lincoln slid smoothly through traffic. I watched the cars around us, and I envied all of those people going about their lives without having to wonder whether the Yakuza had murdered someone they were trying to help.

Sandy sat there rolling the cigar between his fingers, but he didn't say anything else.

"Oh, for God's sake," I said. "Will you light the damn thing? You're driving me nuts with it."

Sandy shot me a rueful grin.

"You won't tell on me?"

"Not me, boss man. I'd never squeal on a living legend."

Sandy produced a lighter from somewhere and took his time about lighting the cigar. As soon as he gave it a puff, Mr. Wu turned his head and gave Sandy a sour look.

"Eyes on the road, Mr. Wu," Sandy chuckled, cracking his window a bit. "We're doing just fine back here."

Sandy sat and smoked quietly for a few moments, and I let him.

"Maybe she's not dead," he sighed after a bit. "Maybe the Yakuza have just grabbed her, and they're holding her somewhere until they get what they want. And we know they don't have what they want yet, because you have it."

"Gee, Sandy, I appreciate the reminder."

"Or maybe she figured out she was in over her head and just went to ground to protect herself."

I thought about the last time I had seen Emma Scott. How frightened she had looked when she gave me those boxes. At the time, I thought she was just a little hysterical and blowing things out of proportion. She was a wealthy woman getting divorced from a powerful husband, sure, but people did that every day without disappearing.

It didn't feel like that to me anymore.

"What am I supposed to do if she *is* dead?" I asked. "Or if she just never comes back and everyone begins to accept that she must be dead? I've still got those documents."

Sandy turned those green eyes on me.

"Can't I just give them to the court then and wash my hands of it all?" I asked.

"No."

The word came out hard, final.

"Your responsibility remains the same even if she's dead, Charlie. Attorney-client privilege attached to those documents the moment she gave them to you. Unless she waives it, it remains. Death doesn't change that. If anything, it makes it more important."

I looked out the window. We were rolling through the nondescript lowlands of Santa Monica now. I could almost smell the Pacific Ocean out there in front of us.

"So, I'm stuck with this stuff."

"You're stuck with it."

"Forever?"

"Until someone with legal authority to waive the privilege does so. That would be her estate, if she dies. You could try to get a court order if you can convince a judge that the privilege should be pierced. But that's a high bar, and you know it."

I did know it. The attorney-client privilege was one of the oldest and most sacred protections in the law. Judges didn't set it aside lightly.

"But let's not get ahead of ourselves," Sandy said, his voice softening slightly. "You have a motion to quash the subpoena to file. That could change everything. So, do the research, prepare the motion, and write the brief. And after that's done and we're waiting for Judge McClanahan to rule, we'll talk through the alternatives you have from there."

"And if she denies the motion?"

"We'll think of something."

"You make it sound simple."

"It's not simple," Sandy said. "But it's what you've got."

He drew on his cigar and exhaled a long puff of smoke toward the front seat which caused Mr. Wu to wrinkle his nose in disgust. I was pretty sure Sandy had done that on purpose.

"If Emma's alive, Sandy, I need to find her. That would get me off the hook."

"We're lawyers, Charlie. Not detectives. I wouldn't have the first idea how to go about doing something like that."

"But you know somebody who does."

A smile slid over Sandy's face.

"Why didn't I think of that myself?"

"It sounds to me like you just did."

He smiled again.

"I'll call Max as soon as I get home."

I retrieved the Mustang, paid the extortionate parking fee it had run up after being parked there for most of the day, and turned north on the PCH toward Malibu.

There was something about driving north on the PCH that always gave me a little lift. Seeing the endless ocean on the left and the mountains on the right, and watching the urban sprawl of LA fall behind me in the rearview mirror, never failed to lighten my load.

I pulled into the driveway at Carbon Beach and killed the engine. The Mustang ticked and settled as I climbed out, stretching muscles that had gotten stiff from too many hours sitting in courtrooms and cars.

Ryan O'Neal stood in his open garage next door, unloading golf clubs from the back of his car. I didn't know Ryan and Farrah very well, although they lived next door. On the PCH side, the fronts of the houses of Carbon Beach were lined up side-by-side like boxcars parked on a siding. The ambiance wasn't exactly conducive to neighbors meeting and chatting. People just parked their cars and hustled inside their houses as fast as they could.

On the beach side, of course, it was a completely different story. I saw Ryan and Farrah there occasionally when we were both out on our decks at the same time. Ryan liked to pound a heavy bag he had hung up out there, and Farrah sunbathed frequently, sometimes topless, which was a considerably more inspiring sight to take in than a sweaty man with boxing gloves flailing away at a leather bag. We weren't exactly friends, but they had always been friendly enough, waving and calling out hellos and good mornings.

Ryan gave me a little half-wave, propped his golf bag against the rear bumper of his car, and pulled a hand towel out of a loop at the top of the bag. He wiped his hands on the towel, threw it over his shoulder, and walked toward my driveway. I didn't remember ever actually having a conversation with Ryan before, but now it looked like I was about to.

Watching him come toward me, it occurred to me that handsome men aged differently from the rest of us. The movie idol good looks of the man who starred in *Love Story* and *Barry Lyndon* had long ago departed and left behind a man who looked like he was uncertain where they had gone.

Ryan had a reputation as a brawler and an angry man. I had no idea whether that was true, but seeing him pounding at the heavy bag on his deck for an hour or so every day did seem to lend a bit of credence to the stories. I wondered if the loss of the quality that had defined him as a movie star might have something to do with that.

"Your friends find you?" Ryan called out.

I had started to push open the gate that led from my driveway into the little front garden of my house, but I stopped and turned back toward Ryan.

"What friends?"

"Three guys were in your driveway when I drove in about an hour ago. They were sitting in a dark-colored SUV of some kind, waiting for you."

"I wasn't expecting anyone," I said. "What did they look like?"

Ryan wiped his face with the small towel he had taken from his golf bag.

"They have to be the only three guys in Malibu wearing black suits," he said. "They're probably the only three guys in Malibu who *own* black suits."

Three men. Waiting in my driveway. All of them wearing black suits.

Uh-oh.

"Can you describe them?"

Ryan shrugged.

"Not really. I mean, they were just sitting there. Didn't say anything to me. They just watched when I pulled into my garage. They gave me the fucking creeps, I tell you."

I kept my face neutral, but my heart hammered.

"Do you remember anything about them other than their suits?"

"Yeah," Ryan said, scratched his chin. "They looked Asian."

Bingo. It looks like we have a winner here.

"Japanese, maybe?" I asked.

"Maybe." Ryan squinted at me. "Some kind of Asian. I really can't tell one from another. Can you?"

My mouth had gone too dry to speak, so I just shook my head.

"They left about thirty minutes ago. Drove off toward Santa Monica."

We must have passed each other on the PCH going in opposite directions. I wondered if they had spotted my Mustang.

"Anyway," Ryan finished, "I'm sure it was nothing sinister. They didn't look like burglars."

Ryan tossed out his signature grin and started to turn away, but then suddenly he stopped and turned back to me.

"Is everything okay, Charlie? You look ... well, a little shaken up."

"Just some work stuff."

Ryan gave me a smile that said he knew bullshit when he heard it, then he nodded and disappeared back into his garage.

I stood there in my driveway staring at my front door. Three men in black suits. Asians. Waiting for me.

Were they Yakuza gangsters? Maybe. Probably, in fact. If they weren't, it would certainly be one hell of a coincidence, wouldn't it?

And right on top of that thought came another one. Sandy's words from our earlier conversation.

The Yakuza don't leave loose ends.

I unlocked the front door and stepped inside, listening.

The house was silent except for the usual rumble of the surf breaking on the beach. I walked over and checked the sliding door out to the deck. Unlocked. I knew I hadn't left it that way. I always locked it.

The men had probably gotten around to the beach side of the house, pulled themselves up onto the deck, and then slipped the lock on the slider.

At a glance, everything looked normal, but I could sense the house had been searched. They wouldn't have had to be particularly thorough about it. Five bankers boxes of documents would take up a lot of room. It's not like I might be keeping them in my sock drawer.

They hadn't found anything, of course, because there was nothing here *to* find. When Sandy suggested Mr. Wu store the boxes for me without telling me where they were, I thought we were just bobbing and weaving with Judge McClanahan and giving me some deniability if she demanded I immediately surrender the documents Emma Scott had given me. It certainly never occurred to me that we might also be hiding them from the Japanese Yakuza.

It bothered me, of course, that when these guys found nothing in the house, they had then decided to sit in my driveway for a while and wait for me to return home. That was pretty brazen, and I had probably been lucky that Ryan happened to drive in from the golf course and flush them out before I turned up.

But it was something even more fundamental about those three men sitting there in my driveway that bothered me most.

The Yakuza knew where I live.

21

I woke the next morning to a gray marine layer that had rolled in overnight and settled over the beach like a blanket. The sun would burn through by noon, but for now, the world outside my window looked muted and distant.

I made breakfast. Scrambled eggs, slightly overdone the way I always made them. Two pieces of toast with butter. Coffee, black. The same breakfast I'd eaten maybe five thousand times in my life. I carried it all out to the deck on a tray and sat down.

The ocean was lost in the fog. I could hear the waves but couldn't see them. Just a gray wall of nothing where the water should be.

I was halfway through my eggs when the phone rang. I went inside and grabbed it on the fourth ring.

"I talked to Max," Sandy said without preamble. "He's willing to do what he can to locate Mrs. Scott, but he's not hopeful. He doesn't have much to go on."

"Well, what does he need?"

"I don't suppose you have anything at all to get him started, do you?"

I thought about it. What did I actually know about Emma Scott? She had come to my house once, and I had been to hers once. She had fed me a tasteless salad and given me five boxes of documents to look at. Then she had disappeared. End of story.

"I've got her address and a telephone number, but that's about it."

"How about a car? A license number, maybe?"

I thought back to that first meeting. Emma calling me from her car, already parked in my driveway, and asking to talk.

"She was driving a black Mercedes when she came to see me. A sedan. Four-door. But she's not driving it now because it's parked in her garage."

"Nothing else?"

"Nothing."

"I doubt even Max can do much with that."

"I've got what I've got," I said, starting to become just a little annoyed that Sandy seemed to be blaming me for not having more. "Anything else, Sandy?"

"I've put your name on the access list for the law library at UCLA," Sandy went on. "You do know where UCLA is, don't you?"

I was pretty much up to my ass with the dry amusement Sandy was sprinkling over everything like salt this morning.

"Yes, Sandy, I know where UCLA is."

"Well, the law library is—"

"Never mind, Sandy. I'm sure I can find it."

"Assuming you can, just go to the main desk and show them some kind of photo ID, and you're in."

"Got it."

"You need to get started on this, Charlie."

"Would today be soon enough?"

"Fine," Sandy said, and hung up. Apparently, he was getting a little sick of me, too. Or maybe he just needed more coffee. I certainly did.

I walked back out onto the deck and dropped into the chair where I had started eating breakfast. My eggs had gone cold. I ate them anyway.

I stared out into the fog, wondering where Emma Scott was and whether she was still alive. Maybe it was time to stop worrying about Emma and start worrying about myself.

The Yakuza knew where I lived, and they thought I had a pile of evidence that could probably take down most of their leadership and half of Hollywood. I was pretty sure they wanted all that evidence back. If I had been them, I sure as hell would have.

I finished my breakfast, then carried my dishes inside, rinsed them off, and dumped them in the drying rack. I showered and changed into a clean Polo shirt and khakis, stuffed a couple of legal pads and a few pens into an old briefcase, and headed off to work.

UCLA sits in the foothills of the Santa Monica Mountains just north of Wilshire Boulevard in Westwood, a neighborhood that feels like a separate city tucked between Beverly Hills and Brentwood. I took the PCH south to Santa Monica, then cut inland on Wilshire and headed east through the commercial district that lined both sides. When a huge Shell station spread out over half a block caught my eye, it occurred to me that I needed gas, but the traffic was heavy and I couldn't get over, so I had to circle the block and enter the station from the back.

I had just gotten out to pump my gas and was feeding my

credit card into the pump when I happened to glance up. My eyes fell on a black Toyota 4Runner that slowed, signaled to turn into the station, then abruptly sped up and kept going east on Wilshire. There was nothing really remarkable about the 4Runner, but the windows were unusually dark, and I couldn't catch even a glimpse of whoever was inside. And then there was the fact that it was a Japanese-manufactured vehicle, of course.

Was I getting a little paranoid? Maybe. But as the old saying goes, even the paranoid sometimes have real enemies.

The more I thought about it, the more sense it made that the Yakuza goons might have me under some kind of at least loose surveillance. After all, they knew now that the boxes of documents Emma Scott had given me to review weren't in the house on Carbon Beach, so where were they?

The obvious answer was that I had stashed them somewhere I went from time to time, and the easiest way to find out where that might be would be to keep an eye on me and see where I went. Of course, they could always grab me and torture it out of me instead, but maybe they preferred a less messy approach to solving the problem. I certainly did.

As I pumped my gas, I eyed the Mustang, and another thought crept into my mind. Was it possible they could have put some kind of electronic tracker in my car and were just sitting out there watching where I went without actually having to keep me in sight? I had seen things like that in the movies, but I wasn't completely certain they actually existed. Still, if they did, my guess was the famously high-tech Japanese would have them in three sizes and six colors, so I couldn't completely rule out the possibility.

Sandy had said that Mr. Wu checked his car weekly for electronics that ought not to be there, didn't he? Maybe I'd ask him to have Mr. Wu check the Mustang, too. Just to be on the safe side.

Just then, the pump clicked off. I returned the nozzle to its holder, closed my gas tank, and accepted the credit card receipt the pump spat out.

The drive from the Shell station to UCLA only took about fifteen minutes with traffic moving at a steady crawl. Just on the other side of the 405, I turned left on Westwood Boulevard and rolled past the old-school movie palaces of Westwood Village to the main entrance to UCLA.

I had no idea where I was going, of course. Regardless of what I told Sandy, the location of UCLA's law school was a complete mystery to me, but I figured if I drove around a while, surely, I would happen onto it.

I didn't. Instead, I wound through miles of streets lined with brick buildings and massive old trees, watching students move between classes in clusters, their backpacks slung over their shoulders and their conversations rising and falling. The whole campus hummed with purpose and youth and energy. I wasn't really jealous of that, was I? Okay ... maybe I was. Just a little.

Eventually, I gave up driving around hoping for the best. When I came to the next parking structure I saw, I pulled in and drove up the ramp until I found a spot on the third level. The garage was dim and cool, and my footsteps echoed on the concrete as I walked to the elevators.

Outside, the campus spread before me like a small city. Brick walkways connected buildings in a variety of architectural styles. Some looked traditional, almost collegiate in the classic sense, with arched doorways and ivy climbing their walls. Others were stark and modern, all glass and concrete and sharp angles.

I stopped a young man who was carrying an armload of textbooks.

"Can you tell me where the law school is?"

He pointed across a broad plaza.

"That way. Past Royce Hall. You'll see it."

There you go. See how easy that was?

I walked in the direction the man had indicated and crossed an open plaza where students sat on benches or sprawled on the grass studying. The sky looked like the inside of a blue lacquered bowl, and the air smelled like eucalyptus and cut grass. The University of Virginia campus had been very pleasant, but this place was on another level entirely. It felt like a movie set being prepared for a film about an impossibly cool university located somewhere in impossibly cool Southern California.

Royce Hall was on my left, a massive Romanesque building with twin towers and ornate archways. It looked like something transplanted from a medieval Italian town square. I passed it and continued north, following the pathways until I spotted a cluster of modern buildings set apart slightly from the main campus.

The law school. There was even a sign that said so.

The complex consisted of several connected structures in the brutalist style popular in the sixties and seventies. Lots of concrete and glass. Lots of hard angles. The buildings looked serious and utilitarian, like they meant business.

I found the entrance and stepped inside. The lobby was cool and quiet. A stylish curved desk made of blond wood that looked vaguely art déco in style occupied the left side of the lobby, and behind it, a pleasant-looking middle-aged woman sat talking on a telephone. A law school with a receptionist? I had seen stranger things, but not many.

I waited until she finished.

"Where is the law library?" I asked.

She pointed toward a hallway.

"Second floor," she smiled. "The elevators are that way."

I found the stairs before I found the elevator, and I took them instead. They were wide and industrial, with metal railings and concrete treads. At the top, I pushed through heavy double doors and found myself in the library.

The space opened up before me in a way I hadn't expected. High ceilings. Rows of books stretching back into shadow. Long tables with green reading lamps. The smell of old paper and leather bindings, and that peculiar mustiness that seemed to permeate every law library I had ever entered.

A few students sat scattered around at the tables, their books spread before them and their highlighters moving across pages of dense text. Nobody looked up when I entered.

I walked to the main desk, where a slightly stout woman with her gray hair in a bun and reading glasses perched on her nose sat working her way through a pile of documents.

"I'm Charlie Trust," I said. "Sandy Bouchier put my name on the access list for the library so I can help him with some research he's doing."

The woman looked up and smiled. It was a nice smile, and the woman looked exactly like you would expect a librarian to look. Was there a factory somewhere out in the Arizona desert where librarians were cranked out from an assembly line, one after another, each birthed from a plastic injection mold to look exactly like the one who had come before? It wouldn't surprise me one bit.

"I need a photo ID, Mr. Trust. A driver's license will be fine."

I handed her mine, and she consulted a list she retrieved from a pigeonhole in front of her. I must have been on it, because she pushed the list back, then copied the details from my license onto a form on a clipboard. She handed the clipboard to me to sign, and then she returned my driver's license and handed me a small, yellow laminated card.

"This will get you in and out and confirm that you have permission to use the library if you're asked for identification. There's a large map showing the location of our major holdings at the card catalogues just behind me. The stacks are open. Restricted reference materials are on the third floor. If you need help finding anything, just ask."

I thanked her and walked into the stacks to find a place to set up shop.

All law libraries are similar, so although I had never been in this one, I knew more or less what I was looking for. Case reports are organized chronologically into those enormous sets of olive-colored books with identical bindings, their spines glinting with titles stamped out in gold foil, that are so beloved by Hollywood set designers because they make such striking backgrounds for lawyer shows on television.

Every law library is built around the case reports from the major appellate courts of the state in which it is located. In California, that would be the California Supreme Court, and all of its decisions are printed in full in a massive set of books called *California Reports*. Most decisions of the lower appellate courts are also reported, but in a separate set of books called *California Appellate Reports*. Trial court decisions are typically not published. Then there are the sets of books dedicated to federal rather than state law. *The Federal Reporter*, the *Federal Supplement*, and the *United States Reports* are the three major ones.

In addition to the case reports, there are other sets of books devoted to codified statutory law and administrative regulations of all kinds. There are also published legislative materials pertaining to the history of most legislation. There are legal encyclopedias like California Jurisprudence that offered descriptive statements of California law derived from statutes and cases, and various local treatises and practice guides. And there are collections of law journals published by law schools all over the country going back for generations.

After that, it gets complicated.

The first table I came to was already crowded with students, and its surface was buried in discarded volumes from various sets of reporters. The second table was a little less crowded, but it was occupied by three students who seemed to know each other pretty well. When I appeared out of the stacks, they all looked at me at the same time. I got the message and moved on.

The third table I found turned out to be the charm. It was off to one side in a sort of vestibule lined with dusty volumes of the *California Reports*. A young woman with a worried look on her face occupied a chair at the far end of the table, and stacked in front of her were what looked more like course books than library research material. She was so absorbed in her studying that she didn't even glance up when I took a chair at the opposite end of the table.

Perfect.

22

I spent the next three days at the UCLA law library trying to remember what they had taught me about doing legal research back at UVA a decade ago. Rather to my surprise, I found I did remember it all pretty well, and I have to admit I enjoyed every moment of researching attorney-client privilege as the courts had applied the law in California.

I know. That sounds like an enormous yawn, doesn't it? But here's the thing. Legal research is more like a treasure hunt than it is a quest for understanding. You're not trying to achieve mastery of a complex concept. It's more like pulling on strings, one after another, until you eventually find one that's tied a case you can use to claim precedent for whatever you're trying to get the judge to do. Then you look at all the cases cited in the one you've found that you like, and you read them, too. After all, what you're doing here is trying to construct a foundation for whatever concept you want to sell the judge that will make your claim seem as solid and as immutable as the pyramids of Egypt.

The process can be a bit of a physical workout, too. For

instance, let's say a law journal article you're reading suggests the idea you're trying to sell the judge was already approved by the California Court of Appeals in a case decided twenty years ago. You have to get up, find the correct volume of the *California Court of Appeals Reports*, and ferry it back to wherever you're working to read that case. Then, when you discover that *Chen v. County of Orange, 116 Cal. Rptr. 2d 786 (Ct. App. 1982),* the case you're reading, approvingly cites *People v. Anderson, 493 P.2d 880 (Cal. 1972)* as support for its decision, you have to get up and find that volume and read that case, too.

And on and on the process goes. You pull on one string until you find another string it's tied to, and then you pull on that one, too, and you keep going until you've built your Egyptian pyramid. Walking back and forth, hour after hour and day after day, lugging those heavy law books, can be a better workout than a day in the gym.

I was willing to bet that eventually computers were going to make the whole process into something entirely different. The first step will be for every law book and case report ever printed to be reduced to digital bits so that you can sit at a keyboard and access anything you want without the physical effort required now to schlep around a library and hunt down all those individual books.

The second step will be for the computers to tell you what is relevant and what isn't, and take you directly to the cases you need without the bother of you having to work out what they are on your own.

And then there will inevitably come the third step. You will be able simply to tell the computer the point you need to brief, and the computer will produce a finished brief without a lawyer having to do any research at all.

Which will quite naturally lead to the fourth step...

Nobody will need real lawyers anymore.

None of us really want to think about that step.

I quickly discovered the case law about attorney-client privilege in California was pretty straightforward and the cases lined up nicely. It was well settled that communication during a preliminary case conference was privileged whether the attorney ultimately agreed to accept the case or not, and it was equally well settled that the term communication embraced both verbal conversations and documentation provided to the attorney by the prospective client.

The claim that Hurter made about the documents constituting stolen property when I appeared before Judge McClanahan in response to her *subpoena duces tecum* was, however, a bit more tricky.

The obvious response was that Hurter had made no showing that the documents Emma had given me really were stolen. He had just thrown out that claim without anything to support it. But as with many things in the workings of our complicated and often obscure system of justice, the obvious response wasn't necessarily the right one.

What, it occurred to me, if I conceded it might make a difference if the documents had indeed been stolen, and then demanded the judge schedule an evidentiary hearing for Hurter to present evidence that they were. That would box her into two alternatives. She could rule that it made no difference to invoking attorney-client privilege whether the documents were stolen or not, and therefore refuse to hold an evidentiary hearing. On the other hand, if she ruled it did make a difference whether they were stolen or not, she could hardly refuse me an evidentiary hearing and simply accept Hurter's bare assertion that the documents actually were stolen.

I figured that was what the motivational manuals called a

win-win, at least for me. The judge would either rule it didn't matter whether the documents were stolen, or she would give me my hearing.

If she did give me my hearing, could Hurter actually produce evidence that might support his stolen documents theory? I had no idea. On the other hand, scheduling and preparing and conducting a hearing like that would take time, probably a month, maybe two. And a lot could change in two months.

Like Sandy said, buy time any way you can. Always buy time.

A story I had heard once suddenly came back to me, and I chuckled to myself. It goes like this.

A criminal was hauled before a powerful king in some ancient land to be punished for his crimes, but before the king could pass sentence, the man dropped to his knees and made one final plea.

"Your Majesty," he cried, "spare me, and I promise that within one year I will teach your horse to talk!

The king thought that over, and then he said, "Very well. One year. But if you have not taught my horse to talk within one year, you will be hanged. Release him!"

The criminal's friends all immediately rushed over and surrounded him.

"You're an idiot," they said. "What do you think you're doing? You can't teach the king's horse to talk."

"Maybe not," the criminal replied, "but a year is a long time. Who knows what will happen in a year? The king may die. Or I may die. Or the kingdom may collapse."

And then the criminal paused and thought about it for a moment, and another possibility occurred to him.

"Or," he added, "the horse *might* talk."

Yeah, it's like that. Exactly like that.

. . .

It took me three days to pull together all the research on the application of the attorney-client privilege in California.

Okay, maybe I could have done it a little faster, but I've already admitted I was enjoying it, haven't I? Maybe I'm really a bit of an academic at heart rather than the kind of lawyer who lives for the heat of the battle, but what were my chances of getting a teaching job at some law school? With the grades I had pulled back in law school, anyone would laugh at the idea. So, it was back to the battle for me, or devote the rest of my career to drafting wills for little old ladies and little old men. Not a hard call, really.

At a little after one o'clock on Monday afternoon, I was finally done with the research. Now all I had to do was draft the Motion to Quash the *subpoena duces tecum*, and write a brief in support of that motion that was long enough and dense enough to guarantee that Judge McClanahan wouldn't read it, but would instead give it to her clerk to research and summarize.

Piece of cake, huh?

I was suddenly really hungry. I hadn't had a decent meal since I'd started the research grind, and I figured I was entitled to one now that I was finished. I wasn't very far away from one of my favorite spots in LA, a place called the Apple Pan, and I decided I'd earned a stop there, so I headed out to the parking structure to retrieve the Mustang.

Now, the Apple Pan has nothing to do with apples. It's a homey little diner on West Pico Boulevard that opened in 1947 and hasn't changed a bit since. You sit at one of the twenty-six stools that faced a U-shaped, Formica-topped counter in a room of lacquered wood, bare brick, and plaid upholstery, and you order a quarter-pound burger with hickory sauce and a slice of apple pie. And I guarantee you that for the next half hour all will be right with the world.

The Apple Pan is a bastion of simplicity and true democracy. Cash only. No credit cards. Counter seating only. No tables. Most any time of the day, you can push through the battered screen door into the little green and white building and find some of the biggest names in Hollywood waiting patiently for one of the twenty-six stools to become vacant. As seats become available, everyone seems to know who's next. And whoever it is, whether it's Harrison Ford or Jose from down at the gas station, that's the guy who gets the seat. No arguments. No attitude.

I was lucky. When I walked in, a couple was just leaving and no one was waiting, so I slid onto one of the two just-vacated stools while the counter in front of me was efficiently cleared by a young Hispanic man wearing a long white apron and a paper counterman's hat. Like almost everyone else, I ordered without bothering with the menu, and the counterman called my order back to the cook while serving up my Diet Coke.

I'd drunk about half of it and was still waiting for my cheeseburger when I felt rather than saw someone sliding onto the empty stool next to me.

"I know you, don't I?" a resonate voice rumbled after a moment or two.

I glanced over, and I found myself looking directly into the eyes of O.J. Simpson. He was immaculately turned out in a dark blue suit, with a snow-white dress shirt, and a red and blue striped silk tie. Suddenly, Simpson snapped his fingers and grinned.

"Yeah, I got it now," he said. "You're Marty Cole's lawyer. He introduced us one night at the Broadway Deli. He called you his courtroom killer."

Then his face split in a warm smile, and he thrust out his hand.

"I'm O. J. Simpson."

"I know," I said as we shook. "And I remember Marty introducing us at the Broadway Deli because he embarrassed me so badly with that courtroom killer thing."

"That was awful. Not that, but what happened to Marty, I mean. Just awful."

I nodded, but I was saved from having to elaborate on Marty's fate, something I most certainly didn't want to do, when the counterman arrived to serve my food. After he did, he took Simpson's order, shouted it back to the grill man, and poured Simpson the cup of coffee he had asked for. Simpson added some milk to the cup from a little metal pitcher on the counter and stirred it.

We made small talk while I ate, and the conversation inevitably drifted to the Lyle and Erik Menendez trial, which would be starting before long. The Menendez brothers had shotgunned their parents to death in the living room of their Beverly Hills mansion back in 1989, and the case had been the talk of LA ever since then.

Sometimes it seemed like people in LA followed the grotesque criminal cases that sprouted here like toadstools after a rainstorm the way people in other cities followed their local sports teams. Particularly when you were a lawyer, a recap of the status of LA's most monstrous pending criminal cases was almost an automatic topic of conversation.

In Dallas, the standard conversation starter might have been, *How about them Cowboys?* In LA , it was usually something more like, *How about those Menendez brothers?*

"Sometimes I really don't understand," O.J. mused. "These two boys everyone thought were perfectly nice kids suddenly turned around and slaughtered their parents. You just never know what kind of violent monsters people are hiding inside themselves, do you?"

The counterman served Simpson's food before I had to respond to that, which was fine by me. Worse, I could see where a conversation about that sort of thing might take us, and the last thing I needed was for the conversation to return to Marty Cole's strange fate. Certainly not when I was in a public place sitting with a well-known public figure and might as well have had a spotlight shining down on me. So, I finished my meal a little faster than I normally would since I wanted to get out of there before Simpson finished and was ready to talk some more.

"Nice to see you, O.J.," I said as I got to my feet and wiped my hands on a napkin.

"Say," he said, "you got a business card on you?"

"A business card?"

It probably sounded to Simpson like I was unfamiliar with the whole concept of business cards, although I was mostly startled by the question. Why did Simpson want my business card?

"Yeah," he answered, almost as if I had asked the question out loud. "Marty recommended you so enthusiastically, I figure I ought to know how to reach you. Who knows? Maybe I'll need a criminal lawyer one of these days."

"I doubt that," I mumbled politely as I extracted a card from my wallet and handed it to Simpson. "Besides, I really don't do much criminal work. With Marty, I was just helping out a friend."

"Well, we're friends now, too, aren't we?"

Simpson waited with a half-smile on his face until I realized he was actually expecting me to answer that.

"Yeah, sure," I said, since it was the only thing I really could say.

"So you'll help me out, too, if I need you. As a friend, I mean."

I fixed a smile on my face and pointed to the business card Simpson was still holding in his hand.

"Now you know how to find me."

That wasn't exactly an answer to Simpson's question, of course, but I figured it was enough of an answer to cover my escape from the Apple Pan.

When I got back to Malibu, I called Sandy to report that I had finished the research and was ready to start writing.

I summarized what the research added up to, and I tried out my idea on him about asking for an evidentiary hearing on Hurter's naked claim that the documents Emma had turned over to me were stolen.

"Why would it make any difference with respect to their privileged status whether they were stolen or not?" he asked.

"I don't think it would, but if the judge doesn't give me the hearing, it has to mean that she's going to rule it doesn't matter whether they were stolen or not. She can't possibly refuse me an evidentiary hearing and then rule that whether they were stolen *does* matter."

"And if she does give you a hearing, do you think Hurter can make a case that they were stolen?"

"Doesn't matter. If she does give me the hearing, I figure that's got to buy us another month, maybe two. We'll think of something."

Sandy chuckled.

"Now you're starting to see the world like I do, my young friend."

I think he meant that as a compliment.

"Let me talk to Pele," Sandy went on, "and I'll arrange for you to use the PC I bought for her office to write the motion and the brief."

"There's something else, Sandy."

I told him the story Ryan O'Neal had related to me about the three Asians in black suits who were waiting for me after the hearing in Judge McClanahan's court, and then finding the back door unlocked and my feeling that the house had been searched.

"Since they know the stuff isn't here now, they've got to be thinking I put it someplace I go at least occasionally," I told Sandy. "I'm getting a little paranoid that they might be following me around to see where that could be."

"Have you noticed anyone following you?"

I told him about the Toyota 4Runner that had behaved suspiciously at the Shell station a few days back.

"I haven't seen it since, but that got me thinking. Is it possible to track a car electronically somehow, or is that just something that happens in the movies?"

"Oh yes, it's certainly possible."

"You said Mr. Wu checks your car for electronics every week. Could you have him check mine, too? I mean, just in case. I don't want to go to Pele's bookstore to work if I'm just going to lead them straight to her."

There was a moment of silence as Sandy chewed that over.

"Mr. Wu will be at your place first thing in the morning," he said. "Do you have a garage?"

"Yes."

"Just let him in through the front then, and he can check the car in the garage without anyone knowing he's doing it."

"You think they might be watching my house as well as tracking my car?"

"These are smart, disciplined guys, Charlie, and I'm certain they have access to the most up-to-date technology. Don't underestimate them."

"Okay."

"I'll ask him to check your house while he's there, too. Can't hurt."

"Okay," I said again, feeling less and less okay the more Sandy talked.

"Don't drive up to Pele's bookstore until Mr. Wu gives you the all clear," he added.

"I won't."

"You're doing good work, my young friend. Keep it up."

And with that, Sandy cut the connection.

23

I hadn't been out of bed for more than a few minutes, and I was standing in the kitchen in my bathrobe, staring at the coffeemaker and willing it to work faster, when the buzzer at the front gate sounded.

I glanced at my watch. Not even seven o'clock.

What the hell?

I walked over to the intercom and pressed the button.

"Yes?"

"I'm here."

Very enlightening.

"Mr. Wu?"

No response.

I opened the front door and trudged out to the gate. Sure enough, Mr. Wu was standing there. He was carrying a black leather briefcase that looked expensive, and he wore the same dark suit and open-necked white shirt I'd seen him wearing the other day. His hair was perfectly in place without a single strand out of order.

He followed me through the front garden and into the house without a word.

"Would you like some coffee?" I asked when we got inside.

"Garage access, please?"

"Through the kitchen."

I pointed to the door that opened into the garage. Mr. Wu nodded once and walked past me. The door closed behind him with barely a sound.

I went back into the bedroom and traded my bathrobe for shorts and a reasonably clean T-shirt. When I returned to the kitchen, the coffee maker had finally finished its work. I pulled a mug out of the cabinet, then I walked over and opened the door to the garage.

All four doors of the Mustang stood open, and the overhead light blazed. Mr. Wu kneeled in the passenger seat. He was leaning down into the footwell holding what looked like a small electronic device in his hand.

"Mr. Wu, would you like coffee?" I called out.

He didn't bother to answer or even to acknowledge that I had spoken.

That was one thing I didn't like about Mr. Wu. He talked too much.

I shrugged and closed the door. I poured myself coffee, walked back through the house to the front gate, and collected the *LA Times* from where the delivery guy had tossed it. Then, I carried both the coffee and the paper out to the deck.

The marine layer had burned off, and the morning was clear and bright. The sky was that perfect shade of blue you only get in Southern California when the offshore winds pushed all the smog somewhere far out over the ocean. The sun was still low above the eastern horizon. It threw long shadows across the beach and turned the water into a sheet of hammered gold.

A handful of seagulls walked along the tide line, poking at seaweed and driftwood, looking for whatever it was gulls looked for. One of them found something interesting and called out with a harsh, scraping squawk, and the others all hustled over to investigate, squabbling and shoving each other like kids fighting over the last cookie.

The view from my deck never got old. The ocean stretched out forever, blue and endless and clean. The waves rolled in with that steady, hypnotic rhythm that made everything else seem insignificant. The air tasted like salt and sunshine. Every morning when I sat out here I felt like I was getting away with something.

This was exactly what I had imagined when I decided to leave Virginia and come west. A different life. A better life. A life where I could sit on a deck overlooking the Pacific Ocean, drinking coffee and reading the morning paper while seagulls argued over breakfast scraps and the world went about its business somewhere else.

And for a few minutes every morning, it actually felt like that life might be real.

I sat down in one of the deck chairs and opened the paper. I worked my way through the front section and just skimmed the headlines. Clinton's transition team, the ongoing situation in Somalia, and the latest developments on the Menendez case. I was already turning to the sports section when Mr. Wu opened the sliding door and stepped out onto the deck.

"No tracker in car."

He stood there with the briefcase in his left hand, perfectly balanced on the balls of his feet.

"I check house now."

"Knock yourself out."

Mr. Wu paused and seemed to consider my choice of words. I thought I saw a puzzled look slide quickly across his generally inscrutable face, but if I had, it was gone almost as soon as it appeared. Maybe Mr. Wu wasn't familiar with that idiom. I wondered for a moment if I ought to explain what it meant, but then he turned away and took his briefcase inside, so I just went back to the *LA Times* and what was left of my coffee and kept my mouth shut.

It took me ten minutes to finish both and go inside for more coffee.

Mr. Wu had placed a black metal box in the middle of the living room floor. It was roughly the size of a car battery, but flatter. It looked military somehow, with riveted seams and a dull, scratched finish that suggested it might have had some hard use. A thin telescoping antenna extended out of the top. It was fully deployed and swaying slightly.

I had no idea what the device was supposed to be doing. Scanning for radio signals? Detecting electronic bugs? Jamming something? For all I knew, it could have been tuned to the morning traffic report.

When I walked into the kitchen to pour more coffee, I found Mr. Wu on his knees with his head in the cabinet underneath the sink. His jacket was off now, draped over one of the kitchen chairs. Whatever he was doing in there involved a small flashlight and what looked like the same handheld device I'd seen him using in the Mustang.

I didn't offer Mr. Wu any coffee. I had learned my lesson.

I took my own coffee back outside to the deck, settled into one of the chairs, and left it to Mr. Wu to do whatever he was doing inside. The sun climbed higher in a sky so blue it hurt to look at. The ocean had gone from gold to dull gray to brilliant turquoise, and the waves just kept rolling in.

A jogger passed on the beach, a woman in bright yellow running shorts and a sports bra. She had earphones on and moved with the easy stride of someone who did this every day. I watched her until she disappeared in the direction of Point Dume.

The seagulls had abandoned their position along the tide line and moved inland. Three of them now perched on the railing of the deck and watched me with flat, black eyes. Their stare was downright unnerving. I had nothing to offer them but coffee, and they didn't seem particularly interested in that. They just sat there, patient as tax collectors.

About twenty minutes later, Mr. Wu stepped outside carrying his briefcase. His jacket was on, perfectly arranged, not a wrinkle visible. I noticed through the sliding glass door that the black box that had been in my living room had disappeared. Presumably packed back into Mr. Wu's briefcase.

"House okay."

He stood there, perfectly balanced as always, looking at me with those unreadable eyes. I suddenly realized how much like the seagulls' eyes they were.

"No bugs or other listening devices?" I said, mostly because I thought I should say something.

"House okay," he repeated. "I go now."

I stood up and walked with him through the house to the front gate. The morning sun was reflecting off the driveway, and I squinted from the glare. Mr. Wu's car sat at the curb, a dark blue Lincoln Town Car identical to Sandy's except for the color.

"Thank you," I said as I opened the gate for him.

Mr. Wu said nothing. He just walked out through the gate with those precise, economical movements he had, opened the Lincoln's door, and slid behind the wheel. I watched him pull away, heading south on the PCH toward Santa Monica, and I closed the gate behind him.

. . .

I gathered my research notes from UCLA and poured myself a bowl of raisin bran. While I ate it and drank another cup of coffee, I thought about the motion to quash and the brief I had to write, and I started making a few notes on a legal pad.

How long was it going to take me to get this written, I wondered. I really hadn't done any legal writing at all since law school, so I knew it might take me a while. Still, the deadline Judge McClanahan had given me was Friday, and the strategy was to file the motion and brief with her at the very last moment, anyway. I should have plenty of time, no matter how slow I was.

At least now I knew I wasn't under any kind of electronic surveillance, so it ought to be safe for me to use the computer at Pele's bookstore without dragging her into any of this.

Or was it? Maybe these guys were old school. What if they were watching the house to see where I went rather than tracking me electronically? If I just drove straight up to Pele's bookstore, I'd still lead them right to her.

I needed to figure out if they were out there somewhere before I went to Pele's, but how could I do that? Just opening the front gate, walking out to the PCH, and looking up and down the road to see if I could spot them would be the jerk move of all time, wouldn't it?

Then I had an idea.

I went out onto the deck and lowered the steps to the beach. If I walked along the beach to a public access corridor, I could come out on the PCH well south of the house and avoid looking like a fool by walking out my own front door and strolling down the highway searching for watchers.

The nearest public access was about a quarter mile to the south, tucked between two houses that would give me at least some cover. The more I thought about it, the better the idea seemed, so I parked my coffee mug on a table on the deck and set off.

The tide was out, and the sand stretched out wide and empty under the morning sun. A few joggers moved off in the distance, and a fat woman who looked vaguely familiar walked toward me dragging a small brown dog along the waterline.

And there were the gulls, of course. There were always the gulls.

A group of maybe twenty strutted along in front of me where the sand met the foam, pecking at whatever the tide washed up, their bodies flashing white in the sunlight. After the woman and her dog passed me, I was close enough to the gulls to register something odd.

One of them was black.

I had lived on Carbon Beach for almost a year, and I had never seen anything like that before. Most of the seagulls I saw were pure white. Occasionally, you might see one that looked a little gray or perhaps mottled brown, but this one was genuinely black. Its feathers gleamed in the sunlight as if they had been painted with glossy enamel.

The flock scattered as I approached, wings beating, voices screaming their usual complaints. All except the black one. It held its ground, standing just above the waterline, and it tracked me with eyes that looked uncomfortably intelligent. When I walked within maybe ten feet of it, it still didn't move. It just stood there and watched me pass.

Now, of course, I don't believe in evil omens. How could I? I'm a university graduate, an alumnus of the University of Virginia School of Law, and a member of three bar associations. If that didn't make me the perfect personification of a twentieth-century rational man, I didn't know what would.

But if I did believe in evil omens, that damned bird would definitely qualify as one.

I told myself I wasn't going to look back, but of course I did. After I was thirty or forty yards further down the beach, I took a quick glance over my shoulder and I saw that the black gull hadn't moved. It was right where it had been when I walked past, and it was still watching me with that same unnerving single-mindedness.

The public access to Carbon Beach was between two huge houses that were probably worth at good ten or fifteen million each. It was nothing but a narrow concrete path about fifty yards long, stretching from the PCH down to the edge of the sand. It was mostly level, but a few steps here and there were needed to account for the difference in elevation between the road and the beach.

I took the last bit at the top slowly and stayed in the shadow of the houses as I emerged onto the side of the PCH. Most of the Carbon Beach houses sat on postage-stamp lots with garages barely big enough for two vehicles. Guests parked on the street. Staff parked on the street. A lot of people parked on the street, so cars lined both curbs as far as I could see.

A white BMW convertible sat directly across from me. Beyond it, a black Mercedes sedan. Then a Ford pickup truck that looked like it belonged to a contractor, a red Mazda Miata, a tan Volvo wagon, and another Mercedes sedan, this one silver.

And on and on, stretching in both directions.

Any one of them could have held someone watching me. Or none of them.

Ryan O'Neal said the guys who had shown up at my house were in a dark-colored SUV, and when they left they had headed in the direction of Santa Monica, but who knew if they had actually gone to Santa Monica. They could have easily turned around, parked three hundred yards down the road, and watched my house from there.

I scanned what I could see of the interiors of the nearest vehicles. Empty. All of them. But the windows reflected the sunlight and made it difficult to see anything clearly beyond the first few cars in either direction.

Across the highway, a man walked a golden retriever, and a woman in running gear stretched against a telephone pole. Three houses down, a landscaper's truck sat with its bed full of equipment while two men in work clothes trimmed hedges.

Normal. Everything looked completely normal.

Which meant exactly nothing.

I turned back and retraced my steps. I had a couple of hours before Pele opened the bookstore for the day, and I knew I really needed to use those couple of hours to sketch out an outline of the motion and the brief I wanted to use her computer to write.

Chasing ghosts up and down the PCH wasn't going to get that done.

24

By one o'clock, I had the motion sketched out as well as a general outline for the supporting brief, and I was ready to write.

I stuffed my notes and all my research into a briefcase and headed out to the Mustang to drive up to Pele's bookstore. I thought about calling first to make sure that Sandy had cleared the way for me to use her computer, but either he had, or he hadn't. Calling first wouldn't serve any purpose if he had, and it wouldn't fix anything if he hadn't. I'd find out soon enough which it was.

Before I started the engine, I wondered again about whether I might be dropping Pele in the middle of this mess just by going up to her bookstore. Right now, the bad guys had no reason to connect me to her, and I wanted to keep it that way. I hadn't seen any signs of physical surveillance, of course, and Mr. Wu hadn't detected any form of electronic surveillance, but that didn't settle the matter for me. In fact, it bothered me a good deal, because it didn't really make any sense.

I had a pile of documents that could blow up Zac Scott and probably take his Yakuza pals down with him, and it stood to reason that they would want to get that stuff away from me before something like that happened. Three Yakuza gangsters had shown up at Carbon Beach and apparently searched my house, and they had found nothing. Was I supposed to believe they had just shrugged and forgotten all about me after that? Of course, they hadn't.

I had something they wanted. Something they had to have, in fact. They either got me to tell them where I had put those documents, which might have been a messy and unhappy process for everyone, particularly me, or they figured out on their own where they were. And the way to figure it out on their own was to keep an eye on me and see where I went.

So where were these guys? I had no idea, and that scared me. They had to be out there somewhere, and not knowing where they were just made it worse.

I was still worrying about that as I backed out of the garage, so instead of turning north on the PCH toward Pele's bookstore, I turned the opposite way, south, toward Santa Monica. I had no idea where I was going, of course, but I figured I'd think of something. And when I got to Topanga Canyon Boulevard, I did.

Topanga Canyon Boulevard is the primary connection between the Valley and the coast for many miles, but it isn't that heavily traveled, particularly not in the middle of a weekday. It isn't actually much of a boulevard either. It's a twisting mountain highway with no cross streets and no places to turn off or stop other than a few scenic lookouts until you get all the way over the mountains and start descending into the San Fernando Valley.

It occurred to me that I could go up a few miles, park at one of those scenic viewpoints, and anyone following me would have to show themselves because there would be no way for them not to. They would have no choice but to drive right by me, and they would stand out like they were driving a float from the Rose Parade.

Turning left off the PCH, I drove up into the Santa Monica Mountains. Sure enough, a couple of miles along, I found a little parking area where tourists could stop and contemplate the beauty of the Pacific Ocean stretching off to the west. I turned in without signaling, pulled to the far side of the lot where I wouldn't be seen by a car coming up from the PCH until they were almost past the entry to the parking area, and shut off the engine.

I had been watching my rearview mirror since I started up Topanga Canyon Boulevard, and the only vehicle I'd seen behind me as I climbed into the mountains was a FedEx van. That couldn't be them, could it? Surely, they wouldn't have mounted a surveillance operation *that* sophisticated.

A minute or so after I parked, the FedEx van passed. It looked legit to me, but what did I know about FedEx vans? So I waited to see what other vehicles were behind it.

And there were none. Not a one. I sat there for a good ten minutes, and not another vehicle passed coming uphill.

Huh.

Was I completely wrong in thinking Zac or his Yakuza pals had me under surveillance, hoping I would lead them to wherever I had stashed Emma's documents? I didn't see how I could be wrong, but plainly, there was no one following me up Topanga Canyon Boulevard.

Maybe Mr. Wu missed some form of electronic surveillance they had put on the Mustang, which would account for why I didn't see any physical surveillance. That seemed unlikely, too, particularly in light of the enormous trust Sandy obviously placed in him, but what other explanation could there be? Either the bad guys had simply lost interest in me, or we had missed something.

I was going around in circles, and I knew it. I had work to do, and I'd had nothing to eat since breakfast, so I was hungry, too. Those were both problems for which I could see immediate solutions. Figuring out what the hell the bad guys were up to didn't come with such an equally straightforward resolution

But I still couldn't get the possibility that somebody was watching me entirely out of my mind.

Instead of driving straight up to Malibu Books when I got down to the commercial area, I parked in front of the Safeway where there were a lot of other cars, grabbed my briefcase, and strolled off into the Country Mart to get myself a turkey club on sourdough. I sat on a bench out by the children's playground to eat it, and as far as I could tell, no Japanese gentlemen in black suits followed me out there.

When I finished eating, I left the gardens of the Country Mart by a different exit, walked through the busiest part of the parking lot I could find, and then abruptly turned and walked straight through the front door of Malibu Books. Pele was sitting behind the front counter reading a book. She looked up, but she didn't smile.

"Charlie."

The big black glasses were perched on the end of her nose, and she wore the same kind of oversized men's clothing she'd had on the first time I met her. Today, it was a faded denim work shirt rolled to the elbows and khakis that looked like they'd been bought in the boys' department.

"I talked to Sandy," she said.

Her voice held no particular warmth, but it wasn't exactly hostile either. More like somewhere in neutral territory.

"He told me you need to use the computer to prepare some documents for court."

"I do, yes." I hesitated. "I hope you don't mind."

Pele shrugged. "Sandy paid for it. I suppose he's entitled to let anyone he wants use it."

"Thank you."

"Does this stuff you're working on have anything to do with that divorce case you mentioned before?"

I nodded. "The woman has put me in a difficult position. She gave me a lot of documents to review, and now the court has subpoenaed those documents. If I turn them over, I'll be breaching attorney-client privilege."

"Why don't you just give them back to her and let her decide what to do with them?"

"I can't. She's gone somewhere, and I don't know how to find her."

Pele hesitated. "We're talking about Emma Scott, I gather, aren't we?"

"How did you know—"

"You asked me if I knew her."

"You said you didn't."

"Yeah, well, I lied."

That was interesting, but I had no idea where Pele was going with this, so I just nodded, stayed quiet, and awaited developments.

"She used to come in here a lot, and we would talk," Pele explained. "Hollywood marriages are always difficult, but hers was particularly difficult."

I nodded some more.

"She told me a lot of things that I consider personal," Pele added. "I didn't want you to ask me what she had told me and then have to tell you I didn't want to say, so I thought it was better just to say I didn't know her."

"Can you tell me what you think of her without violating any confidences?"

"I like her. She's smart, and she's a lot tougher than you probably think she is."

That was interesting. Particularly because I already thought Emma was plenty tough.

"Look, Pele, I know you weren't very happy about me asking you to smooth the way for me to meet Sandy, but Emma's really dumped me in it whether she intended to or not. Sandy has helped me to keep my head above water. I don't know what I would have done without him."

"You don't owe me any explanation, Charlie. Whatever involvement you and Sandy have is none of my business."

"I'm just saying that I don't want—"

"Let's just move on," Pele interrupted. "Each of us is uncomfortable talking about Emma for different reasons, so let's stop. Want to talk about the computer instead?"

"Okay. The computer it is."

"Sandy thought he was helping me run the store better by buying a computer for me, but he doesn't really understand that I like this place the way it is. I don't really *want* to run it better."

I didn't understand that either, but I thought it was better under the circumstances just to nod some more and look friendly rather than argue about it.

"I've never actually used the computer myself," she said. "I didn't want to invest the time it would take for me to learn how."

I nodded again. That had been working fine for me so far, so I figured I'd just stick with it.

"I'll show you where it is," Pele finished, "but then you're on your own."

She walked past me and opened a narrow doorway I hadn't noticed on my previous visits. I followed her through it into a small office that looked like it had once been a storage closet. A wooden desk sat pushed against one wall, its surface buried under stacks of invoices, book catalogs, and what could easily have been a month of unopened mail. A small window high on the back wall let in a square of pale afternoon light.

The computer sat on an old-fashioned typing table with a brown Formica top that had probably once held an actual typewriter since it looked well used. The surface was scratched and stained, and I could see several rings from coffee cups and what might have been cigarette burns along one edge. I pulled over a typist's chair, one of those rolling jobs with a padded seat and a back that adjusted up and down, and sat. The padding had compressed years ago into something approximating hardened cardboard.

"Do you know how long you're going to be?" Pele asked.

"I'll be a while. I've got to prepare both a motion and a brief in support of the motion. The brief's going to be pretty long."

I pointed at my briefcase sitting at my feet.

"I've done all the research," I said. "Now I've got to do the writing. It could take a couple of days. Maybe more. Is that a problem?"

"No problem. I'll get you a key so you can come early or stay late if you want to. No reason for you to depend on me."

I wondered if there was a subtext to that comment, but I wasn't about to ask.

The computer was a Dell. The tower sat on the floor under the typing table, and the keyboard and a fourteen-inch monitor in a beige plastic case were on the typing table. The monitor looked enormous on that little table. A cable ran from the back of the computer tower on the floor to a dot matrix printer sitting next to it. I didn't recognize the brand, but at least its paper feed was already loaded up with continuous form paper curling out of a box and attached at the perforations.

I pressed the green power button on the front of the tower

and heard an encouraging whirring noise. The monitor flickered, glowed for a moment, then settled into displaying white text on a black background. According to the startup screen, the computer was running Windows 3.0.

I had seen the new version of Windows advertised, but I'd never actually used it. Back at Pritchard, Wells and Monroe, we'd had computers running an earlier version that was barely more sophisticated than DOS. Everything appeared as text in monochrome lists. This was different. There were all sorts of graphics rather than just lines of text. Little pictures represented all the programs and the files.

Very cool indeed.

"Do you know if there's a word processing program?" I asked, glancing at Pele.

She just looked at me.

"You're on your own, man, like I already told you. I've never even turned this thing on."

The little chime back at the front door rang.

"Customers," Pele said. "Gotta go. Can't take a chance on them escaping without buying something."

And then she disappeared back through the little door to the front of the store, leaving me alone with the computer.

I turned back to the monitor and started clicking through the icons and examining what each one represented. File Manager. Control Panel. Games. Then there, tucked in among the others, was something called Microsoft Office. That sounded promising.

I double-clicked the icon and watched while the screen changed. Soon a fresh set of icons appeared. Excel. PowerPoint. And a third application called Word.

Bingo.

I opened Word, and the screen filled with a blank white page. A cursor blinked in the upper-left corner of the page. The toolbar across the top showed buttons for common functions. Font. Font size. Bold. Italic. Underline. Save. Print.

I'd never used Microsoft Word before, but it looked a lot like the program called WordPerfect that we had used back at Pritchard, Wells and Monroe. How hard could a new word processing program be for a highly educated guy like me to figure out?

Plenty hard, as it turned out.

25

Software and computers are supposed to make our lives easier and more productive, aren't they?

So who designs this stuff? And whoever it is, why do they make everything so damned difficult? Are they just showing us how much smarter than us they are, or is it that they're simply too dumb to find a more natural way to make computers work?

I was still fiddling with Word's settings, changing the font style and size, getting the paragraphing set up correctly for a legal document, and trying to make the damn margins stay where I put them when Pele came back about an hour later.

She brought me a cup of coffee and put the yellow mug down on the table right next to the keyboard. Was it a peace offering? I certainly hoped so.

"One cup of terrible coffee," she said. "Black, right?"

"Right. Thank you."

She looked over my shoulder at the monitor.

"How's it going?"

"Slowly," I admitted. "I haven't even started the writing.

Maybe you did the right thing by not investing your time in learning how to do this stuff."

"Is it really that difficult?"

"Not difficult, exactly. Just confusing. The way it works isn't always entirely logical."

"Then it would probably be a piece of cake for me. I'm not entirely logical either."

I chuckled, as I gathered I was expected to, but I made no comment. I knew a trap when I saw one.

"Sandy thinks the world of you," Pele said. "I swear I don't know what he sees that I'm missing."

I didn't know what to say to that either. I assumed she was joking, but then I noticed she wasn't smiling, so maybe not.

Pele took a key out of her pocket and laid it on the typing table next to the coffee.

"I've got to leave early today, but stay as long as you like. I'll lock the front door behind me and put out the closed sign when I go, so you shouldn't be disturbed. Actually, as few customers as I've had today, I could leave the front door wide open and you probably wouldn't be disturbed."

I chuckled again and continued to keep any specific comments to myself. Why change a winning policy?

"Anyway," Pele finished, "just lock up when you go."

"I will. And thanks for the coffee. You're getting better at it. This isn't terrible coffee at all. It's just pretty bad coffee."

Pele smiled. Actually smiled.

Maybe I was making some progress toward peace here after all. We live in hope, huh?

"See you tomorrow?" Pele asked as she started back to the front of the store.

"Count on it," I said.

. . .

I turned back to the computer and spent another thirty minutes wrestling with fonts and margins and paragraph spacing. Word kept wanting to do things its own way, and it reformatted what I'd just set up the moment I turned my back on it. But eventually I got everything configured the way I wanted it, or at least close enough.

I typed a few lines of random nonsense into the template I'd constructed. Legal gibberish. Placeholder text. I hit return a few times, added some paragraph breaks, then scrolled back up to check the formatting.

Everything stayed exactly where I'd put it.

Hallelujah!

I declared victory, leaned back in the typist's chair, and lifted the yellow mug to my lips. The coffee was lukewarm now, but I drank it anyway.

It honestly wasn't terrible coffee. To be entirely fair, it really wasn't half bad. Maybe I should tell Pele that, or maybe it would be better to keep the banter going. The terrible coffee joke had become a thing between us, a small ritual that put at least one aspect of our relationship on solid and predictable ground. Disturbing that probably wouldn't be wise.

My eyes drifted around the cramped office while I finished the coffee. Pele wasn't exactly a model of organization and efficiency. Stacks of paper teetered on every available surface, books were piled on the floor, and a calendar from 1991 still hung on one wall. Pele had said she wasn't entirely logical, and from what I could see here, there was a lot of support for that claim.

I noticed some bankers boxes shoved back in one corner that looked similar to the ones I had taken from Emma Scott's garage. They were even sealed up with packing tape exactly the same way I had sealed those boxes before putting them in the Mustang's trunk.

I looked closer.

There were five of them.

Dear God, please don't tell me...

I stood up and walked over to where the boxes were stacked. They weren't similar. They were identical to the ones I'd taken from Emma's garage. For a moment, I refused to accept what I was looking at. My brain simply wouldn't process it. But then I had to.

These were Emma's five boxes of documents. Right here in Pele's office at Malibu Books. This was where Mr. Wu had taken the boxes when he collected them from the trunk of my Mustang at Sandy's house.

Oh, shit.

I ran my hands over the boxes. The packing tape was still intact on all of them, so at least it didn't appear that anyone had opened them and examined the contents. I lifted the top box off one of the stacks and put it on the floor. I reached to peel back the packing tape, but then I stopped.

How was I going to explain to Pele what I was doing if she walked in while I had the box open? I would have to tell her what these boxes were and how they came to be in her office, wouldn't I? And that seemed to me to be a really lousy idea.

I didn't want Pele connected with any of this, and I couldn't imagine why Sandy had let Mr. Wu store this stuff in her office. The only thing for me to do was to get the boxes out and take them somewhere else before anyone found out, and before Pele realized they were here.

Pele had told me she was leaving early today, hadn't she? Maybe that would give me a chance to fix this before anyone was the wiser. I put the box I had moved to the floor back on the stack where I had found it.

And then I went back to the work I was doing on Pele's computer, and I waited.

. . .

An hour or so later, I heard Pele call out from the front of the store.

"Goodnight, Charlie. Don't forget to lock up."

"I'm on it," I called back.

I gave it a few minutes and then went out to the front to check. Pele was gone, the CLOSED sign was out, and the front door was locked. I sat on the stool behind the counter and dialed Sandy's number on the store's telephone. Sandy picked up on the second ring.

"Did you finish the motion and brief already?" he asked before I could say anything about Emma's boxes.

"I've barely started. I spent most of the day trying to figure out how to make the damn computer work."

"Get used to it, pal. Trying to make computers work is going to be the future for young guys like you." Sandy paused. "Old guys like me don't have to worry. It's not our problem. It's yours."

"I wasn't calling about the motion."

"Oh?"

"I need to ask you something."

"Okay."

"Do you know?"

"Do I know what?"

"Where Mr. Wu put those boxes of documents that you had him take out of the trunk of my Mustang."

"The stuff Emma Scott gave you to look at?"

"Yes."

"I told him not to tell me where he had taken them."

"Well, I'm going to tell you."

"Look, Charlie, I really don't think that's a very good—

"They're here," I interrupted.

"Here?"

"At Pele's bookstore. In her office."

That brought a silence.

"You can't be serious," Sandy eventually said.

"I can be, and I am."

A longer silence came after that, and it stretched on for a while. I could hear Sandy breathing, and I could almost hear him thinking through the implications.

"Charlie, listen to me very carefully. Don't touch those boxes."

"I've got to get them out of here before Pele discovers what they are. Or worse, Zac and his pals find out that they're here. I don't want any of this stuff to be connected to Pele in any way. And neither do you."

"I said, don't touch the boxes. You still need to be able to tell Judge McClanahan that you don't have them and don't know where they are."

"But if Pele—"

"I'll arrange for the boxes to be taken somewhere else tonight."

"Where?"

Sandy's voice carried a note of dry amusement when he answered.

"I don't want to know, and neither do you."

"So how are you going—"

"I'll send Mr. Wu. I'm sure he'll be able to think of someplace to put them."

"Oh, sure. And he did such a bang-up job the first time you asked him to take them someplace, what could possibly go wrong?"

Sandy said nothing, but then I hadn't expected him to say anything.

"Can I put another question to you?" I asked.

"Sure."

"Why do you always call him Mr. Wu?"

"Because that's his name."

"Doesn't he have a first name?"

Sandy hesitated. Then he said, "Willie."

I burst out laughing.

"*Willie Wu?* Are you being serious?"

"Now you know why I always call him Mr. Wu. And I would strongly advise you to do the same."

After I hung up, I went back to Pele's office and eyed the boxes. If Mr. Wu was going to disappear them, there was something I wanted to do first.

I started going through the cabinets and drawers in Pele's office, but I stopped when I found what I was looking for. A roll of packing tape similar to the tape I had used to seal the boxes when I had collected them from Emma's garage.

I set the five boxes out on the floor in a straight line and methodically peeled the packing tape off each one. I sorted quickly through the contents of every box and collected the Japanese language documents. If there was really a connection between Zac Scott and the Yakuza, it seemed a reasonable guess that there would be something about it in the Japanese-language documents he had.

It took a while to get through all five boxes, but when I was done, I had collected thirty or forty foreign-language documents that varied from a single page to maybe a dozen pages stapled together. They made a stack about three inches high. I put the documents I had collected into my briefcase and started sealing up the boxes again with packing tape. I had just finished when I heard knocking at the front door. When I let Mr. Wu in, he just walked straight past me without a word, went into Pele's office, and emerged with one of the five boxes.

"Do you want some help with those?" I asked.

Mr. Wu didn't answer. He didn't even acknowledge that I had spoken to him. And I just stood and watched as he walked back and forth between Pele's office and the dark blue Lincoln Town Car he had parked at the curb right in front of the bookstore. One by one, the five boxes disappeared into the Town Car's cavernous trunk. Then Mr. Wu got in, started the car, and drove south on the PCH toward Santa Monica. And he had never spoken even a single word.

Sometimes I thought Mr. Wu really didn't like me very much. Other times, I decided Mr. Wu really didn't like *anyone* very much. I had no idea which one it was, but there was something about Mr. Wu that made me want to avoid turning him into an enemy, and I wondered if there was anything I could do to improve the dynamic between us.

Maybe I should start calling him Willie.

Or maybe not.

After Mr. Wu left, I called Sandy again.

"*Willie Wu*, Sandy?" I was still laughing. "You've got to be pulling my leg."

"I already regret I told you that. Please just forget it."

I chuckled again, and then I got to the reason I had called him back.

"I took the Japanese-language documents out of the boxes before Mr. Wu collected them. Do you know anybody I can trust to translate them and then keep their mouth shut?"

"Call Max. He probably knows a guy, and if he doesn't, he always knows a guy who knows a guy."

Sandy rattled off a telephone number, and I wrote it on a pad by the telephone.

After Sandy and I hung up, I dialed the number he had given me for Max. Max answered so quickly I wondered if he'd been sitting there with one hand on the telephone just waiting for me to call. I told him about the Japanese-language documents I needed translated, and that the translation had to be done by someone who could be relied on to keep their mouth shut about the contents. Max told me he could take care of that. He gave me an address and asked me to send the documents to him by one of the local courier services.

I went back to Pele's office and shut down the computer. Then I collected my briefcase and walked around the bookshop shutting off the lights. When I was done, I locked up and walked out to the Mustang.

The parking lot was considerably emptier than it had been when I had arrived in the afternoon. Most of the cars in the lot now were lumped up at the other end by the Baja Cantina. I wondered if Larry Hagman was warming his usual stool at the end of the bar, and I thought for just a minute about going inside and having one of those big margaritas they served up, but I decided just to go on home instead.

I was tired. I'd been trying hard to do the legal work I had to get done while bobbing and weaving around to flush out the Yakuza goons I was pretty sure had to be out there someplace watching me. The fact that I had never picked up a sign of even a single person with any interest in me, let alone spotted Japanese guys stalking me through the mean streets of Malibu, just made me even more tired.

But when I got back to where I had parked the Mustang, my adrenaline started to flow again.

Just three spaces over from my car was a black Toyota 4Runner.

There appeared to be no one inside the 4Runner, certainly not three Japanese guys in matching black suits, but the vehicle was exactly like the one I had seen at the gas station in Brentwood. And it was exactly like the one Ryan O'Neal said my visitors were in when they were sitting in my driveway at Carbon Beach.

Was it just a coincidence?

Maybe.

But maybe not.

26

I left Carbon Beach for the bookstore a little early the next morning since I was anxious to get stuck into writing the motion and the brief as soon as I could.

The black Toyota 4Runner that was parked near me when I left the bookstore last night was still on my mind, of course, and I looked up and down the PCH when I backed out of the garage. I saw nothing suspicious.

On my way to Malibu Books, I stopped at a small copy shop in a strip mall on the PCH that was wedged between a nail salon and a real estate office. Inside, fluorescent lights buzzed overhead, and the air smelled like toner and paper. The first thing I did was make a set of copies of all the foreign language documents I'd collected from Emma's boxes. The machine hummed and clicked, spitting out page after page while I stood there watching. When I finished, I found a large brown envelope in the shop's inventory of supplies, sealed the originals in it, and addressed it to Max using the address he'd dictated to me over the phone.

The kid behind the counter was maybe twenty. He had a

nose ring and was wearing a grungy T-shirt touting some rock band called Nirvana. I had never heard of them, and that made me feel like I was about a hundred years old.

"Guaranteed delivery by end of business today," the kid said, tossing the big envelope into a gray plastic bin behind him with a practiced flip of his wrist.

I left the shop feeling lighter. One task completed. That was progress, at least of a sort.

Coffee was next on my list. I spotted that place called Starbucks that had opened the year before and pulled in. It appeared to be hanging in there, but I was still sure it would disappear pretty soon. How many people were willing to pay four dollars for coffee, for Pete's sake? But the parking lot was full, so maybe I was wrong. This was Malibu, after all. People around here thought nothing of paying four dollars for water. I ordered a large drip coffee and carried it back to the Mustang.

When I got to Malibu Books, I looked around the parking lot for Toyota 4Runners but, happily, saw none. Pele hadn't arrived yet, so I let myself in with the key she had given me and headed straight into her cramped office. The computer sat waiting for me on its typing table, and I settled into the uncomfortable chair, powered up the machine, and opened Word.

And for the next two days, that was pretty much the way I stayed.

The writing consumed me in a way I hadn't expected. I started with the motion itself, which was straightforward enough. It was a simple request asking Judge McClanahan to quash the subpoena she had issued for the documents Emma Scott had given me because the documents in question were protected by the attorney-client privilege.

The twist, of course, was my request for an evidentiary hearing on Brian Hurter's claim that the documents were stolen if Judge McClanahan determined that the source of the documents was relevant in any way to their protection under attorney-client privilege. Eleven pages in all. Standard formatting. Clear arguments supported by basic case citations.

But the brief was a different deal altogether.

The brief required me to take everything I'd learned during those three days at the UCLA law library and transform it into something persuasive. I had to build an argument the way you might build a wall, brick by brick, each case citation fitting precisely into place, each legal principle supported by the one that came before.

I found myself enjoying the process. The research phase had been a treasure hunt, pulling strings until I found the cases I needed. But this was different. This was construction. Creation.

I started with the foundation. California law was crystal clear that communications between an attorney and a prospective client during preliminary case conferences were privileged. I cited *People v. Jackson*, then built outward from there, adding *In re Mitchell et al*, and *Roberts v. City of Industry*. Each case brought additional weight. Each citation built the argument and made it stronger.

Whether documents provided during those preliminary conferences enjoyed the same protection as the oral communications required more careful handling. I found a nice progression through the cases, starting with older decisions and working forward to more recent ones, that showed the courts had consistently extended the protection of privilege to include materials turned over during initial consultations.

Then came the tricky part. Hurter's claim that Emma's documents were stolen property.

I devoted a major section of the brief to that, maybe thirty pages. My first argument, of course, was that the source of the documents was irrelevant for purposes of applying attorney-client privilege. My second argument was that the documents weren't stolen at all, but were copies of documents that Emma Scott had been given in the ordinary course of helping to manage the couple's joint affairs. And my third was that, if Judge McClanahan decided the source of the documents could be relevant, then an evidentiary hearing was mandatory so Hurter could prove his naked assertion that the documents were stolen.

Every lawyer who had ever been in a courtroom had drummed into him the same story teaching him how to make arguments in the alternative.

Say, for example, you're defending a claim that your client's dog has bitten somebody. Here's your defense. Your first argument is that your client's dog doesn't bite. Your second argument, in the alternative, is that your client's dog was tied up that night. And your third alternative argument?

'My client doesn't have a dog, Your Honor.'

No wonder everybody hates lawyers, huh?

The argument I wanted to make to Judge McClanahan flowed nicely onto the page. One point led naturally to the next. I could see the structure taking shape, solid and immutable, just as Sandy had told me back during my research phase that it had to be.

The writing itself proved satisfying, too, and in ways I'd long forgotten. Each paragraph had a beginning and an end. Each section built toward a conclusion. The whole thing existed as a complete work, self-contained, something I could hold in my hands when I finished.

Maybe I really had missed my calling. Maybe I was an academic rather than a courtroom warrior. It didn't really matter. With my law school grades, no university would ever be crazy enough to hire me to teach anything.

On the second afternoon, I was deep into the final section when Pele appeared in the doorway with a mug of fresh coffee.

"Still at it?"

I nodded without looking away from the screen.

"Almost done."

She set the mug down next to the keyboard and glanced at the monitor.

"How many pages is that thing?"

"Sixty-three so far. I figure I'll finish at seventy-five, maybe eighty."

"Jesus. Who's going to read all that?"

"The judge's clerk. That's the point. Make it long enough that McClanahan has to hand it off to someone else to have it summarized for her, which will draw the whole process out and buy me at least another week to figure out what to do next."

Pele shook her head.

"Lawyers."

But she was smiling when she said it.

I finished the brief on Thursday afternoon. Eighty-three pages, all in, it turned out to be. That ought to keep the judge and her clerks busy for a few days.

When I went back and read it one more time from the beginning, I had to admit I was pretty pleased with myself. It was really decent work, and holding the completed brief there in my hands made me feel like I had done something worth doing.

I collected the pages and stapled them together, then I walked out front where Pele was perched on a stool behind the counter and held it up.

"Done," I said. "Hallelujah."

Pele smiled and mimed applause.

"Do you get a raise now?" she asked.

That got a chuckle out of me.

"Can I use your phone?" I asked, pointing to the telephone on the counter in front of her.

When she picked it up and set it in front of me, I dialed Sandy to tell him I was done.

"You're telling me you want me to review the motion and the brief before you file them?" Sandy asked.

"Well ... yeah."

"Are they any good?"

"Yes," I said. "They are."

"And you're happy with them?"

"Yes."

"Then why in the hell would you need my opinion. Anyway, I hate reading stuff like that."

I could hear shuffling papers in the background. Sandy was probably working on something of his own, and the last thing he needed was eighty-three pages of my legal brilliance cluttering up his afternoon.

"You did ask for the evidentiary hearing on whether the documents were stolen, didn't you?" he asked.

"I did."

"Then just file it."

"I still need to bring it to you first."

"Why?"

"You have to sign it."

That stopped the paper shuffling.

"In court," I reminded him, "you told Judge McClanahan the motion hadn't been filed yet because you were supposed to do it and you forgot. Remember?"

I heard a grunt.

"Ah, yes," Sandy said. "The distinguished but slightly senile old man excuse. Works every time."

"So these filings are in your name, and your signature is required on both the motion and the brief before I can file them."

More paper shuffling. I could picture Sandy in his study, his massive mahogany desk covered with documents, those fighter-pilot eyes scanning the file for whatever case he was working on now.

"When are you planning to file?"

"Friday afternoon. Right before the courthouse closes. That way they can't possibly get to it until Monday at the earliest."

"Good man."

"I learned from the best."

Sandy laughed at that, but it was a dry sound, and it came through the phone line like sandpaper rubbing on wood.

"Bring them by tomorrow afternoon on your way to the courthouse. Say around three? That should leave you plenty of time to get to Santa Monica before Judge McClanahan shuts down for the day."

"Three o'clock tomorrow it is."

"And Charlie?"

"Yeah?"

"I'm proud to be working with you, my young friend."

The line went dead before I could respond. Which was probably a good thing, since I had no idea what to say.

I hung up and looked at Pele, who had been watching me with mild amusement while I talked to Sandy.

"All set?" she asked.

"All set. I'll file this stuff tomorrow afternoon."

"Then what?"

That was the question, wasn't it? What happened after I filed the motion?

Would Judge McClanahan quash the subpoena and tell Hurter I didn't have to produce Emma's documents? Or would she just brush my arguments aside and demand that I produce Emma's documents regardless? Or would she split the baby, give me half of what I had asked for, and grant the evidentiary hearing on whether the documents were actually stolen?

And regardless of how the judge ruled on my motion, what would happen then?

Would Emma turn up and let me extract myself from all this by returning the documents to her, or would she remain on the run somewhere and leave me stuck with defending myself against all the people who were lining up to grab them? And what about the Yakuza thugs who were hovering somewhere out there like a sinister Greek chorus? Would they just keep watching from a distance, or would they make some kind of move?

The simple truth was that I had absolutely no idea what was likely to happen after I filed the motion and the brief, so I had to settle for giving Pele a generic response.

"Then I wait," I said. "And hope."

"Hope for what?"

"That the horse might talk."

Pele gave me a look that suggested she thought I'd finally lost my mind.

"Never mind," I said. "Old lawyer joke."

"You want more coffee?"

I glanced at my watch. It was a little after four. I was tired. I should probably head back to Carbon Beach and unwind and get a good night's sleep before going to see Judge McClanahan tomorrow, but the truth was I just didn't feel like going back to that empty house yet.

"Sure," I said. "Why not?"

Pele slid off the stool and disappeared into the back room. I heard the coffee maker gurgling to life, a familiar sound that had become part of the rhythm of the past few days.

Working in Pele's cramped office and drinking her increasingly less terrible coffee had developed into a comfortable and familiar pattern. And it was a pattern I had come to like a lot.

When Pele returned with two mugs, she handed me one and leaned against the counter.

"So what's next for you?" she asked. "After all this is over, I mean?"

I wrapped my hands around the warm mug and considered the question.

"Honestly? I have no idea."

"Want to buy a bookstore?"

I chuckled.

"Not a bad idea. Does it come with a computer?"

"Indeed, it does. A computer, and some really terrible coffee."

All of a sudden, a feeling came over me that I liked. Something good was happening here. I didn't want to put a name to it yet, and honestly, I couldn't do that even if I had wanted to because I had no idea what it was. But it *was* something good.

That much, at least, I was sure of.

Well ... pretty sure.

27

Friday afternoon, I drove to Sandy's place on North Rockingham carrying the motion and brief.

It was a California afternoon right out of some cheesy television show, and I lowered the top on the Mustang so I could enjoy it to the fullest. The marine layer had burned off, and the sky was that perfect shade of blue that made the whole world feel sharper and clearer.

Mr. Wu opened the door when I rang the bell. He stood there in his dark suit, expressionless as always, and then he stepped aside without a word. Now that I knew what his first name was, it was all I could do not to greet him with a cheery, *Hello, Willie!* But something told me that might be a bad idea.

I followed him silently back through the house to Sandy's study, but when Mr. Wu opened the door for me, I discovered I wasn't Sandy's only visitor.

Sandy was behind his massive mahogany desk as usual, those green eyes sharp as broken glass, but Max Furman occupied one of the uncomfortable chairs facing the desk, and he turned halfway around to watch me enter. He looked exactly the same as he did when I met him in that shabby office on Normandie. The same blue sport coat over a black shirt. The same slicked-back hair held down by something greasy.

"Charlie," Sandy said. "Good timing. Max just got here himself."

"I've got those translations you wanted," Max said.

He gestured toward a manila folder sitting on the edge of Sandy's desk.

I put the motion and brief I'd brought for Sandy to sign on the desk, then I picked up Max's folder, settled into the other chair in front of Sandy's desk, and opened it. Inside were photocopies of the foreign language documents from Emma's stash that I'd sent to him, each one now accompanied by a typed English translation stapled to it.

Sandy leaned back in his chair, and from somewhere he produced one of those cigars Pele had forbidden him to smoke. He stuck it in the corner of his mouth and chewed absently at it, but I noticed he didn't light it.

"What's the executive summary?" I asked, flipping through the pages in the folder.

Max settled back in his chair.

"The documents you sent me concern financing agreements, mostly," he said. "Contracts between Zachariah Scott's production companies and various Japanese investors. Pretty standard stuff. And there's also some correspondence about payment schedules, production budgets, and that sort of thing."

I scanned the first translation. It was exactly what Max had said. A straightforward agreement between Scott Productions and something called Pacific Media Holdings to finance a television series called 'Metro Squad.' Terms, conditions, delivery dates. Nothing remarkable.

"That's it?" I said. "Just financing agreements?"

"Just financing agreements," Max confirmed.

I kept reading. The second document was similar. So was the third. All legitimate business deals on their face. Professional. Properly structured.

Out of the corner of my eye, I could see Sandy flipping through the motion and brief while I read. When I heard his fountain pen scratching across the signature lines, I shifted my full attention back to the folder of translations.

"I don't get it," I said, looking up at Max. "These appear to be completely ordinary."

"As they do to me," he said. "My guess is these documents are the public face of the operation. They're the legitimate framework that makes everything else possible."

I nodded and thought about that.

"I don't know what's in the rest of the documents Emma Scott left with you," Max went on. "But I can guess. Wire transfer records. Bank statements. Invoices that don't match these contracts. Payment schedules that don't line up with the production budgets outlined in these agreements. That sort of thing?"

When I stayed silent, Max gestured at the folder I was holding.

"Those Japanese financing agreements are the foundation," he said. "They establish the relationship. They create the paper trails that make Scott's production companies look like routine businesses that just happen to attract a lot of international investment. But underneath all that is where the transactions that really matter are done. Payments that exceed the amounts specified in contracts. Money moving to offshore accounts. Funds distributed to shell companies that don't actually do any work."

Sandy shifted the cigar from one side of his mouth to the other, but he said nothing.

"The agreements you're holding are what Scott shows the

IRS," Max added. "What he shows anyone who asks questions. Clean, professional, completely legal."

"But the rest of Emma's documents show what's really happening," I said.

"Exactly," Max said. "Large-scale money laundering through Scott's production companies. The Yakuza puts dirty money in through these legitimate investment channels, Scott runs it through his operations, and clean money comes out the other side. Of course, Scott takes a cut for providing the service."

I looked down at the translations again. Financing agreements for 'Metro Squad,' 'Pacific Dreams,' and 'Street Justice.' All hit shows produced by Scott's production companies. All funded largely by funds coming from Japanese investors.

Was it possible that at least some of the sources for the tens of millions those Japanese investors were pumping into American television production were possibly a little dubious? Of course it was.

"These contracts are the quid pro quo," Max said. "The Yakuza finances Scott's shows, and in return Scott launders the Yakuza's money for them on the side."

Sandy pushed the signed motion and brief back across the desk toward me.

"Now you understand what you're sitting on," he said.

I did. But I wished I didn't.

I drove over to the Santa Monica Courthouse a little after four that afternoon with the signed motion and brief.

The parking garage swallowed the Mustang into its cool concrete belly. I grabbed my briefcase, stuck everything into it, and headed for the elevators. When neither one showed up for a couple of minutes, I got impatient and took the stairs instead.

The courthouse lobby was nearly empty at this hour on a Friday afternoon. A few lawyers hurried past, clutching files and heading for the exit. A janitor pushed a wide dust mop across the linoleum. The security guards at the metal detector looked bored.

When I got up to Room 111, the courtroom door was standing open, but the lights were off inside. The bench sat empty, chairs pushed back from the counsel tables. I walked down the hallway behind the bench toward where I thought Judge McClanahan's chambers probably were.

The door at the end of the hallway was half open. I couldn't see inside, but I could hear voices, low and indistinct. A woman laughed at something. Papers rustled.

I knocked on the door frame.

"Come in."

Judge McClanahan sat behind a desk that looked like it might have been government issue when Roosevelt was president. Teddy, not Franklin. It had a metal frame with a fake wood veneer top, and it was scratched and dented from what looked like decades of hard use. Behind her, sagging bookshelves held rows of California Reports and Federal Supplements, their spines cracked and worn.

The judge wore reading glasses pushed up on her forehead and had a pen in one hand. She wore a sensible navy-blue dress that buttoned up the front and a pair of pearl earrings. Stacks of files covered most of the desk's surface, and her black robe hung on a coat rack in the corner. Without the robe, she looked smaller somehow, more human.

"Mr. Trust." She set down the pen. "I had about decided you were going to miss your deadline."

"No, ma'am. Still got almost an hour."

I held up the motion and brief.

She gestured toward a chair across from her desk, and I sat.

The chair was upholstered in cracked brown vinyl and uncomfortable as hell. I set my briefcase on the floor and placed the documents on her desk.

Judge McClanahan picked up the motion first. She skimmed through it, her eyes moving quickly across the pages. Then she set it down and lifted the brief. The weight of it made her eyebrows rise.

"An evidentiary hearing? Seriously?"

"Yes, ma'am."

She flipped through the pages, not reading, just gauging the length.

"This must be eighty pages."

"Eighty-three, Your Honor."

"Mr. Trust, I'll be honest with you. Do you really think I'm going to read eighty-three pages about attorney-client privilege?"

"No, ma'am. I expect you'll have your clerk read it and prepare a summary."

A smile flickered across her face, there and gone.

"At least you're honest." She set the brief down. "Walk me through this evidentiary hearing business."

I leaned forward slightly.

"Mr. Hurter claims the documents are stolen property. But that's just a naked assertion. He hasn't offered any evidence to support it. If the court finds that the source of the documents matters with respect to attorney-client privilege, then basic due process requires an evidentiary hearing where Mr. Hurter's claim can be presented, and I will have an opportunity to respond to it."

"And if I decide the source doesn't matter?"

"Then the hearing's unnecessary. The documents are privileged regardless of where they came from."

Judge McClanahan studied me for a moment. Those dark eyes were sharp and evaluating.

"So either I quash the subpoena outright, or I give you your hearing."

"Yes, ma'am."

"Clever."

I said nothing.

"Have you provided copies of the motion and brief to Mr. Hurter?"

"I have copies in my car that I'll get to his office as soon as I leave here."

"Today?"

"Yes, ma'am."

She gave me another one of those evaluating looks.

"Of course," she said, "it's almost five o'clock on a Friday afternoon now, so they won't arrive at his office until well after business hours, will they?"

I struggled to keep my face neutral.

"But they will be delivered today, Your Honor. Which conforms to the deadline you set."

It took every ounce of self-control I possessed not to smile.

Judge McClanahan sighed and leaned back in her chair. It creaked under her shift in weight.

"You know what the hardest part of being a judge is, Mr. Trust? It's not the complicated legal questions. It's not the heavy caseload. It's dealing with lawyers."

She picked up her pen and tapped it against the brief.

"Sometimes I feel like a kindergarten teacher in a home for wayward children."

At that, I did permit myself a small smile.

Judge McClanahan dropped the pen and folded her hands on top of the documents.

"I'll put my clerk to work on this on Monday morning. I'll try to have a ruling by the end of next week."

"Thank you, Your Honor."

"Don't thank me yet. You might not like what I decide."

"Yes, ma'am."

She stood, which meant I stood, too. She extended her hand across the desk, and we shook. Her grip was firm and dry.

"One more thing, Mr. Trust."

"Yes?"

"I was truly amazed to see Sandy Bouchier in my humble little court last week."

"Yes, ma'am?"

"You're working with him now?"

"Well ... in a way, yes."

"That's quite an honor. I have to say I envy you."

I just nodded and did my best to produce a humble and self-effacing smile.

"Tell Mr. Bouchier I said hello. And tell him I still remember that ACLU fundraiser in 1978 when he told the governor exactly what he thought of his prison policies. Best speech I ever heard."

"I'll tell him."

She smiled then, a real smile that transformed her face.

"Now get out of here before I change my mind and rule against you right now."

I grabbed my briefcase and headed for the door.

Walking back to my car, I suddenly felt at loose ends, and it wasn't entirely a good feeling.

For a while now, I had been wrestling with Emma Scott's boxes of documents, and then for the last week, I had been completely absorbed in writing the motion and the brief I had just filed with Judge McClanahan. So what was left for me to do now?

Nothing, really. Just wait.

Just wait for the judge's ruling on whether I had to turn all Emma's documents over to her regardless of my conviction that I was compelled by attorney-client privilege to protect them.

Just wait for Emma Scott to put an end to her disappearing act and surface so that I could give her the documents back and extract myself from this whole mess.

Just wait for the Yakuza to show up and kill me because of what I knew about the large-scale money laundering operations they were conducting through Zac Scott's production companies.

Okay, maybe not that.

The fact remained that I had been single-mindedly barreling down a road for weeks at top speed, and now here I was at a complete standstill. Silent, unmoving, lifeless. Waiting for something to happen.

I didn't like it much.

Last week, I had been asking myself if I was really cut out to fight battles like this. Now I was asking myself if I was really cut out *not* to fight battles like this.

Stop it, Charlie.

You just filed a goddamn brief. You have not reached a watershed moment of philosophical insight.

When I got back to the Mustang, I sat in the driver's seat for a moment without starting the engine, trying to decide what to do now.

I still had to get the copies of the motion and brief to Hurter today like I had promised the judge, of course, but that was just a matter of dropping the envelop off at some copy shop and arranging for a local courier to deliver it.

After that, what I really needed was a drink and a good dinner to write *finished* to a damned successful week.

That was when an idea occurred to me

Maybe I could get Pele to share that drink and that dinner. Why not? We had settled into a comfortable relationship during the time I was working in her office at the bookstore, hadn't we? It had started feeling almost like we were an old married couple sharing a space and time.

But maybe I was getting ahead of myself here. Yes, Pele and I had gotten along pretty well all week, but I had learned when I asked her to introduce me to Sandy that Pele was wary of people she thought might be trading on their relationship for what she saw as ulterior motives.

Maybe she would see an unexpected, even an unwanted dinner invitation now in that same light. Maybe she would even see an invitation from me as pushy, and then it would undo all the progress we seemed to have made at getting back to a comfortable relationship after she jumped to the conclusion that I was using her to meet Sandy.

I sighed. It could just as easily go either way, couldn't it?

Probably the safest thing for me to do, I decided, was just to go home, get a Budweiser out of the refrigerator, and make myself a sandwich. So I started the Mustang, put it in gear, and headed for the PCH.

After all, I had an ocean to watch and some gulls to hang out with, didn't I?

28

The next week passed slowly. Mostly because I had to spend it doing something I really wasn't very good at.

Waiting for something to happen.

Waiting for Judge McClanahan to rule. Waiting for Emma Scott to reappear. Waiting for the Yakuza to make their move.

I walked on the beach every evening, which helped. There was a big storm somewhere off the coast, and the surf was spectacular. Set after set of huge waves rolled in and broke on the beach with a sound like volleys of exploding artillery shells. When the tide was high, the powerful surf drove all the way across the sand to where the houses stood. It broke right up against the line of decks along the sea, decks that now looked impossibly flimsy facing the power of the Pacific Ocean.

I tried at least to pretend to be productive, too. The straightest road out of this whole mess for me was for me simply to decline to represent Emma Scott and return her files to her, but I couldn't do that until she reappeared or somebody found her. Max was supposedly trying to locate her, but I hadn't heard from him, so either he hadn't, or maybe he had given up.

I developed a regular routine. Every morning over breakfast, I read through the crime reports in the Metro section of the *LA Times*, hoping not to see a story about Emma's body being found. I didn't.

Then, just after breakfast, I called Emma's house, and around noon I called Harry's apartment in New York. Later in the day, I made occasional calls to Harry's toy phone and I called the Beverly Hills Hotel a few times, too, just to see if Harry might have checked back in. I even drove over to Emma's house a couple of times and walked around it to see if there were any signs of life.

None of these undertakings achieved anything. I found no sign of either Emma or Harry anywhere.

I dropped into Malibu Books one afternoon pretending I was there to buy another couple of Raymond Chandler books, but I think Pele saw straight through me. Oh, she happily sold me the books, of course. When you're a merchant, sentimentality ranks below making sales in your universe of emotions. But I'm sure Pele could tell that I was anxious and edgy, less interested in buying books than I was in just having something to do to pass the time.

It was Thursday afternoon, nearly a week after I had filed the motion and the brief with Judge McClanahan, when the buzzer at the front gate sounded. When I went out to answer it, I found Sandy and Max standing quietly waiting for me. Somehow, I knew immediately why they were there, and I decided there was no reason not to get right to the point.

"Emma's dead, isn't she?"

"Let's go inside," Sandy said. "We need to talk."

I led them through the house and out onto the back deck. We pushed the chairs around and sat down. Nobody said anything for a while. We all just sat there and watched the ocean.

The surf was running very high. Massive walls of water marched in from the horizon, building higher as they approached the shore. Each wave rose like a mountain, turned glassy and green at the crest, then collapsed in an explosion that broke over us like thunder.

Six white seagulls perched on the deck railing just out of reach of the spray. They watched both the three of us and the surf with that eerie stillness gulls had, heads turning very slowly in unison like spectators at a tennis match.

I half expected to see the black gull again that I'd spotted on the beach a few days back. Now that I knew Emma was dead, it seemed appropriate that the black gull would show up again to bookend the dire omen it had seemed to be forecasting back then, but it was nowhere in sight.

Did that mean the gull hadn't been an evil omen after all? Or did it mean the evil thing it was foretelling had yet to occur? Now *that* was a scary thought.

The silence stretched on. Sandy sat with his hands folded in his lap, looking out at the water. Max slouched in his chair, one leg crossed over the other, his face as unreadable as ever.

I was getting better at waiting, but my impatience eventually won out.

"Tell me," I said.

And then Max did.

"You know I've been trying to locate Emma?"

I nodded. "When I didn't hear from you, I decided you weren't getting anywhere."

"I wasn't. Until yesterday."

I said nothing. I just waited for Max to get on with it, but he seemed strangely reluctant for some reason. Something was coming. Something even bigger than Emma's death, but I couldn't imagine what it might be.

"I put out the word to my law enforcement contacts around California," Max explained. "I asked them to keep me in the loop if they stumbled over any suspicious deaths of women in the right age group."

The surf thundered against the beach. One of the seagulls lifted off the railing and headed for the PCH. Maybe he had some place he had to go. Maybe he was just getting the hell out of there while the getting was good.

"A couple of days ago," Max continued, "a cop I know down in Laguna Beach called me. He said they had a middle-aged woman dead in an apartment down there."

Max paused. I waited.

"Then yesterday he called back. He told me they had identified the woman's body through her fingerprints. Apparently, she was in the system because she had once applied for a concealed carry permit."

Another pause. Longer this time.

"The body is Emma Scott," Max said. "There's absolutely no doubt about it."

I let Max's words hang in the air for a moment. I had been expecting something like this for days, of course, maybe for weeks, but hearing it now hit me harder than I had thought it would.

"How did she die?"

Max and Sandy exchanged a look.

"She was murdered," Max said. "A single gunshot to the head."

I nodded slowly. That made sense. The Yakuza was cleaning up loose ends.

"Do they have anything that points to her killers?"

Another look passed between Max and Sandy. Whatever

was coming, they had thoroughly discussed it. Maybe they had even argued about what to tell me. Max was being extraordinarily careful with his words.

"The Laguna Beach police are calling it a murder-suicide," Max said.

For a moment, I blanked.

"A what?"

My brain simply refused to process what Max had just said into a coherent thought. Murder-suicide? Emma was murdered. Emma was a suicide. The words didn't fit together.

"You mean Emma was a suicide?"

"No," Max said. "Emma was the murder."

He fell silent and exchanged another look with Sandy.

Max was obviously reluctant to say something, but what was it?

And then he just told me.

"The suicide was your friend Harry Wells."

Has someone ever said something to you that made so little sense the words might as well have been from a dead language you had never heard before? Yes, it was just like that. The words Max used sounded like actual words, and the sentence he spoke sounded like an ordinary sentence, but what he had said didn't convey any coherent thought to me.

We sat in silence for several minutes after that. I was trying to get my mind around what I just heard, and Sandy and Max let me have the space to do it.

The five gulls that remained lined up along the railing of the deck watched me carefully. Their heads rotated slowly from side to side, but their expressionless black eyes never left me. They seemed to be waiting to see what I would say next.

Before I said anything, I needed to make certain I really had understood what Max had just told me.

"You're saying the cops told you Harry Wells and Emma Scott were in an apartment in Laguna Beach together?"

Max nodded.

"And that Harry shot Emma in the head, and then committed suicide."

Max nodded again.

I studied both of their faces. Sandy's green eyes watched me with his usual sharp intelligence, but there was something else there now, too. Something that looked a lot like warmth and concern.

I shifted my eyes back to Max.

"You don't look like you think that's what actually happened."

"No," Max said. "I don't."

Another wave crashed against the beach. The gulls along the railing didn't even flinch.

"My friend down there sent me the preliminary police report." Max shifted in his chair. "Somebody did a pretty good job of making it look like a murder-suicide, but it was just pretty good, not perfect. They were both murdered. There's no doubt in my mind about that."

"So you're saying the Laguna Beach cops are going to reopen the case as a double murder?"

Max's expression didn't change.

"No. They're keeping it down as a murder-suicide."

I stared at him. "But you just said—"

"Cops like closed cases," Max interrupted. "Cops don't like open cases with no suspects."

I nodded slowly.

Sandy leaned forward in his chair.

"The Laguna Beach Police Department is small. Maybe thirty officers total. They don't have the resources for a major investigation, especially not one connected to a big-time Hollywood producer about whom there are whispers of connections to organized crime. A murder-suicide is simple. Clean. No follow-up required."

"So they're just going to let it go," I said. "Even though they know."

"They don't *know*," Max said. "They have some doubts. But doubts aren't the same as evidence. And without evidence, they've got nothing to work with, anyway."

The surf kept pounding. The gulls kept watching. And somewhere in Laguna Beach, Harry Wells and Emma Scott lay in a morgue while the cops said their deaths didn't matter enough to investigate properly.

I thought about Harry sitting on this very deck just a few weeks ago, drinking Coke and complaining about the music business. I thought about Emma in my living room, nervous and desperate, asking me to help her.

And now they were both dead.

"When did this happen?" I asked.

"A couple of weeks ago," Max said. "Give or take a few days."

Two weeks. Right around the time Emma stopped answering her telephone. Right around the time I broke into her house and found the place had been searched.

"Where in Laguna Beach?"

"A small apartment complex up the hill from the beach. The kind of place where people rent vacation apartments by the week. They pay cash, no questions asked."

I tried to picture it. Harry and Emma hiding out together in some little apartment. Why? What were they doing there?

"How did the cops find them?"

"Anonymous tip," Max said.

"Anonymous tip," I repeated.

We all knew what that meant. Whoever killed them had

called it in themselves. Partly to make sure the bodies were found before decomposition made it hard to read the way the scene had been staged. And partly to send a message. But a message to whom?

Why, to me, of course.

"What do you know about the scene?" I asked Max.

Max pulled a small notebook from his jacket pocket and flipped it open.

"Harry was found in a chair facing the television. Single gunshot wound to the temple. The gun was on the floor next to the chair. His prints were on it."

"And Emma?"

"On the floor near the bedroom door. Single gunshot to the back of the head. Execution style."

I wanted to say something, but I had no idea what.

"The story the scene tells," Max continued, "is that Harry shot Emma, then sat down and shot himself."

"But you don't think that's what happened."

"No."

"What makes you so sure?"

Max closed the notebook.

"The angles are wrong on the blood spatter patterns. They don't match. And Harry's gunshot wound shows contact burns that look a little too perfect. Like someone pressed the gun against his temple to make sure the powder residue transferred."

"Could the cops see all that?"

"If they looked hard enough, they could. But as I said, they're not looking all that hard. They've already got a theory of the case, and they like the one they have just fine."

I was seized by a sudden feeling that I had to move, so I pushed myself to my feet and walked to the railing. The gulls scattered, and I stood there looking out at the ocean. After a long moment, I turned around, leaned back against the railing, and folded my arms.

"Do you have any idea what Harry was doing in Laguna Beach with Emma?" Sandy asked.

I shook my head.

"You don't think they were lovers?" he pressed.

"No," I shook my head again. "I know I'm not the world's most sensitive guy when it comes to relationship stuff, but I think I would have picked that up if it were true. And I never got the slightest hint of it from either of them."

"Then you think your friend was just trying to protect Emma."

"That sounds exactly like something Harry would do. He didn't have many friends, but he really cared about the ones he did have. Harry was probably trying to make sure Emma stayed safe, but she knew so much about Zac's business that she had become a threat to a lot of people. When the Yakuza found her somehow, poor old Harry was just in the way."

I walked back over and sat down again.

"Well," I said, "at least I guess that simplifies things now."

Sandy just looked at me. "What are you talking about?"

"The Yakuza has taken a big step toward eliminating the risk all this has created for them. They've only got to take care of one more detail, and then they'll be completely in the clear."

"And what is that detail?" Sandy asked.

"Me," I said.

Max reached under his jacket, pulled a black, medium-frame semi-automatic pistol from a belt holster, and placed it on the side table next to me.

"Take it," he said. "I've got a lot of them."

I recognized the gun as a Glock, probably a second generation Glock 19. I picked it up and pushed the magazine release. After the magazine dropped into my hand, I ejected the round in the chamber, caught it, and pressed it back into the top of the magazine.

"I guess that answers my question," Max said.

"What question is that?"

"Whether you know enough about guns not to shoot yourself in the foot."

I shrugged. "I used to go to the range a little."

Sandy cleared his throat.

"You're welcome to stay with me, Charlie," he said. "At least until this blows over."

"It's not going to blow over. Not until I put an end to it."

Sandy and Max exchanged that look again.

"And how do you figure on doing that, Charlie?" Sandy asked.

I thought about it for a moment and then decided to tell both of them the absolute truth.

"I have no fucking clue."

29

Harry's body was released the following week.

Nobody else stepped forward to claim it, so I did. Somebody had to, and it looked like that somebody would have to be me. Harry was divorced. He had no children. His parents were long dead. There was no one else. As his former divorce attorney, I knew that all too well.

Max stepped in to help me make the arrangements.

"When you're as old as I am," he said, "you have a lot of experience with this stuff."

Max knew a few people. Of course, he did. He was able to arrange a plot at Forest Lawn Memorial Park in Glendale. The Disneyland of the Dead, they called it around Hollywood. Humphrey Bogart was buried there. Bette David. Walt Disney. Errol Flynn. Spencer Tracy. Clark Gable. A whole constellation of stars from the golden age of Hollywood.

Harry would have loved knowing he ended up there. The golden age might be over for everyone else, but now Harry was part of it for all eternity.

The burial was scheduled for Tuesday morning at eleven.

I drove out early. I took Malibu Canyon Road past Pepperdine University and crossed the Santa Monica Mountains. When I got to the Ventura Freeway, I turned right and headed east through the San Fernando Valley. The morning sun hit the windshield hard, and I lowered the visor to block the glare. Forest Lawn sat in the hills above Glendale, sprawling across the landscape like a manicured park. Green lawns. Sculpted hedges. White monuments rising against a painfully blue sky.

The place looked more like a resort than a cemetery. Walking paths wound between sections with names like Whispering Pines and Sunset Slope. Classical statuary dotted the grounds. Everything was perfectly maintained, perfectly peaceful, and perfectly fake.

I found the gravesite without much trouble. A simple rectangular hole in the earth. A mound of dirt covered with green felt. A few folding chairs set up under a white canopy.

And six people waiting.

Six.

For a man who had written music for some of the biggest television shows ever. For a man whose themes people hummed without even knowing his name. For a man who had spent forty years in an industry that claimed to value loyalty and friendship above all else.

Six people.

I recognized only two of them. Sandy and Max stood off to one side, both in dark suits. Sandy looked even more like Abraham Lincoln than usual. Max had slicked his hair back extra carefully and wore a black tie for the occasion.

The other four were strangers. An elderly couple who might have once been Harry's neighbors somewhere. A middle-aged woman in a flowered dress clutching a tissue. And a young man in his twenties wearing an inexpensive suit that fit him poorly. Maybe some kid Harry had mentored somewhere along the way.

That was it. That was the crowd that turned out to say goodbye to Harry.

The minister appeared a few minutes before eleven. He was young, maybe thirty, with carefully styled hair and a practiced expression of solemn concern. He carried a leather folder and positioned himself at the head of the grave.

The hearse arrived right on time. The casket was simple. Dark wood with brass handles. Nothing elaborate. The funeral home guys transferred it onto the lowering device with practiced efficiency.

The minister opened his folder and began to read. They were just some standard words about eternal rest and loving memory. He didn't know Harry. He couldn't have. Everything he said could have applied to anyone.

I stopped listening and let my eyes drift across the cemetery. Rows of headstones marched across the perfectly trimmed grass. Marble angels. Stone crosses. Flat bronze plaques embedded in the lawn. Out there, the golden age of Hollywood slept beneath this perfectly tended lawn.

Now Harry was joining them.

But Harry wasn't like them, I thought. Harry wasn't a star. Harry was the guy who made the stars possible. The guy who created the music that made people feel things while they watched those stars on their television screens. The guy nobody remembered.

The minister finished his reading. One of the funeral home workers pressed a button, and the casket began its slow descent into the earth. The mechanism hummed quietly.

Nobody cried. The elderly couple held hands. The woman

in the flowered dress dabbed at her eyes but produced no actual tears. The young man stared at the descending casket with a blank expression.

The industry had already erased Harry. He was no longer a player. Showing up at his funeral did nobody any good. Worse, the murder-suicide thing made him an embarrassment, and Hollywood folks didn't like to be embarrassed by association.

Better to stay away. Better to pretend they had never known him at all.

The casket reached the bottom of the grave. The humming stopped. The minister closed his folder and made a small gesture that I interpreted as permission to leave.

The elderly couple turned and walked away first. The woman in the flowered dress followed. The young man lingered for a moment, then he left too.

Sandy and Max came over to where I stood.

"You did good, Charlie," Sandy said. "Harry would have appreciated this."

I nodded but said nothing.

We all stood there in silence for a few minutes. The funeral home workers waited at a discreet distance, ready to fill in the grave the moment we left. I thought about Harry sitting with me on the deck at Carbon Beach. Harry laughing at my Budweiser. Harry mourning the film and television going corporate. Harry telling me Emma Scott needed someone she could trust.

I thought about Harry trying to protect Emma, and getting killed for his trouble.

I reached into my jacket pocket and pulled out one of the cards I'd had printed with my name and Harry's address on it. I walked over to the edge of the grave and tossed it in.

The card fluttered down and landed on top of the casket.

"Thanks for the loan of the house, Harry," I said quietly. "I'll try not to get killed in it."

Sandy touched my shoulder.

"Time to go, Charlie."

We walked back to where we parked the cars. The morning sun had climbed higher now and turned the cemetery into a sea of green and white shimmering beneath a perfect blue sky. It was beautiful. It was peaceful. It was empty.

I got into the Mustang and sat there for a moment before starting the engine. Through the windshield, I could see the funeral home workers already moving in with shovels.

The golden age was over.

And now, so was Harry.

Something made me think of F. Scott Fitzgerald's final epitaph for Jay Gatsby. *The poor son of a bitch*, somebody had said of him as they tossed a little dirt on his coffin.

Emma Scott's funeral was, by contrast, the most lavish kind of Hollywood production.

Of course, it was.

Zac Scott was a player, and the fact that he had filed for divorce from Emma was quickly glossed over in an outpouring of faux compassion for the loss of his wife. Especially in such a tawdry way. A murder-suicide. How tragic. How terrible. The poor woman.

Emma was buried at Westwood Memorial, which sits tucked behind a strip of office buildings on Glendale Avenue in Westwood Village. The cemetery occupies maybe an acre, maybe less, and it is surrounded by high walls that separate it from the commercial development pressing in on all sides. You could walk past it a hundred times and never even know it's there.

But everyone in Hollywood knew it was there.

Marilyn Monroe rested in a crypt in the wall, and her grave drew pilgrims from around the world. Natalie Wood was there. Truman Capote, too. Even Darryl Zanuck, the godfather of the Hollywood studio system. A whole collection of legends packed into one tiny space like sardines in a very expensive tin can.

The funeral was scheduled for two in the afternoon on Thursday.

I drove over early and parked on a side street. The cemetery opened onto Glendale Avenue through an archway in the wall. I walked under it and found myself in a surprisingly intimate space. Green lawn. Scattered trees. Crypts built into the walls that surrounded the property on all sides.

And at least five hundred people.

They filled every inch of available space. Suits and dresses in blacks and grays and tasteful navy blues. Sunglasses despite the overcast sky. Conversations conducted in hushed tones that somehow still managed to convey urgency and importance.

The mortuary building sat at the far end of the cemetery, a small Spanish-style structure with a red tile roof. It was nowhere near big enough to hold this crowd, so they had erected a huge white tent on the lawn. Rows of folding chairs filled the tent's interior, but even it couldn't accommodate everyone and people milled around outside the tent, clustering in groups, exchanging air kisses and carefully calibrated expressions of sympathy.

I spotted Sandy near the entrance to the tent. Mr. Wu stood beside him, perfectly still, hands clasped in front of him. Sandy had insisted Mr. Wu come along as a sort of bodyguard.

I thought that was silly, but I didn't want to argue.

I made my way over to them through the crowd.

"Charlie." Sandy gripped my hand. "This is quite the spectacle, isn't it?"

"Harry would have been jealous."

Sandy's green eyes crinkled at the corners. "From what you've told me about Harry," he said, "I think he would have been disgusted."

Mr. Wu said nothing. He just scanned the crowd with those flat, calculating eyes, watching everyone and everything.

A murmur rippled through the assembled mourners. Heads turned. Conversations paused.

Zac Scott had arrived.

He moved through the crowd like royalty, which in a way, I guess he was. Tall. Slim. He had that Cary Grant thing working overtime. He wore a perfectly tailored black suit, a crisp white shirt, and a black silk tie. His silver hair caught what little light filtered through the overcast sky.

People parted for him. Hands reached out to touch his arm. Voices offered condolences, which he acknowledged with small nods and tight smiles.

He was grieving, that expression said. But he was bearing up. Being strong. The way men of his generation were taught to do.

What a performance.

I had to hand it to the guy. He knew how to look good even if he had to stand on his wife's dead body to do it.

The funeral director appeared and guided everyone toward the tent. The chairs filled quickly. The overflow crowd pressed in around the edges, standing room only.

I ended up near the back with Sandy and Mr. Wu. From there, I could see everything.

The service began.

But there was no minister this time. No young man with a leather folder reading generic words about eternal rest.

Zac Scott presided.

He stood at the front of the tent beside a photograph of Emma. She looked younger in the picture. Happier. The woman I had met on my deck had been anxious and frightened. The woman in this photograph smiled like she believed the world might actually be a good place.

Zac Scott began to speak.

His voice carried across the tent without any need for amplification. Rich. Resonant. Perfectly modulated. An actor's voice. A performer's voice.

"Emma was the love of my life," he said.

The crowd murmured its approval.

"We met back when she was singing in clubs in the Valley. I heard her voice, and I knew immediately that I had found something precious. Something rare."

He paused. Let the moment breathe.

"Our marriage wasn't perfect. What marriage is? But through all the challenges, all the difficulties, I never stopped loving her."

I glanced at Sandy. His expression remained neutral, but those green eyes had turned hard.

Scott continued. He spoke about Emma's kindness. Her generosity. Her support of his work. He told an anecdote about a party they had thrown in the eighties when one of his shows had been nominated for an Emmy. Emma had insisted on cooking everything herself instead of hiring caterers.

The crowd laughed at the appropriate moment.

He told another story about a vacation they had taken in Europe. How Emma had gotten them hopelessly lost in the streets of Rome, but instead of being frustrated, she'd turned it into an adventure.

More appreciative murmurs from the assembled mourners.

Everything Scott said was polished. Articulate. Perfectly pitched to elicit the desired emotional response.

And all of it was about him.

How Emma had supported him. How Emma had made his life better. How Emma had helped his career. How Emma had stood by him. He never mentioned what Emma might have wanted for herself. What dreams she might have had beyond being Mrs. Zachariah Scott.

The performance stretched on for maybe twenty minutes. Scott's voice never wavered. His composure never cracked. He was the grieving widower, dignified in his sorrow, generous in his remembrances.

When he finished, he stood for a moment in silence. Then, he placed one hand on the photograph of Emma, bowed his head, and stepped away.

The crowd rose to its feet in spontaneous applause.

I stayed seated.

Sandy glanced over at me.

"Not impressed?"

"He's good," I admitted. "I'll give him that."

"He's very good," Sandy said. "That's what makes him so dangerous."

The service concluded, and the crowd began to disperse. People clustered in small groups on the lawn and continued conversations that had nothing to do with Emma Scott and everything to do with deals and projects. They were playing the eternal Hollywood status game. Who was up, and who was down.

Zac Scott held court near the tent entrance. A sort of receiving line spontaneously developed. People waited their turn to offer him condolences, and to be seen paying their respects to one of the most powerful men in television.

I watched Zac work the line. A hand on someone's shoulder here. A warm smile there. The perfect word for each person, always calibrated to their importance in his world.

"You want to get out of here?" Sandy asked.

I nodded.

We made our way toward the exit. As we passed near Scott's receiving line, he spotted me.

Our eyes met for just a moment.

His expression didn't change. That practiced smile remained in place. But something flickered in his eyes. Recognition. Assessment. Calculation.

He knew who I was.

And he knew what I had.

Then someone else claimed his attention, and the moment passed.

When we walked through the archway and back out onto Glendale Avenue, the noise of traffic replaced the hushed conversations. The ordinary world resumed.

"Well," Sandy said as we stood on the sidewalk. "That was something."

"Yeah," I said. "It was something."

Mr. Wu had already disappeared. I spotted the dark blue Lincoln Town Car pulling away from the curb half a block down.

"You want a ride back to Malibu?" Sandy asked.

"I've got the Mustang."

"Of course you do."

Sandy started to turn away, then stopped.

"Charlie?"

"Yeah?"

"Be careful. Scott's not going to let this go. And neither are his friends."

"I know."

"Do you?" Sandy's green eyes were fixed on mine. "Because I'm not sure you do. This isn't about winning a motion in front of Judge McClanahan anymore. This is about survival now. Your survival."

"I know that, Sandy."

Sandy studied me for another moment, then nodded.

"Call me if you need anything. Anything at all."

He walked off down the street toward where Mr. Wu waited with the Lincoln.

I stood there alone on the sidewalk, thinking about Emma's funeral. About Zac Scott's performance. About Harry's pathetic six mourners at Forest Lawn.

The golden age was definitely over.

And here I was right in the middle of whatever came next.

I was walking to my car when Zac Scott suddenly appeared on the sidewalk right in front of me. He was alone. He had emerged from some hidden access to the cemetery that I didn't even know existed, but then Zac Scott doubtless knew about entrances and exits from all sorts of places that I didn't even know existed.

"We need to talk," he said when I reached him.

I kept walking.

"Please," he said. "It would be to your advantage as well as mine."

I stopped and turned back and just stood looking at him for a moment.

"You don't really want to do this on a public sidewalk in Westwood right after your wife's funeral, do you?"

"No, I don't. Would you come to my office tomorrow? Say, around ten?"

"No."

He nodded slowly as if that were exactly what he had expected me to say.

"All right," he said. "Then I'll come to you. I'll be at your house tomorrow at eleven."

"You don't know where I live."

He chuckled. "Of course I do."

"I might not be there."

"Oh, I think you will be, Charlie," Zac Scott chuckled again. "You want to hear what I've got to say. You wouldn't miss it for the world."

Then he turned on his heel and walked back toward the cemetery without another word.

When I got into the Mustang, I just sat there for a moment. You had to marvel at how fast the world turned, didn't you?

One day, I was having a beer with my landlord and agreeing to talk, just to talk, to a friend of his about her divorce. Now, only a few weeks later, here I was living in a dead man's house with a loaded Glock next to the bed in case the same Yakuza thugs who killed the woman he asked me to talk to, and then him, decided I had to go as well.

Now that Harry was dead, I assumed that whoever was administering his estate would want me out of the house as soon as possible. I couldn't help but wonder what would come first. My eviction from Harry's house, or the Yakuza showing up to kill me, too? The more I thought about that, the more certain I became that it might well be a close call.

But who really cared? Other than me, of course.

The most terrifying fact about the universe is not that it is hostile, but that it is indifferent.

Stanley Kubrick was generally credited with that line, so it seemed appropriate to me that it would drift to the surface of my memory at a Hollywood funeral.

Good one, Stan. You nailed it, baby.

Then I started the Mustang, turned west on Wilshire Boulevard, and rolled slowly toward the universal and immutable indifference of the Pacific Ocean.

30

At exactly eleven the next morning, the buzzer at the front gate sounded.

I had been sitting on the deck all morning, watching the ocean and drinking coffee, and had built up enough caffeine-driven courage that I had half convinced myself not to answer the gate if Zac actually showed up. But now that he was here, and exactly on time to the minute no less, my resolve crumbled.

"Good morning!" he sang out when I opened the gate.

Zac had his Cary Grant shtick cranked up to full volume, and he looked as if he were dressed for a GQ fashion shoot. He was a prince of the city, and I was nobody, and he wanted to make certain I understood the importance of that distinction.

I was certain he was the only man within twenty miles of Carbon Beach who at that moment was wearing a hand-tailored suit that cost more than a small car, and a perfectly pressed, show-white dress shirt. His one concession to Malibu was that he wasn't wearing a tie. That was something, I guess.

I turned without a word and led him into the house. Inside, I pointed to a couch and seated myself on the couch opposite.

"Say what you've got to say and get out. I've got things to do."

Okay, maybe that wasn't the most hospitable greeting I could have offered, but this son of a bitch either arranged for Emma and Harry to be murdered or, at the very least, he let them be murdered. I was damned if I saw any reason to pretend to courtesy I neither felt nor thought he deserved. And I sure as hell wasn't in the mood to serve him coffee and settle in for a nice chat.

"We don't have to be enemies, Charlie."

"Actually, we do. And when did I give you permission to call me by my first name?"

Zac shook his head and looked away.

"I thought now that this was all over," he said, "that maybe we could get everything cleaned up without the need for any more personal conflict."

"All over? What do you mean *all over*?"

"Emma is no longer alive, so the attorney-client privilege you cited to keep from returning my documents is no longer an issue."

"Like hell it isn't. The courts have consistently held that the attorney-client privilege survives the death of the client. I'm sure Mr. Hurter can explain that to you if you need him to. Surely he's aware of it."

"Actually, that's not entirely correct."

I just looked at him.

"As I understand it, the privilege does indeed survive the death of the client. That much is certainly true. But after the client's death, the power to assert or waive that privilege passes to the personal representative of the decedent. That is to say, it passes to the executor of their estate."

Suddenly, I saw where this was going. I didn't like it, but I saw it.

Sure enough, before I could gather myself to say anything, Zac unleashed a nasty-looking grin and delivered his big news.

"I'm the executor of Emma's estate, so the power to exercise or waive her attorney-client privilege now passes to me."

He flipped open a leather portfolio he had been carrying under his arm and slid a document across the coffee table between us. I didn't pick it up or touch it, although I suppose that was a childish gesture on my part, but I did glance down to see what it was.

I found myself looking at the first page of a document that bore the title Letters Testamentary. I hadn't done particularly well on the wills and estates section of the California bar exam, but even I knew what that was. It was the notice issued by a California court of the formal appointment of an executor to administer the estate of a decedent. And I certainly didn't need to read this notice to realize who the executor was in this case.

"You didn't waste any time," I said.

"And while you're reviewing documents," Zac said, "here's another one for you."

He slid a second document across the table, and it came to rest next to the first one.

"This is being filed with Judge McClanahan right about now by a clerk from Brian Hurter's office. Since she hasn't yet ruled on your motion to quash the subpoena for all those documents Emma stole from me, we thought it was appropriate to notify her that your motion was now moot. I told Hurter I'd be happy to take care of serving a copy of our motion on you myself since I was coming out here anyway."

I didn't take the bait on the stolen documents gibe, but I did pick up the second set of papers Zac pushed across the table. I had worked damn hard on the motion to quash and the brief in support of it, and I certainly wanted to see what Zac's attorney had to say about it.

I found myself skimming through a request that my motion to quash be dismissed on the grounds that Emma's death had rendered it moot. The request made the argument that the power to assert or waive attorney-client privilege had passed to Emma's executor upon her death, and Zac, as the duly appointed personal representative, was waiving the privilege entirely.

Gosh, what a surprise, huh?

Since the privilege had now been waived, Zac asked Judge McClanahan to enforce her original *subpoena duces tecum* and compel me to produce all the documents in dispute immediately and without any further delay. The Letters Testamentary affirming Zac's appointment were duly attached as an exhibit, as was an affidavit from him formally waiving the attorney-privilege I had relied on in refusing to surrender the documents. All very neat.

"I think I have a week under the rules of procedure to respond to this, don't I?" I asked when I had finished skimming and dropped Zac's filing back on the coffee table.

"Why bother? There's really no response you can make."

"I guess we'll see about that, won't we?"

Zac sat and shook his head very slowly.

"What's the point of drawing all this out, Charlie?"

There he went, calling me Charlie again. I considered reminding him that I preferred Mr. Trust, at least coming from somebody responsible for murdering two of my friends, but then I just let it go. I was getting tired of all this. I was getting tired of a lot of things.

"Have you read the stuff Emma gave you?"

I said nothing.

"I guess that means you *have* read it, doesn't it?"

I said nothing.

"That's really too bad."

"What do you mean?"

"After such knowledge, what forgiveness?"

I recognized the quotation, but I wasn't given to quoting T.S. Eliot, or to hanging around with people who did, so I wasn't entirely certain what Zac was on about. But I was pretty sure I didn't want him to explain it to me.

"Are we done here?" I asked instead.

"Look, why don't you just turn those documents over to me right now?" he asked. "Then we can forget about all this unpleasantness. After that, you'll be completely out of it, and you can just go back to whatever you were doing before. Why keep fighting a battle you've already lost for somebody who's dead and doesn't give a damn anymore one way or another?"

Yep, that was one of the things right there that I was getting tired of, all right. If I had to keep dealing with these smug, entitled Hollywood assholes, the risk of my eventually cracking and going postal on the lot of them was building up steam every day.

I got to my feet.

"I will file my response as I am entitled to under the California Rules of Procedure, and then we will wait for Judge McClanahan to rule. When she does rule, I'll decide what I'll do in response to her ruling, whatever it turns out to be."

Zac remained seated on my couch.

"You're a very stubborn man, Charlie Trust.

"That's what my mother used to say."

"Did she really?"

"No."

Then, I pointed my forefinger at Zac.

"Get up," I said. "We're done here, and you're leaving."

Zac made a point of rising very slowly. Speaking of childish.

"You're making a mistake," he said.

"That wouldn't surprise me. I've made a lot of them. And I'll probably make more in the future."

"It doesn't have to go down this way."

"Yes," I said, "it does."

I walked over and held the front door open, and I kept holding it open until Zac walked out through it. Then I closed it. Probably a little harder than I really needed to.

I was so angry when Zac left that I just stood there in the living room and stared out at the ocean for a while.

Not angry at Zac so much as angry at myself. I had accepted the inferior role in which he had cast me, and I had just stood around while he crapped all over me. The response he really deserved was a smack in the mouth, but I had shied away from delivering it.

Had I been a little cowed by his prince of the city act? Maybe. On the other hand, I knew it wasn't actually an act. When it came to Hollywood, Zac *was* a prince of the city, and I was just a guy who had scraped his way through a second-tier law school.

Eventually, I got tired of standing there, and I pulled open the sliding door to the deck. I walked over to the beach stairs, unwrapped the rope from the cleat, and lowered them down to the sand.

Farrah Fawcett was stretched out on a chaise lounge on her deck next door wearing a black bikini. She lifted her head when she heard the pulley squeaking and gave me a little wave. I waved back and walked down the steps to the beach. Did I mention Farrah was wearing a black bikini?

The surf had calmed since the big swells earlier in the week. Now the waves were coming in steady and clean, maybe three feet at the break, peeling left down the beach in long, glassy lines. They were the kind of waves that brought surfers out at dawn.

A handful of gulls worked the tide-line. They walked with their usual jerky, mechanical gait, heads bobbing, beaks stabbing at kelp and driftwood. Beyond them, the Pacific stretched out flat and silver under high clouds that had moved in overnight.

I turned left and walked down the beach toward the public access walkway. I had no destination in mind, but the idea of movement was very appealing right then since every step increased the distance between me and Zac Scott's smug face, his perfectly tailored suit, and his goddamned T.S. Eliot.

A jogger passed going the other direction, earphones on, lost in whatever music drove her forward. Two small children played at the water's edge while their mother watched from a beach towel, her face buried in a paperback. The sand was firm and cool under my bare feet. I let the rhythm of walking clear my head.

When I reached the public access, I turned around and headed back the way I had come. I made it maybe a hundred yards up the beach when I noticed the gulls.

A flock of a dozen or so had gathered behind me. They followed at a respectful distance, maybe twenty feet back, squawking to each other in that harsh gull language that always sounded like they were having an argument.

I stopped. They stopped.

I walked. They walked.

I picked up my pace. So did they.

The whole thing felt absurd. I'd somehow acquired an

entourage of scavenging seabirds who had nothing better to do on a Friday than trail me along Carbon Beach.

When I got back to Harry's house, I made some coffee that I didn't really want and took a mug of it out to the deck to drink. Farrah had gone inside, so I was on my own now.

Except for my gull entourage, of course. They had assembled themselves in a neat line on the railing and were watching me intently, their heads twisting first one way and then the other while their black eyes stayed fixed on me. They seemed really curious to see what I was going to do next.

I knew just how they felt.

I finished the coffee while I thought about it some more. We were coming to an end here. I could feel it, even if I didn't know what that end was likely to be.

Finally, I looked at the gulls and said, "I think I need to sit down with Sandy and talk about all this, don't you?"

Squawk.

"Maybe I'll take those court filings that Zac served on me over to Sandy right now and see what he thinks. about them."

Squawk, squawk, squawk.

I was glad they agreed with me.

Mr. Wu met me at the door when I arrived at Sandy's Brentwood estate. He stood there in his dark suit, expressionless as always, then stepped aside without a word.

I followed him through the house to Sandy's study. When he opened the doors, I saw Sandy sitting behind his massive mahogany desk, those green eyes sharp as broken glass even at eighty years old.

"Coffee?" Sandy asked as I dropped into one of the uncomfortable chairs facing his desk.

"I'm already wired."

I pulled the Letters Testamentary and the copy of Zac's filing with Judge McClanahan out of my briefcase.

"Zac Scott came to see me this morning," I said.

Sandy's eyebrows rose.

"What did he want?"

"He wants me to turn over Emma's documents to him. He seems to think I no longer have any choice."

I pushed the Letters Testamentary and the copy of Zac's filing with Judge McClanahan across the desk to Sandy. He picked them up and began to read.

For a while, the only sound in the room was the pages turning and the ticking of an antique clock on one of the bookshelves.

Sandy finished the first document and moved on to the second. Outside the window, a gardener's leaf blower roared to life, and then faded as the man moved past the window and off into another section of the grounds.

When Sandy had finished reading, he set the papers down and leaned back in his chair.

"Well, now," he said. "That looks like checkmate to me."

"It's not fair, Sandy."

"No, it isn't. But he's right on the law."

"The bastard might as well have killed Emma himself, and now, because somebody did it for him, he's going to get away with everything. If I give him those documents, they'll never be seen again."

"You've got no choice," Sandy said. "If you don't give the documents to him, the judge will order you to turn them over."

"That doesn't mean I have to do it."

Sandy leaned forward and fixed those green eyes on me.

"Of course, you do. There are times to take principled stands, Charlie, but this isn't one of them. Why would you risk being held in contempt of court for refusing to surrender those documents when there's no longer anything to protect? Your client is dead. You're not protecting her now."

"I'm protecting the truth."

"No, you're not." Sandy's voice went flat. "You're protecting your ego. You just don't want to let this prick get on top of you."

Maybe he had me there. I didn't want to think that was all there was to it, but maybe Sandy was right.

Or maybe he wasn't.

"I'm going to tell Judge McClanahan that I'm filing a response to Zac. That will buy me another week to think about everything. Besides, you never know what a judge is going to do."

"I know what this one is going to do," Sandy said. "And so do you."

31

I was eating a bowl of raisin bran the next morning when the telephone rang. I wanted to ignore it, but ignoring a ringing telephone was something I had a hard time doing. I know. I really ought to learn, shouldn't I?

"Hello."

"I think we should try this again."

I took the receiver away from my ear and stared at it like a man posing for a New Yorker cartoon. It was a silly gesture, particularly since there was no one around to see it, but I did it anyway.

"Zac?" I asked.

"Have you given any more thought to what I said yesterday?"

"None at all. I've notified Judge McClanahan's clerk that I will be responding to your filing within the period allowed me."

"That doesn't make any sense, Charlie."

"I thought I asked you to call me Mr. Trust."

There was a silence after that. Zac didn't say anything else, and neither did I.

I almost hung up, but I didn't. I didn't want Zac to think he had driven me into a petulant gesture like hanging up on him, but there was something more than that, too. I had to admit I was curious. Zac had a specific reason for reopening a discussion I thought was dead and buried, and I wanted to know what that reason was.

So I let him tell me.

"Look," he said. "I gain absolutely nothing by getting Judge McClanahan to hold you in contempt. Why would you even risk something like that? You gain nothing either, and you'd probably end up permanently damaging your career for no reason."

I said nothing.

"I've got an idea how we can both get ourselves out of all this without going to war. Want to hear it?"

I said nothing.

"Come around to my house this afternoon. Say, about four? I'll lay it all out for you."

"If you have something to say to me, Zac, just say it right now."

"Nope. This is my party, and I'll give it the way I like. I want us to sit down face-to-face, and then I'll tell you how we're going to end this. 739 Bel Air Road. You know where that is?"

"I don't need to know where it is. I'm not coming."

Zac chuckled.

"Oh, I think you are. You're a smart man, Charlie Trust. You know perfectly well you're driving a car that's headed straight for a brick wall. You need an off-ramp here just as much as I do. Maybe more. I'm prepared to give you one, and you're not even going to let me tell you what it is? You're way too smart for that."

I said nothing.

"Four o'clock," Zac repeated. "Don't be late."

Then he chuckled again and hung up.

I hated him for that chuckle.

I left Malibu around three to give myself plenty of time to find Zac's place before four.

The Mustang's engine rumbled to life, and I backed out of the garage, pausing to look up and down the PCH in both directions. No black Toyota 4Runners. No suspicious vehicles at all. I counted that as a good start.

The marine layer had burned off, and the afternoon sun etched the world in sharp relief. I headed south on the PCH toward Santa Monica, then cut inland on Sunset Boulevard. Sunset through Pacific Palisades and Brentwood is all manicured lawns and high hedges hiding houses I knew I would never be able to afford. The traffic moved in fits and starts over the 405 and then crawled past UCLA.

Bel Air Road runs northwest off Sunset Boulevard from the intersection of Sunset and Beverly Glen into Bel Air through what is known as East Gate. And a very impressive gate it is. A matched pair of decorative iron barriers hangs from a massive black iron frame topped by a giant lantern, and right next to them is what appears to be a neatly landscaped security post built of white stucco with a red-tiled roof.

If you don't know any better, it looks as if you need some kind of official credentials to pass through the gate into Bel Air, or at least be cleared through by a resident, but that isn't so. The security post is unmanned. Bel Air Road is a public street, and anyone can drive through. It just doesn't look like it.

Some say Bel Air is the most exclusive residential area in America, but that isn't so either. No credentials are required to become a resident of Bel Air other than the possession of large amounts of ready cash. Anyone can buy a house in Bel Air if they have the minimum of ten million dollars or so that's needed to acquire even the most modest of the properties there.

There are fewer than seven thousand residents in the six and a half square miles that comprise Bel Air, which gives the area one of the lowest population densities of any urban area in America. Over the years, Bel Air has boasted residents ranging from Elizabeth Taylor and Clint Eastwood to Alfred Hitchcock and Zsa Zsa Gabor. Howard Hughes once lived there, and Ronald and Nancy Reagan have lived there ever since they left the White House in 1989.

I spotted East Gate on my left and turned into Bel Air Road. I followed the street as it climbed into the hills, winding between estates hidden behind high walls and protected by sturdy gates.

Large trees formed a thick canopy overhead and filtered the harsh sunlight into soft, dappled patterns that fell across the pavement with a delicate tranquility. Everything felt hushed and far removed from the chaos of the rest of the world. It was as if I had driven into a nature reserve for the extremely wealthy.

I kept an eye on the house numbers that appeared on the gateposts and mailboxes I passed. As the Mustang followed the curves of the road and climbed higher and higher into the hills, I watched the numbers grow larger.

659 Bel Air Road.

723 Bel Air Road.

733 Bel Air Road.

And then I came to 739.

Two massive stone pillars flanked the driveway of 739 Bel Air Road, each one topped with an ornate iron lantern, and a heavy gate stretched between them. It was wrought iron painted glossy black with gold accents worked into an elaborate pattern. Through the bars, I could see a cobblestone driveway that curved uphill and disappeared behind a wall of meticulously trimmed hedges.

Beyond the hedges, I could catch just a glimpse of the house. White stucco walls. Red tile roof. Multiple levels rising up the hillside. Arched windows caught the afternoon light. The place looked like a Spanish castle transported from somewhere in the Mediterranean and plunked down here among the eucalyptus trees.

A security camera mounted on the left pillar pointed down to the place where I had stopped. A polished brass intercom panel was inset flush with the stone on a smaller pillar next to the driveway, and I sat there looking at it for a moment while the engine of the Mustang ticked quietly. From somewhere in the trees, a bird called out, sharp and insistent.

Was I really going to do this?

Yes, I eventually admitted to myself, I really was going to do this. I reached out and pressed the intercom button.

Nothing happened for maybe ten seconds. Then a voice crackled through the speaker, male and professional.

"Yes?"

"Charlie Trust. I think Zac is expecting me."

"One moment."

The connection went silent. I sat there with my hand on the steering wheel, looking up at the camera lens. I didn't smile.

Another ten seconds passed.

Then, the gate began to move. It glided open slowly, smoothly, and without a sound. The mechanism that powered it must have been expensive as hell because I couldn't hear even the slightest whisper of hydraulics or motors.

The gate stopped moving when it had opened wide enough for a car to pass through.

I shifted into gear and drove forward onto Zac Scott's cobblestone driveway.

Behind me, the gate glided silently closed again.

The house's front door opened as I got out of the Mustang. When I glanced over to see who was waiting for me, I froze with my hand resting on the car's door handle.

The man holding the door looked distinctly Japanese. And he was wearing a black suit.

Uh-oh.

But then I took a more careful look and decided that I had nothing to worry about.

The man didn't appear to be a threat to anybody. He was slightly built, almost elfin, and his body language was entirely self-effacing. He wore heavy-framed black glasses that had slipped down to the end of his nose and he reached down and pressed them back up with his forefinger while I watched. He looked less like a Yakuza gangster than he did a Japanese Woody Allen.

"Please come in, sir," he said.

The man spoke in a soft, even deferential tone of voice, and he had no accent at all. Was he actually Japanese? Maybe I was wrong. For all I knew, the guy was really from Encino.

When I stepped inside, he closed the door behind me.

"Mr. Scott is waiting for you in the library," he said. "Please follow me."

He moved off down a hallway that ran to the left, and I followed.

Waiting for me in the library, huh? I rather liked the sound of that.

Mr. Scott worked in a library. I worked at my dining room table. But it was all pretty much the same thing, wasn't it?

No, actually it wasn't.

32

I stepped through the door my escort held open, and he closed it quietly behind me.

If this was the library, it wasn't at all what I expected. No dark wood paneling. No leather-bound volumes arranged by color. No Persian rugs or oil paintings of dead ancestors.

Instead, the room was stark and modern with an industrial look to it. Floor-to-ceiling windows along one wall gave onto a view west toward Pacific Palisades, and I could just see sunlight glinting on the ocean off in the distance. The floor was gray painted concrete that had been etched to look old and pitted from hard wear, and there were stainless steel shelves on the wall opposite the windows that held just enough books to justify calling the room a library. A glass and chrome desk had been positioned with its back to the windows to catch the natural light.

Zac was sitting behind that desk. He was wearing a perfectly pressed white dress shirt with the sleeves rolled up to his elbows in what I figured was a carefully calculated gesture of informality. I suppose he intended dialing back the Cary

Grant shtick to be some sort of conciliatory gesture. Now we were just a couple of guys having a friendly conversation on equal terms.

But we weren't on equal terms, and I doubted this was going to be a friendly conversation.

Zac stood and walked around the desk, but instead of greeting me and shaking hands, he stopped in front of the desk and leaned back against it. He folded his arms across his chest and stayed where he was, just looking at me.

He didn't offer me a seat. I didn't take one.

"What is this proposal you have to end all this?" I asked.

Zac tilted his head slightly.

"Actually," he said, "I lied about that. I don't have one."

"Then what am I doing here?"

"My friends want to have a little talk with you. They think maybe they can persuade you that you're handling this all wrong."

"What friends?"

Zac pointed past me toward the door through which I had entered the library.

"Them."

When I looked where he was pointing, I realized the door to the library had opened again so quietly I hadn't even heard it. Woody Allen was standing there with what appeared to be something like a smile on his face. He still didn't look like anyone I needed to worry about.

But the two guys who were with him now were a different story. They were both huge and fleshy. They looked like two Japanese sumo wrestlers moonlighting as mob muscle.

The Sumo Brothers wore black suits with white shirts open at the neck, but the men's size and the way they were dressed weren't the things that struck me most about their appearance. I would have to say the most memorable thing about them were the two semi-automatic pistols they carried in their hands, and the way both of them had those pistols pointed directly at my chest.

When someone points a pistol at you, you look at it, because right at that moment, the only thing you're thinking about is whether the damned thing is going to go off. So that's where I looked, at the pistols, and that was when I realized there was something strange about them. Both of their barrels seemed unnaturally long and heavy.

Noise suppressors, I realized almost immediately. There were noise suppressors screwed onto the barrels of both pistols.

The Sumo Brothers weren't holding pistols on me just for their intimidation value, were they? You didn't bother to put a noise suppressor on the barrel of a pistol unless you intended to use it and you were concerned about the noise it would make when you did.

Uh-oh.

"You're wasting your time," I said to Zac. "I don't have what you're looking for."

"I don't care. I've done what they asked me to do. I'm out of this. You're their problem now, not mine."

That didn't strike me as particularly good news.

"Please turn around and face me, Mr. Trust," Woody Allen asked from behind me.

The two silenced pistols the Sumo Brothers were holding made any request from Woody Allen pretty much nonnegotiable, so I did what he told me to do and turned around. Then I just stood there looking at Woody Allen, and he just looked back at me, his face flat as a dinner plate.

"This isn't going to do you any good," I told him.

"What isn't?"

"Whatever you plan to do now."

"Why is it you think we're here, Mr. Trust?"

"You want the same thing Zac wants. The boxes of documents Emma Scott gave me to review. He's tried to get his hands on them, and he's failed, but now you probably think you can muscle me into giving them to you."

I tried to read the look I saw on Woody Allen's face, but I couldn't.

"Do you somehow imagine we're going to torture you until you give up those documents?" he asked.

"It doesn't matter."

"It doesn't?"

Woody Allen seemed genuinely bemused by my response, as well he might have been.

"Well ... yes, I guess it does matter," I said. "To me at least. The idea of being tortured isn't exceptionally appealing. But what I meant was that it doesn't matter to *you*, because you're not going to get the documents that way. I don't have them any longer, and I don't know where they are. No matter what you do to me, I can't help you."

"Go ahead," Woody Allen said.

"What?"

I couldn't see what he meant by *go ahead*, but then I realized he wasn't speaking to me. He was speaking to the Sumo Brothers. And I realized that because the two men immediately began to move.

They split apart, circled around me, and took up positions near where Zac was still leaning against his desk behind me. I was extremely pleased that their guns were no longer pointed at my chest, but considerably less pleased that they were now no doubt pointed at my back. So I started to turn to see if they were.

That was when Woody Allen raised both his hands, held

them toward me palms out, and said, "Please don't move, Mr. Trust. Just stay where you are and keep looking at me."

In the movies, firing a pistol with a noise suppressor renders it virtually silent, but nothing is further from the truth.

Discharging a pistol in an enclosed room is still a noisy business even with a noise suppressor. So when I heard a sound behind me like a very heavy book being dropped from about head height onto the floor, a sound that was immediately followed by the mechanical ratcheting of a pistol's cycling action and the rattle of an ejected cartridge hitting the floor, I knew that one of the men had fired his pistol.

My heart rate instantly spiked. Had I been shot? I couldn't feel anything, but I instinctively ran a quick system check on myself. I could detect nothing amiss. So, maybe I hadn't been shot after all. Did the shooter miss, or did he fire at something else?

Despite Woody Allen's insistence that I face him, I half turned and looked over my shoulder. Thinking back later, I wondered what I expected to see. Whatever it was, it certainly wasn't what I actually did see.

Zac Scott was lying on his face on the floor in front of his desk. Bright arterial blood was pulsing onto his artfully pitted concrete floor from what appeared to be a large exit wound just behind his left eye.

While I watched, one of the two Sumo Brothers bent over Zac. Taking care to avoid contact with the pooling blood, he wrapped Zac's right hand around his pistol, pointed it at a couch across the room, and pressed Zac's right index finger against the trigger.

There was another sound, like another heavy book being dropped, another sound of the pistol's action cycling, and another rattle from another cartridge being ejected. Then the man unscrewed the noise suppressor from the barrel of the pistol, slipped it into his jacket pocket, and stood up. I noticed he had left the pistol in Zac's hand when he did.

"In exactly one hour," Woody Allen said in that soft, accent-less voice of his, "the police will receive an anonymous call that a body has been discovered here at Mr. Scott's residence. I'm sure their response time will be very quick, probably only a few minutes. After all," he smiled, "this is Bel Air."

My heart was still racing, but I tore my eyes away from Zac Scott bleeding out on his study floor and looked back at Woody Allen.

"They'll never believe this was a suicide," I said.

"Oh, I think they will, Mr. Trust. I have no doubt the police will quickly conclude that they are looking at a suicide. A man distraught over the murder of his wife has decided he can't continue to live? One shot was a contact wound to his right temple. A second shot, no doubt the result of a muscle spasm when he fell to the floor, went into the couch. The gunshot residue on his right hand marks him as having pulled the trigger."

"You're not giving the cops enough credit."

"And you're giving them too *much* credit. After all, there's nothing to suggest that anyone else was even in the house, although sadly, all the security cameras were turned off for some reason. So, what explanation could there be *other* than suicide?"

"Does that mean you're going to kill me, too, to keep me from telling the cops what really happened?"

"I had rather assumed you would use that hour before I make my call to remove yourself from the scene, Mr. Trust. There's absolutely nothing to indicate you were ever here. No security camera footage. No witnesses. Why would you want to be here to tell anyone anything?"

Why, indeed? That made more sense to me than I really wanted it to.

"Besides," he continued, "what could you tell the police even if you did inform them this wasn't actually a suicide? That there were three mysterious men here dressed in black suits who appeared to you to be of Japanese appearance, and that one of us murdered Zac Scott and made it look like a suicide? You can't identify us. I doubt you can even describe us well enough for your description to be of any value to the police. After all, we all look pretty much alike to you, don't we, Mr. Trust?"

He had me there.

"You'd only end up making yourself a figure of suspicion," he finished, "and for no reason at all."

"It sounds to me like you think you've got this all figured out."

"It sounds that way to me, too. May we therefore agree that this unhappy conflict is now at an end and we can all simply go our separate ways?"

"You know I've been through the documents I was given by Emma Scott. Are you asking me to forget what I saw there and never tell anyone?"

"It doesn't matter to me in the slightest," Woody Allen shrugged. "The only two people on earth who can directly tie the money passing through Zac Scott's companies to us are Zac Scott and Emma Scott, both of whom are now tragically deceased."

And then, unexpectedly, Woody Allen suddenly grinned.

"All you can tell anyone, Mr. Trust, is that you saw some documents that show Zac Scott was very skilled at raising international investment capital, and that he was engaged in all sorts of schemes to avoid paying taxes on the profits he earned from that capital. A Hollywood producer who is dodging taxes? I'm shocked. Tell the *LA Times*, for all I care. I doubt that's nearly interesting enough for them even to bother reporting it."

I glanced over my shoulder at Zac again. The blood had pooled around his head, but it was no longer pulsing from the wound. I suppose eventually a body simply runs out of blood and stops bleeding, and that appeared to be exactly what was happening to Zac Scott.

I pointed to a chair across the room.

"May I?" I asked Woody Allen. "I'm starting to feel a little shaky here."

"By all means," he said.

He walked with me, and we both took seats in red leather chairs arranged around a glass and steel coffee table while the Sumo Brothers took up posts just inside the library door. We sat in silence for a while. I willed my heart rate back toward normal and tried to wrap my mind around everything that had just happened.

Eventually, Woody Allen broke the silence.

"You see, Mr. Trust, we've had a good run, but as the saying goes, all good things eventually come to an end."

He shrugged.

"We have a lot of excellent alternatives. America is a wonderful country for us. The only loyalty most people have here is to money, and we have plenty of that, so there's always a deal to be done. Mr. Scott's domestic problems made him yesterday's deal, so we've been forced to terminate our arrangement with him. Permanently. Tomorrow, we'll move along to something else."

"Then that's it? You're letting me go?"

"Why would we do anything else, Mr. Trust? You're no longer any threat to us. We're businessmen, not monsters."

"Emma Scott and Harry Wells might argue that point with you, but you've made sure they can't argue about anything with anyone anymore."

To my surprise, Woody Allen actually looked abashed at that.

"I regret very much that occurred. Two of our younger men got carried away and exceeded their instructions. I can assure you they have been appropriately disciplined."

He shrugged.

"Kids," Woody Allen added after a moment. "What are you going to do?"

I said nothing. I had no idea what to say to that.

"Are you okay to drive now?" Woody Allen inquired solicitously after a bit.

"Yes, I think I probably am."

"Then may I respectfully suggest you get in your car and do so. I have a telephone call to make. If you leave now, by my calculations, you should be back home in Malibu about the time I make it."

I sat for a moment and considered my alternatives.

I couldn't think of any.

So I stood up, walked out of the study without looking back, and left Zachariah Scott's house through the front door.

Then I got into my Mustang, started it, and drove back to Malibu.

33

The next morning, Zac Scott's death was on the front page of the *LA Times*. Above the fold, no less. Of course, it was.

I read the story while eating what had become my habitual bowl of raisin bran. And drinking coffee. A great deal of coffee. I had been out on the deck until after midnight last night, just watching the surf pound the beach, drinking Budweiser, and thinking about everything that had happened. A lot had happened, and that called for a lot of Budweiser. Which was why I needed a lot of coffee this morning.

The *Times* was circumspect in relating the circumstances of Zac Scott's death. They didn't come right out and say he had committed suicide. They just referred to his sudden death without mentioning a specific cause. Regardless, anyone who knew how to read between the lines, and that included absolutely everybody in Hollywood, knew exactly what the paper was really saying.

Later that morning, I went for a walk on the beach, then I came back and sat on the deck for a while, watching the surf, and thinking about nothing at all. When the telephone rang a little after noon, I considered just ignoring it, but I almost always consider ignoring it, and I almost never do.

"Hello."

"Hey, young man," Sandy said. "I've been wondering when you were going to call me."

I had been wondering when I was going to call Sandy, too, but I hadn't decided what I was going to tell him, so I hadn't done it yet.

"You got anything to tell me?" he asked.

I did, and I didn't.

"It seems to me," I said, "the more important question is whether there's anything you really want to know."

"It wasn't suicide, was it?" he asked, sliding right by my question.

"No, it wasn't."

"Our Yakuza friends were responsible?"

"Yes."

"And how is it that you're so sure of that?"

"Because I was there."

A short silence fell after that, as well it might have.

"Maybe you should come around later and have a drink with me," Sandy said after the silence had stretched on for a bit. "We've obviously got some stuff to talk about. Say, around six?"

"I'll check my calendar and see if I'm available."

Sandy chuckled.

And then he hung up.

Sandy opened the front door himself when I arrived. I didn't recall him ever doing that before, but this time he did, and Mr. Wu was nowhere to be seen. He led me back to his study, handed me a glass of what I assumed was one of his usual single malts, and pointed me to one of the chairs in front of his desk.

"So you were there, were you?" he asked as if our telephone conversation of nearly six hours before was simply continuing uninterrupted.

I nodded.

"Tell me about it," he said.

And so I did.

He listened without comment as I told him about Zac's summons to his house in Bel Air, being confronted by Woody Allen and the Sumo Brothers after I arrived, and then becoming a mute witness to Zac's murder.

"I gather that little show was meant to be a message for you," Sandy said.

"I'd say so," I nodded. "And if it was, then message received."

"Well, I'm not sure what difference that makes. The whole matter is moot now. Both the petitioner and the respondent are dead, so the divorce action that sucked you into this in the first place is over. I'm sure Zac's attorneys will withdraw the petition, and then Judge McClanahan will dismiss your subpoena and everything connected with it. You're off the hook."

"But I'm still the proud possessor of five boxes full of documents that could blow up Hollywood."

"You're sure about that? It sounds to me like your Yakuza pals have a good point. Without either Zac or Emma to authenticate the stuff and tie it all together, all you've got are copies of some records that suggest Zac was engaged in a little tax chiseling. That's not going to shock anybody."

"It's still a big loose end for me, Sandy. Those documents aren't going anywhere unless I do something with them."

Abruptly, Sandy got to his feet.

"Grab your drink, kid, and come with me."

Before I could ask him where we were going, he had picked up the whisky bottle and his glass and was halfway out of the study, so I just got up with my glass and followed him. He led me down a hallway, across a room I'd never been in before, and through a door that took us out the back of his house.

I found myself standing on what had probably once been an elegant brick patio, although now it seemed a bit neglected. The old red brick pavers had cracked and shifted in several places leaving them uneven, and a few weeds even sprouted between them here and there. The patio was shaded by large trees, and beyond them Sandy's perfectly tended lawn rolled out to the thick hedges that surrounded his property.

The strangest thing about the patio to me, however, was that its far side was anchored by a big barbecue pit constructed of the same red brick, and standing in front of it was Mr. Wu tending a large fire burning in the central box of the pit. There were all sorts of things I had difficulty imagining, but Sandy Bouchier flipping burgers on a barbecue grill would have been right at the top of my list of the most inconceivable of all.

"Are we going to have a cookout?" I asked Sandy.

"In a manner of speaking," he replied, and pointed off to the side of the barbecue pit.

That was when I saw them. Five bankers boxes neatly arranged in a straight line. The five boxes that had spawned the murders of three people, and created so much personal difficulty for me.

And suddenly I realized what we were doing there.

"You can't do this, Sandy. You'll be destroying evidence."

"Evidence in what? There's no longer a cause of action pending."

"Maybe not, but there's still evidence here that Zac committed all kinds of crimes. Certainly tax evasion. Probably money laundering and other more serious crimes, too."

"You can't prosecute a dead man, kid. If Zachariah Scott did commit any of those crimes, the crimes died with him."

I could see where Sandy was going with this, and I didn't much like it.

"The way it looks to me now, Charlie, all of this stuff is nothing but your personal albatross. And it's time to kill it and bury it once and for all."

Sandy pointed to two red cedar chairs with a table between them.

"Sit down and finish your drink. You've earned a little peace."

I sat, and Sandy took the other chair for himself. Then he put the whisky bottle and his glass on the little table between us, and he called out, "Go ahead, Mr. Wu."

We watched Mr. Wu work his way through all five of the bankers boxes, methodically shoveling everything in them into the fire in the barbecue pit. And when he was done, he broke down the five boxes and burned them, too. An hour later, nothing was left of the boxes of documents Emma Scott had given me other than what I remembered about them.

"And that," Sandy said as we watched the last of the fire burn down, "is that."

I have to admit that drinking good whisky while watching Mr. Wu turn the past into ashes was a wonderfully fulfilling way to spend an hour or so. If you ever get the chance to do something similar yourself, I recommend you grab it. Nothing is more cleansing to a man's soul than seeing his troubles reduced to ashes.

I left shortly after that to drive back to Malibu, but Sandy had one more surprise in store for me before I did.

He walked me out to the front door when I left and handed me a large manila envelope just before I stepped outside.

"Read this later," he said, "and tell me what you think."

"What is it?"

"Never mind that now. Read it tomorrow."

Tomorrow it would be.

On the way home, I stopped at a little taco stand I knew in Santa Monica and picked up a bag of beef and chicken tacos. When I got back to Malibu, I grabbed a Budweiser out of the refrigerator and took it and the tacos out to the deck. Passing through the kitchen, I dropped Sandy's envelope on the kitchen table and forgot all about it.

I sat there on the deck for the next couple of hours watching the surf, eating the tacos, and stuffing the wrappers back in the paper bag. Except for one quick trip to the refrigerator for another Budweiser, I hardly moved.

A flock of gulls perched along the railing of the deck to watch me, and I liked that. It felt like a gathering of old friends. The moment a bit of something consumable hit the deck, one of the gulls would swoop in and scoop it up. In the spirit of the moment, I made sure I dropped enough debris from my tacos on the deck to keep my friends happy.

A heavy weight had lifted from my soul, and that made for a fine night out there on the deck. Just me, my pals the gulls, a couple of Budweisers, and a big bag of tacos.

The moon hanging above the water looked so big I could almost reach out and touch it. I felt the warm wind on my skin, watched the surf roll in, and smelled the salt in the spray

It was California at the height of its powers.

34

It wasn't until I was in the kitchen waiting for the coffee to finish dripping the next morning that I remembered Sandy's envelope.

It was lying there on the kitchen table, so I opened it and scanned the contents while I was drinking my first cup of coffee. The document that I found inside appeared to be a partnership agreement of some kind, and I wondered why Sandy had given it to me for review. Surely, he was at least as qualified as I was, probably more so, to assess a simple partnership agreement.

Then I noticed the name under which the new partnership would operate.

Bouchier and Trust
Attorneys at Law

I sank into a chair right there at the kitchen table and read through the rest of the agreement with growing astonishment.

. . .

Sandy answered the telephone on the second ring.

"So," he asked before I could say a word, "what do you think?"

"I think you must be out of your mind."

He chuckled.

"Sandy, I'm flattered all to hell, of course, but I'm also just a schnook who barely scraped through a second-tier law school, and you're a fucking legend. The two of us practicing law together sounds like somebody's idea of a bad sitcom on a cable television network nobody watches anymore."

He chuckled again.

"I've enjoyed the experience of working with you over the past few weeks, Charlie. To be honest, it's given me new life, and I want to keep that going. Besides, I've learned that you're a deeply decent man, and the law needs all the decent men it can find. I don't want to let one get away."

"Then you're serious about this?"

"I'm absolutely serious."

"But, Sandy, I don't have any clients, and I've got no idea how to find any."

"Oh, I've got plenty of clients. People track me down all the time with pleas that I take over what seem to be hopeless criminal cases or civil liberties cases no one else wants to take. What I don't have is the energy or the years left to represent those clients the way they deserve to be represented. That's where you come in."

"I don't know what to say, Sandy."

"Then just say yes. I own a little building in Hollywood that's right behind Musso and Frank's. There's a tenant on the ground floor that calls itself an erotic lingerie shop, but the upper two floors are empty. I thought I'd have them remodeled into offices for us. There's something about capping off my legal career by practicing law above an erotic lingerie shop that I find extremely appealing."

I had to laugh.

"If you come to your senses and change your mind, Sandy, just call me back and tell me. No hard feelings. Honest."

"Then you're in?"

When one of the legendary names in the law asks you to become his partner, what else can you say?

"Damn right, I'm in."

"Wonderful. I'll start planning the remodeling. Let's have dinner in a couple of days and talk about the details. Say, Musso's on Friday?"

Musso and Frank's was one of my favorite places in Los Angeles, if not in the entire world. It was the oldest restaurant in Hollywood, having been in the same location on Hollywood Boulevard since the twenties. Almost every major American writer from Scott Fitzgerald to Raymond Chandler had gotten stinking drunk at its bar, and Hollywood stars from Charlie Chaplin to Clint Eastwood had sprawled in its red faux-leather booths night after night. The martinis were legendary, and I had done my share to keep that legend alive.

"Fine," I said. "Musso's on Friday."

"Tell you what. Why don't you meet me a little early, and we'll walk over and look at the building before dinner? It's just a few doors away. Six o'clock, okay?"

"Fine," I said again.

I was still so flabbergasted that short answers were pretty much the most I could manage right then.

For the rest of the day, I wandered around the house in something of a daze. Was I really going to become law partners with the living legend Sandy Bouchier? That was hard for me to wrap my mind around.

Eventually, I got restless and took a walk on the beach, and of course, I told my gull pals the great news. They hardly seemed to believe it at first, but then I convinced them it was true, and they were as overwhelmed as I was. They squawked the good news back and forth to each other in obvious excitement, and a few flew off to spread the word.

But when the telephone rang a little after four that afternoon, I wasn't really surprised.

I couldn't blame Sandy for changing his mind. He had proposed the partnership in what was doubtless a burst of pure sentimentality, but when I accepted, he soon realized what he had done and came to his senses. How could I blame him for that?

I took a deep breath and answered.

"Sandy?"

There was only silence on the phone.

"Hello?" I said. "Is that you, Sandy?"

"Uh..."

The voice I heard was male, but it sounded far younger than Sandy's, and the pitch was higher.

"Is this Charles Trust I am speaking to?" the voice asked.

Definitely not Sandy then.

"Charlie Trust," I said. "Yes, that's me."

"My name is Jackson Young. I'm an attorney with Rosenthal, Massey, and Taylor."

"Yes?

"We're a law firm here in Los Angeles."

"Yes?"

"Our offices are in Century City."

"Of course they are."

"Uh..."

He hesitated again, and then he finally got to the point.

"Our firm represents the estate of Harry Wells, and the probate court has appointed us as Mr. Wells' executor under his will."

I was almost relieved. When a lawyer you've never heard of from a law firm you're unfamiliar with telephones out of the blue, it's never with good news. But this was a call that I knew was coming sooner or later, so I was glad to get it over with and have everything settled.

"I've been waiting for your call," I said.

"You have?" The man sounded genuinely puzzled.

"Of course, I have. It was very generous of Harry to let me stay here for so long, but I knew whoever was administering his estate would ask me to vacate the house. I'm certainly prepared to do so whenever you require it. Can I just ask you how long I have?"

"How long do you have to do what?"

"To vacate Harry's house. Isn't that why you're calling? To ask me to vacate the house?"

"Oh no, sir. Nothing like that. I just need to know when you can come to our offices to sign the necessary paperwork."

"Paperwork? For what? What are you talking about?"

I wondered if this was what Sandy heard when he talked to me on the telephone? A young lawyer doing his best, but making a muddle of providing a clear and concise explanation of what he wanted.

"I'm so sorry, sir," Jackson Young said. "I'm really not explaining this very clearly, am I?"

"I regret to say you are not."

"Then let me try again. Mr. Wells' will includes a specific bequest to you of the house, and I have been asked to arrange for you to sign the paperwork involved in implementing that bequest."

"The house?"

"Yes."

"What house?"

"The one Mr. Wells owns in Malibu. The one where I understand you've been staying."

"Harry left me this house?"

"Yes."

"You can't be serious."

"I'm completely serious."

"Harry left me this house?"

"Yes, sir. That's what I've been trying to tell you."

"Are you fucking kidding me?"

I was in shock. The conversation went on for a bit after that, but I can't remember much of what was said other than that we agreed that I would come to the law firm's offices in Century City tomorrow and sign the documents needed for them to transfer the deed for the Carbon Beach house into my name.

After I hung up, I just stood there for a moment with no idea what to do next. Then I did what I generally do these days when I have no idea what to do next. I got a cold Budweiser out the refrigerator, took it out to the deck, and flopped into one of the deck chairs to watch the surf while I drank it.

A man in gray sweats was ambling along down at the water line following close behind a golden retriever trotting in front of him. I popped the tab on the Budweiser and watched them pass while I took a long pull.

The dog made a dutiful effort to lunge at the occasional gull that ventured too close, but his heart didn't seem to be in it. The man was overweight and middle aged. He was keeping up with the dog, but his heart didn't seem to be in that either. Both of them looked as if their minds were on something else altogether.

And, boy, did I know how that felt. I was looking at the surf and the dog and the man, but all I could really see was the same thought running through my mind over and over as if it were spelled out in lights on one of those moving signs in Times Square.

Are you fucking kidding me?

Yesterday, I was an unemployed squatter living in a borrowed house. Today, I'm law partners with one of America's most celebrated attorneys, and the owner of a home on one of America's most beautiful beaches.

Are you fucking kidding me?

Go west, young man, Horace Greeley famously exhorted the young and the restless just after the end of the Civil War, and for a hundred and fifty years Americans had been doing exactly that. We had headed west in a never-ending procession, every one of us looking for something.

And now I was one of those who had actually found something.

I was as lucky as the guy from Pennsylvania who drove his pick into the ground and discovered gold, or the young woman from Nebraska who turned up at the right audition and become a movie star.

It had been a mad and magnificent parade, one as American as the proverbial apple pie, and now it had defined my life just as it had defined the lives of so many who had come before me.

Call whatever had brought me here fate or fortune or chance or luck. Call it anything you like, but maybe, against all odds, I had actually come to the place where I belong.

And then, right on top of that thought, a different one shouldered it aside.

Perhaps I should call Pele and see if she'll have some tacos with me at the Baja Cantina tonight so I can share my good news with her.

We'd had a comfortable relationship when I worked on the motion and brief at her bookstore, hadn't we? There was even something in the air then that felt very much like a sense of inevitability about us being there together.

I weigh up my prospects and decide I probably have only about a 50-50 shot, but I doubt there will ever be a better day in my entire life to take a 50-50 shot.

Perhaps I'm pushing my luck a little, but I've always believed you've got to bid up your cards, and maybe my run of good fortune will stretch far enough to bring me just one more win.

I put my Budweiser down on the little table next to the deck chair and stand up. Then I take a deep breath and go inside to call Pele and find out.

Wish me luck.

A Note
FROM JAKE NEEDHAM

I hope you enjoyed CONTEMPT OF COURT.

If you would consider recommending it to other readers, I'd be honored. When you post a short review on Amazon for a book you like, you help me a lot with reaching new readers.

Your review doesn't have to be long. Just a couple of sentences will do the job. What really counts is the rating you give the book and the fact that you took the time to recommend it.

Just go to the CONTEMPT OF COURT page on Amazon and scroll down to the *Write a Customer Review* button. It's on the left side, just below the graphic showing the ratings the title has received so far.

A Preview

The Charlie Trust series Book 1

Have you read the first title of the Charlie Trust legal thrillers, the book that introduced Charlie Trust?

CHAPTER ONE

Los Angeles, 1992

Los Angeles is a hallucination. It's what Robert Parker called a dwindled fragment of the last and greatest of all human dreams. It's the place where reality runs out of room.

I don't really think about that very much. A hallucination, if that's what it is, will do me fine. I've had enough of reality for a while. That's why I'm here.

My name is Charlie Trust, and I'm a recovering lawyer.

That makes it sound a little like we're kicking off an AA meeting, doesn't it? Twelve steps? Could be more. I really don't know *how* many steps it takes to recover and repair your soul when you start to feel it shriveling up and turning black, but I'm trying to find out.

It would probably be easier for guys like me if we did have a place like AA. Maybe a church basement somewhere in which we could all sit in a circle, drink crummy coffee, and talk about our struggles to other lawyers who are also trying to recover from whatever stretch they served in the perdition of our shared profession. But we don't have anything like that. Each of us is on his own.

And that's why I have to make do now with living on Carbon Beach in Malibu.

Stop laughing. I can hear you. Stop it.

The house I'm living in isn't mine anyway, of course. A man I had brought through the fires of a particularly gruesome divorce had a house here he didn't live in very much anymore.

When he discovered I needed a place to go while I got myself together and tried to figure out what came next after eight years of divorce lawyering, he told me the house was mine for as long as I wanted it. Sometimes you have friends you don't even know you have.

Carbon Beach is referred to by the locals as Billionaire's Beach. The houses, if you can speak of structures that sell for the prices these do using a pedestrian term like *houses*, are shoved up against each other on a narrow strip of land sandwiched between the Pacific Ocean and the Pacific Coast Highway. On my right, a modernist glass fortress reflects the sunset. On my left, a Cape Cod-style mansion with weathered gray shingles and white trim looks almost humble despite its eight-figure price tag.

But here's the thing. It's not just money that bathes Carbon Beach in such a golden light. There's a a fair measure of glamor, too. After all, Malibu is Hollywood on the sand.

Farrah Fawcett and Ryan O'Neal live right next door to me. We aren't pals exactly, but usually Ryan waves when he sees me out walking on the beach, and they always nod and smile when we're both on our back decks at the same time. Farrah sunbathes on their deck most days, generally topless, so I'm out on my deck quite a lot.

A dozen houses or so down the beach is another actor named Martin Cole. He's one of those guys you see on television all the time, mostly in cop shows. You probably don't know his name, but you would recognize his face anywhere. I've gotten to know Marty a lot better than I have Ryan and Farrah. Sometimes he even accompanies me on my evening strolls along the beach.

I kicked off my shoes and let my toes sink into the cool sand. A jogger in designer workout gear padded past and tossed me one of the crisp nods that passes for a friendly greeting around here. Just on the other side of the houses lining the beach I could hear the traffic roaring along the PCH. The constant background hum of tires on asphalt mixed with the noise of the surf on the beach was the backing track for daily life in Malibu.

I walked up the beach along the water's edge as I did almost every evening, and almost every evening it gave me the same feeling. I was teetering here on a narrow ledge between two worlds. Off to my right were concrete, internal combustion engines, and almost unimaginable wealth. Off to my left was the endless Pacific Ocean, unchanged since before human beings existed.

"You're on private property," a man's voice called down to me from the deck of one of the modern boxes of glass and steel I was passing.

I raised a hand in acknowledgment without lifting my eyes from the lines of breakers pounding in toward the beach.

"Below the high tide line is public access," I called back. "And I'm below it."

I could feel the homeowner's annoyance at my very existence radiating across the sand, but he said nothing else.

The tide was coming in, eating away at the narrow strip of sand that belonged to the public. Soon, there would be none of it left, no space remaining between private property and the ocean. The metaphor wasn't lost on me.

A child's laughter cut through the sound of the surf, a rare sound on this beach where the median age seemed to be well north of sixty. I spotted a family up ahead of me setting up on the sand. My guess was they were most likely guests of someone who lived here.

Public access to beaches was an article of faith in California, but the access to Carbon Beach wasn't easy to find, and visitors seldom made their way onto this stretch of sand. Those who did were usually encouraged by the security patrol to move along somewhere else, or badgered by one of the residents until they left. The public wasn't welcome on Carbon Beach. That was the way the people who lived here wanted it. And the people who lived on Carbon Beach were accustomed to getting exactly what they wanted.

I dug my toes deeper into the sand and breathed in the salt air. The houses along this beach represented more wealth than most people would encounter in a dozen lifetimes, all crammed onto a narrow strip between civilization and wilderness. So, I asked myself for at least the hundredth time, what the hell was a small-time Virginia divorce lawyer doing in a place like this?

I had been an average student, and that was being generous. I'd squeaked into UVA Law by the skin of my teeth with my LSAT score just barely above the cutoff. How I had graduated remained one of life's great mysteries. Every exam had been a battle, and every legal research paper a war of attrition. But after managing to keep my head above water for three years, somehow, I eventually walked with the rest of my class up onto that stage. They gave me a diploma, and with every step I took to get off the stage again, I wondered if they would realize their mistake and tackle me before I could.

The Virginia Bar Exam was my personal Everest, but once again, I had passed, somehow. When I went looking for a job, I found out quickly enough that average Joes with average records from average law schools weren't exactly the toast of the town. When I landed at Pritchard, Wells & Monroe in Arlington, a modest-sized local firm in the suburbs of Washington, DC, I felt like I had hit the lottery. I thought maybe I had my feet on solid ground at last. I was a real lawyer with a real office, even if my office was a closet with one small, very dirty window that looked out at two diuretic pigeons and a brick wall.

"Hey, Trust! I got another one for you."

That was Cliff Monroe's standard greeting each time he dumped another divorce file on my desk. No one else at the firm would touch divorce cases. Real lawyers handled corporate matters, led real estate transactions, settled tax disputes, and did estate planning. Divorce cases were the firm's redheaded stepchild, and I was the kid's duly designated caretaker.

For eight years, I did the job they paid me to do. I just kept my head down and got on with it. For those eight long years, I watched a never-ending parade of people who had once whispered *I love you* to each other scream about who would get the blue chair. For eight years, I calculated child support payments while parents used their kids as bargaining chips. For eight years, I divided assets that had once been the fabric of shared dreams.

And every minute of those eight years sucked.

There was the tech executive who changed the passwords for all his bank accounts the day before filing, leaving his wife of twenty years without access to a penny. There was the kindergarten teacher who poisoned her husband's dog because he loved it more than her. There was the couple who fought for three months over a blender neither of them wanted, just so the other couldn't have it.

It was soul-deadening stuff. I started having trouble sleeping. I drank too much and dated women I hated on sight. I was becoming someone I didn't recognize, someone I didn't much like.

I turned around and walked back the way I had come, splashing along the water's edge and letting the cold Pacific pool around my feet. The sun was setting now, painting the sky with those streaks of orange and pink and yellow that always left me a little breathless. How had I ended up here, so far from the sad and sterile rooms where I had presided over the dissolution of so many lives? I was in a place I hadn't earned, in a world where I obviously didn't belong. Yet somehow, here I was.

The crashing waves pushed the tides of cold water up the sand, erasing my footprints almost as soon as I made them. If only I could wash clean the past so easily. Maybe I could, if I did it right. After all, that's why I was here, living in a borrowed house on Carbon Beach. I was washing away the memory of all those things I didn't want to remember.

When I reached the wooden steps that led up to the back deck of my borrowed mansion, I stood for a moment and watched the last sunlight of the day slide into the ocean. I call the house a mansion, but I'm really only joking. It's a long way from actually being one. If this house were anywhere in the country other than on the beach in Malibu, it would probably be considered downright shabby.

It's an older house of no particular style, nothing at all like the architectural excesses with which it shares the beach. Constructed of weathered white clapboard that had seen decades of salt spray and sunshine, the design is deliberately plain, functional, and entirely without the architectural flourishes that embellish its neighbors.

The house sits there like an old beach bum who grabbed his spot on the sand long before the billionaires arrived with their entourages of architects and contractors and designers. I remembered a guy I had known in high school who laughingly described his parents' home as shabby genteel. I had smiled automatically at the phrase, but I'd never really understood before what it actually meant. Now I did.

The house belonged to a man named Harry Wells, who was a successful composer of music for television and movies.

He lived in New York, mostly, but when he and his wife had called it a day, she moved back to Lexington, Virginia, where she had been born. That was where she had filed for divorce, and that was why Harry had ended up as my client.

She was angry, and it was an angry divorce, but I got Harry through it without him taking too many hits below the waterline. He and I got on well, even settling into a kind of friendship.

He actually thanked me when it was all over and insisted on taking me to dinner. That all by itself was memorable, but during that dinner, in a moment of weakness, I had admitted to Harry how fed up I was with doing divorces. And that was even more memorable, because it eventually changed everything for me.

I thought being a lawyer would be something bigger than this, I told him. *I want my life to add up to more than negotiating divorce settlements.*

That was when Harry told me he had a house in Malibu that he seldom used anymore. He owned it in the name of a production company through which some of his television music was licensed, so its existence had never come up in the negotiations over the divorce. I had never heard anything about it before, and I should have, but I just nodded and didn't ask any questions.

"You kept me sane through this," Harry said. "Anytime you want to go out there, just let me know. You can use the house for as long as you like."

Truth was, I had never really seen myself as a beach guy, so I thanked him and said I would keep that in mind, but I doubted I would. I didn't surf, I swam badly, and as for sitting in the sun, forget it. My pale Virginia skin turned lobster red in an hour. The beach had always been a place other people went on vacation, not somewhere I belonged.

But that was before my mother died.

The call came on a Tuesday. Stage four pancreatic cancer, discovered too late. Six weeks later, she was gone. We had never been particularly close. Her disapproval of most of the choices I had made in my life had, brick by brick, built a wall between us. But her death threw me more than I expected.

The surprise inheritance she left threw me even more. It wasn't a fortune by any means, but it wasn't pennies either. It was enough that I could look at my soul-crushing job and finally say what I'd wanted to say for nearly as long as I could remember.

I don't have to do this anymore.

I figured the money would buy me at least a couple of years of peace. No more screaming couples, no more calculating who got how much of the pension fund, no more explaining to kids why mommy and daddy couldn't live together anymore. Then I could figure out what came next.

I quit on a Friday. By Monday, I'd already forgotten the names of clients whose divorces had consumed my waking thoughts for years.

And that was when I called Harry Wells and asked if the offer to use his house in Malibu was still good.

It was.

I climbed the steps to the deck and unlocked the sliding glass door. The house was cool and quiet. It smelled faintly of lemon furniture polish. I grabbed a beer from the refrigerator, walked back outside, and flopped into one of the deck chairs.

The darkness was gathering now, and the stars were just starting to pop out above me. I took a long pull from my beer.

This wasn't my world. These weren't my people. I was just visiting, a temporary interloper in the land of the beautiful and wealthy. But I was still happy as hell to be sitting there right then, listening to the ocean and wondering what in the world I was going to do now that I had stopped being a lawyer, since that was the only thing on this earth I had ever really been.

I had lived in Malibu for nearly six months now, and I had settled into a rhythm that felt suspiciously like contentment. My days had a pleasant, aimless quality that would have horrified my former colleagues at Pritchard, Wells & Monroe. No billable hours, no client emergencies, no ringing telephones, and no partners breathing down my neck about cases that made my skin crawl.

Most mornings, I would wake shortly after sunrise, make coffee, and walk the beach for a while. At midday, I often drove my Mustang down to the Malibu Country Mart. That car had been my one splurge since arriving. It was a cherry-red 1969 convertible with a rebuilt engine and more personality than most of the attorneys I had worked with back in Virginia. Something about the rumble of its big V8 and the way it held the curves of the Pacific Coast Highway as it snaked along the coast made me feel like I'd bought a better life along with it.

The Country Mart became my unofficial headquarters. I'd grab a sandwich from the deli, find an empty bench in the garden area, and settle in for the afternoon show. The place was an endless parade of wealth and glamor, all generously displayed. Yummy mummies in expensive linen pants and oversized sunglasses laughed and gossiped with each other, their diamond earrings flashing in the sun as they followed their children around the garden. They would sip from tall glasses of strange-colored juices while their children, all sun-bleached hair and expensive sneakers, scrambled over the playground equipment.

"Sweetie, be careful!" one would call out, never actually looking up from her conversation about the new yoga instructor or which private school had the better college acceptance rates.

I sat and watched, eating my ham and cheese on sourdough and thinking about how different this world was from the grim conference rooms where I once mediated property disputes between couples who had loved each other until they didn't anymore. Here, sitting in the garden of the Malibu Country Mart bathed in the golden light of California, all that misery now seemed a long way away.

Evenings were for the Baja Cantina, a Mexican joint where the margaritas came strong and the clientele came famous. Larry Hagman held court most nights at the end of the bar surrounded by his usual entourage. J.R. Ewing in the flesh, though considerably more likable. After a while, Hagman even began to nod in my direction occasionally, a casual acknowledgment that I had become a fixture of sorts there, too.

I would nurse my drink and listen to the conversations drifting around me about upcoming pilots, troubled productions, and other industry gossip. Occasionally, someone would strike up a conversation, assuming I was *in the business* or I wouldn't have been there. Most of the time, I let them believe whatever they wanted. It was easier than explaining that I was really a burned-out divorce lawyer from Virginia squatting in somebody else's beach house.

The truth was, I was living a borrowed life, and I knew it, but I certainly wasn't complaining. Some nights, driving home on the coast highway in my Mustang with the top down, the ocean breeze blowing through my hair, and the radio playing classic rock, I'd think, *this is what they mean when they talk about California dreaming.*

And for now, that was good enough for me.

In Malibu, in 1991, we were living the golden times. Of course, we didn't know it then. No one ever knows it when they are.

Somewhere in the back of our minds, we probably

suspected it was all too good to last. One day, surely we realized it would all have to come to an end.

And then, just like that, on the 29th of April, 1992, it did.

It's available at all Amazon stores worldwide
in both e-book and paperback editions.

THE CHARLIE TRUST LEGAL THRILLERS

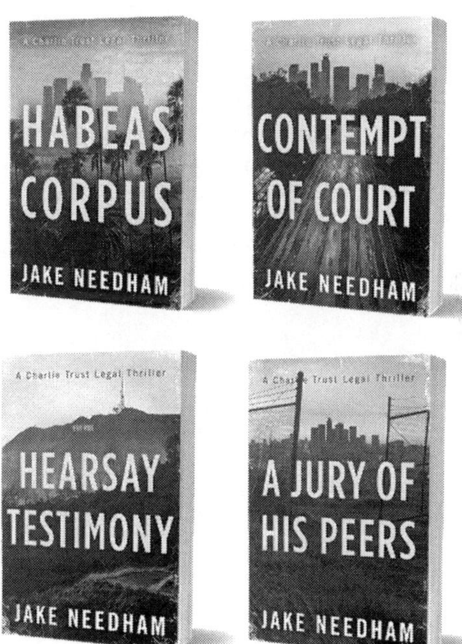

Los Angeles, 1992

Charlie Trust is a Budweiser kind of guy living in a champagne world. After grinding away his soul as a divorce attorney in Virginia, he's found the ultimate escape: a borrowed house on Malibu's exclusive Carbon Beach.

His plan is simple. Drink beer, drive his cherry-red '69 Mustang, watch the Pacific Ocean, and figure out what to do with the rest of his life. He has no clients, no office, and absolutely no desire ever to practice law again.

But — wouldn't you know it? — that's not exactly how things work out for him.

Set against the backdrop of Malibu, California, in the uneasy spring of 1992, during the time of the LA Riots, the **Charlie Trust Legal Thrillers** blend legal intrigue with California noir for fans of Michael Connelly's 'The Lincoln Lawyer.'

They're available at all Amazon stores worldwide in both e-book and paperback editions.

HABEAS CORPUS - book 1

CONTEMPT OF COURT - book 2

HEARSAY TESTIMONY - book 3

A JURY OF HIS PEERS - book 4

If you enjoyed reading the Charlie Trust novels,
there are sixteen more
great mysteries and thrillers
from
Jake Needham.

THE INSPECTOR SAMUEL TAY NOVELS

The Inspector Samuel Tay Novels

Samuel Tay is a little overweight, a little lonely, a little cranky, and he smokes way too much. He's worked almost his entire life as a senior homicide detective in Singapore CID, and he's the best investigator anyone there has ever seen.

THE AMBASSADOR'S WIFE - Book 1

THE UMBRELLA MAN - Book 2

THE DEAD AMERICAN - Book 3

THE GIRL IN THE WINDOW - Book 4

AND BROTHER IT'S STARTING TO RAIN - Book 5

MONGKOK STATION - Book 6

WHO THE HELL IS HARRY BLACK? - Book 7

THE DETECTIVE GONE GRAY - Book 8

GOODBYE, MR. BOOGIE - Book 9

THE JACK SHEPHERD NOVELS

Jack Shepherd was a well-connected lawyer in Washington DC until he tossed it all in for the quiet life of a business school professor at Chulalongkorn University in Bangkok.

It was a pretty good gig until the university discovered the kind of notorious people Shepherd had gotten involved with in his law practice. That was when they suggested he'd probably be happier somewhere else.

These days, Shepherd lives and works in Hong Kong where he's the kind of lawyer people call a troubleshooter. At least that's what they call him when they're being polite.

Shepherd is the guy people go to when they have a problem too ugly to tell anyone else about. He locates the trouble, and he shoots it.

Neat, huh? If life were only that simple...

LAUNDRY MAN - Book 1

KILLING PLATO - Book 2

A WORLD OF TROUBLE - Book 3

THE KING OF MACAU - Book 4

DON'T GET CAUGHT - Book 5

THE NINETEEN - Book 6

And a Stand Alone Novel

“THE BIG MANGO is a classic!”
-- Crime Reads

THE BIG MANGO: A Heist Novel

is available at Amazon in both
e-book and a paperback formats

Meet Jake Needham

Jake Needham is an American lawyer who became a screen and television writer through a series of coincidences too ridiculous for anyone to believe. When he realized how little he liked movies and television, he started writing crime novels.

Jake and his wife, a prematurely retired concert pianist, have lived in Bangkok for over thirty years. He has published seventeen novels that have collectively sold over a million copies.

He is a three-time finalist for the Barry Award for the Paperback Mystery of the Year and once a finalist for the International Thriller Writers' Award for Ebook Thriller of the Year. In 2024, he won the Barry Award for Best Paperback Mystery of the Year for the seventh book in the Inspector Samuel Tay series, WHO THE HELL IS HARRY BLACK?

Every month or two, Jake sends out one of his famous *Letters from Asia* to those readers who have asked to receive them. If you want to be one of those readers who receive Jake's letters, go to this web address and give him the email address you would like for him to use:

www.JakeNeedhamNovels.com/letter-to-readers

Ebook edition ISBN 978-616-629-913-7

Trade paper edition ISBN 978-616-629-944-1

Made in United States
Orlando, FL
03 March 2026

78981615R10210